BY
ALEXANDER GORDON SMITH

THE DEVIL'S ENGINE

LLWALKERS

THE
DEVIL'S
ENGINE

HELL

LKERS

ALEXANDER GORDON SMITH

FARRAR STRAUS GIROUX
NEW YORK

Farrar Straus Giroux Books for Young Readers
An imprint of Macmillan Publishing Group, LLC
175 Fifth Avenue, New York, NY 10010

Printed in the United States of America
Designed by Andrew Arnold
First edition, 2017

1 3 5 7 9 10 8 6 4 2

fiercereads.com

Library of Congress Cataloging-in-Publication Data

Names: Smith, Alexander Gordon, 1979– author.
Title: The devil's engine: hellwalkers / Alexander Gordon Smith.
Description: First edition. | New York : Farrar Straus Giroux, 2017. |
  Series: The Devil's Engine ; 3 | Summary: After Marlow makes a deal with
  the Devil to get himself and Pan released from Hell, war breaks out and
  the friends have only each other, and hope, to combat demonic creatures
  and monsters.
Identifiers: LCCN 2017001322 (print) | LCCN 2017030098 (ebook) | ISBN
  9780374301750 (Ebook) | ISBN 9780374301743 (hardcover)
Subjects: | CYAC: Science fiction. | Demonology—Fiction. |
  Monsters—Fiction. | Hell—Fiction. | Horror stories.
Classification: LCC PZ7.S6423 (ebook) | LCC PZ7.S6423 Hg 2017 (print) |
  DDC [Fic]—dc23
LC record available at https://lccn.loc.gov/2017001322

Our books may be purchased in bulk for promotional, educational, or
business use. Please contact your local bookseller or Macmillan Corporate
and Premium Sales Department at (800) 221-7945, ext. 5442, or by e-mail
at MacmillanSpecialMarkets@macmillan.com.

To Beki, my awesome wife.

If I had to walk through hell with anyone, it would be you.

Not that I'm saying our marriage is like hell or anything—

it's amazing, and I love you and our girls so much.

Honestly, it's not like hell at all, that's just the name of the book.

I was trying to be clever.

Can I start over?

PART I
WILD DREAMS
TORMENT ME

WELCOME TO HELL

Open your eyes.

The easiest thing in the world, and the hardest.

Hardest because Marlow knew he wasn't *in* the world anymore. He was somewhere else, somewhere far worse.

Open your eyes.

He didn't even feel like he had eyes to open. He couldn't sense anything, not the beating of his heart, not the weight of his flesh, not the pressure of his eyelids. There was literally nothing left of him, just a lost soul adrift in the ash that had once been his body.

Open your eyes.

He didn't want to, because if he opened them then he would know for sure where he was. There would be no going back. He would be able to see exactly where this journey had led him. With his eyes closed, though, there was no hiding from where it had all begun.

He could see himself now, just a kid back on Staten Island, a kid with no memories of childhood, kicked out of school for being an asshole, for burning all his bridges. Yeah, Marlow Green: big, bad hellraiser.

He saw the day he'd left school, stumbling into an underground parking lot, stumbling into a war. Hell had come to Staten Island that day, and somehow—despite his cowardice, despite the fact he'd always put himself first—he'd done his part to send it back.

Open your eyes.

That first battle had opened his eyes—opened them to a world that he never could have imagined, a world where demons were real, where hell was real. He'd been recruited into one of the armies fighting this war, the Fist. He'd become a soldier—a true Hellraiser—alongside Herc, Truck, Night, and the enigmatic leader, Sheppel Ostheim. Not to mention Pan, a Hellraiser for four years, ever since Herc had rescued her from juvie for killing a guy who'd attacked her. Through them he'd learned about a weapon, something ancient and something evil.

The Devil's Engine.

Make a deal with the Engine and you could have anything you wanted—money, fame, and power beyond your wildest dreams. The Fist had been using this machine to turn its army into superheroes, giving them powers like invisibility, strength, speed, even invulnerability. And all it asked in return was your soul. Because once your contract was up, the demons came for you.

They came to drag you to hell.

Marlow had thought the risk was worth it, because it wasn't like your contract couldn't be cracked. The lawyers for the Fist—quantum mathematicians armed with the world's best technology—could undo the Hellraisers' deals with the Engine, they could free you up to fight another day. And the cost of not fighting the war . . . That was unthinkable. Because on the other side of this battle was a group called the Circle, armed with an Engine of their own, and all they wanted was to open the gates of hell and flood the streets with blood.

Not good.

Open your eyes.

He hadn't opened his eyes, though. He'd been blind to the

truth. The Fist had destroyed half of New York trying to get hold of the Circle's Engine, trying to end the war once and for all. But at the last minute they'd been betrayed—betrayed by the person Marlow had trusted most, his best friend, Charlie. Charlie had been working for the Circle all along, for their commander in chief, Mammon. He'd found a way inside the Fist's Engine, and he'd opened the door to their enemies. Mammon had obliterated most of the Fist in one blood-soaked swoop, and he had control of both Engines. As far as Marlow had known, as far as any of them had known, it was only a matter of time before Mammon united the Engines and opened the gateway to hell.

There had still been hope, though. One last chance to find the Engines, to win the war. And they did it. Together, he and Herc and Pan and the others had found the physical location of the Engine—inside the world's largest graveyard, beneath the streets of Paris. They'd found it, they'd entered it, and they'd been about to destroy it.

Except Mammon was already there, Mammon and Charlie and their army.

And they were already destroying it.

Open your eyes.

It had been too late to open them, too late to see what was really going on. Ostheim had always said that they were fighting to save the world, that Mammon was the bad guy. But Ostheim had been lying. *He* was the true force of evil, and they'd been doing his bidding. He'd followed them to the Engine, finally revealing his true form—a demonic creature of immense power. And right there, Ostheim had killed Mammon and taken control of the Engine.

And now the barrier between this world and the realm of the demons was about to crumble.

Open your eyes.

There had been no time to think, no time to see. They'd been so desperate to fix their mistakes, to undo the harm they'd caused, that they'd done exactly what Ostheim had wanted them to do. Mammon's dying gift to them had been a name: Meridiana, his sister. They'd fled the Engine and found her in Venice, a crazy woman stuck in a loop of time who had managed to build an Engine of her own. She'd offered to make them one final contract for powers to use in the fight against Ostheim—an unbreakable contract for a single soul—but Marlow and Pan had fallen into the Engine together, and made a deal side by side.

Armed with the ability to travel through space and time, they had found their way back to the Engine, to an instant in time where Mammon couldn't find them—an instant in time where they could pull the bastard machine to pieces. Meridiana had told them to find the heart of the Engine and destroy it. But their contract was corrupted, it was already unraveling, the demons were on their way.

It was over.

Open your eyes.

Why, though? Why would he do that? Why would he want to see? The demons had taken Pan first, had pulled her to pieces and dragged her soul into the molten earth. Then they'd come for him.

They'd shredded him.

Devoured him.

His soul had been ripped out of his body, pulled through the void, up and up and up and into the darkness.

Into *this* darkness. Endless, unfathomable.

This was hell, he knew—an eternity of nothing.

And he couldn't even scream.

"Marlow?"

The word was a whisper, right into his ear. He tried to turn his head, reached out for it with arms he didn't have. He wanted to laugh, wanted to cry, wanted to speak, but he could do nothing but listen, willing the voice to speak again. An eternity seemed to pass before it did.

"Marlow?"

Not a whisper this time but a voice, Pan's voice.

And she sounded pissed.

"Marlow," she said again. "You idiot."

Pan? he tried to say.

"Marlow, just open your eyes," said Pan. "You're not going to believe this."

Open your eyes.

The easiest thing in the world, the hardest thing in the world.

Just open your eyes, Marlow, he told himself.

And he did.

BORN AGAIN

This being hell, Marlow expected to see fire.

But when he opened his eyes, there was only snow.

It fell all around him, a blizzard of white against the dark, so furious that he had to screw his eyes shut again. He tried to lift a hand to his face but there was still that gaping absence where his body had once been.

"Open your eyes," said Pan, her voice grainy, like an old gramophone recording.

He did as she said and saw the snow again—only it wasn't snow, it was something else, something almost like static.

What's going on? he wanted to ask, but his lips were numb. Everything was numb. *Pan? I'm scared.*

He *was* scared. Not the adrenaline bomb of combat, not the cold-sweat shakes of a nightmare. This fear was so much older, and so much worse.

"Can you see me?" said Pan.

The snow was clearing, sunlight starting to burn through it. Marlow could just about make out shapes there, a person. The relief of it, of not being blind, of not being helpless in the dark, was almost as bright as the light. He lifted a hand again and was surprised this time to feel it respond.

What's going on? he tried to say, but what came out of his disobedient mouth was more, *Atooingon.* He tried to move his arm, tried to control it, grabbing hold of a fistful of what could have been dirt. He managed to blink, and again, each time the world swimming further into focus. There was a person there, sitting to his side, just a silhouette against the sky. He reached for her, and when the person slapped his hand away—hard—he pursed his lips and spat out a word.

"Pan."

He blinked again and suddenly the world was crystal clear. It was Pan, but she was different, somehow. He couldn't work out what it was because the sky behind her was so bright, shrouding her face with shadow.

"Marlow," she said, chewing on the word.

He looked down the length of his body. Most of his body, that was, because right now he ended at the knees.

He swore, a depth charge of panic exploding inside him. He tried to sit up but couldn't lift his head more than a couple of inches off the floor before his stomach muscles gave out. His mind was full of the demons who had torn him to bloody ribbons and he was lost in the memory of their fury, all teeth and claws and heat. They'd taken his feet, and what else? He groaned, staring at his legs—only to see that they were longer now, down to his shins.

They were growing.

"What the . . ."

Pan laughed, a sound as strange as birdsong. He peered down at his ankles as they materialized from nothing—or maybe not quite from nothing. He could see tiny threads being drawn from the ground around him, as thin as silk, white and red and earth-colored. They were being pulled into his flesh, knitted together into meat and bone.

"What's going on, Pan?" he asked. The words were still mangled, like he had a mouthful of caramel, but they were louder now. He coughed, testing the power of his lungs and sensing

9

no sign of his asthma. His legs had sprouted two feet, and they in turn were dividing into toes. He wiggled them and they responded, even as the last few threads spiraled around one another to form his nails.

His stomach cramped and he rolled onto his side, waiting for the agony to pulse its way out of him. Down here he could see that the ground wasn't made of gravel at all, it was bits and pieces of what could only be broken bone, fractured skull, powdered flesh. Ribbons of skin and muscle seemed to hold it all together. He could make out the gaping hole of an eye socket, hundreds of scattered teeth. He blew at a dusting of ash and saw a tube, made of glass and filled with a liquid that was almost black—a spatter of silver spots swimming in it. There was something else there, too, pieces of dark metal woven into the organic. They were moving, ever so subtly, the machinations of an Engine.

They were there in him, too, delicate traces of gunmetal gray and copper in his flesh. He held up his arm and they glinted in the light. Even now tiny filaments of metal and flesh were settling into whorls and shapes, like tribal tattoos. There was a sudden urge to dig in his nails and tear them out but he clamped his teeth together and forced himself to breathe. He traced his fingers along his forearm, feeling the tickle. Then he patted his hands down the length of his body to make sure everything was where it was supposed to be.

It was, and it was right there in the open for anyone to see.

Because he was stark naked.

"Oh," he said, slapping his hands to his crotch. His stomach muscles fluttered, threatening to cramp again. "Sorry."

Pan shrugged, circling him. When she caught the light he suddenly saw what it was about her that seemed different. Her body was too thin, hunched over like an arthritic old lady's. She was wearing a faded summer dress, something that might once have had flowers on it, but the skin on her legs looked too loose, as if she were wearing leg warmers. The sun shone through them, revealing crooked bones. She circled him, stalking like a vulture, making guttural noises in her throat as if trying to dislodge a string of meat.

"Pan," Marlow said. He put his knuckles to his mouth, chewing on skin that tasted like machine oil. "What's going on?"

"You really need me to tell you?" she said in that not-quite-right voice, staring over his shoulder. Her mouth curled into a tight smile, her eyes as big as moons as she said, "Look."

He did. They were halfway up a mountain of dead things, forged of bones packed so tightly together that they were as hard as concrete. Scraps of flesh and hair were caught between them, like an abattoir floor. More of those tubes and mechanical parts were embedded in the decay, and the ground beneath him seemed to thrum. Above him a lightning rod of black metal jutted up from the top of the mountain, piercing a sky that was too bright and too dark at the same time.

In front of him, too close for comfort, was a sheer cliff edge. Over it, stretching as far as he could see, was a landscape of ruin and decay. There were other mountains out there, towering cairns that might have been made up of human remains like the one he was sitting on, those antennae pointing skyward. They had to be a thousand yards tall, maybe twice that, maybe ten times that. It was impossible to tell because the air was thick with dust, great clouds of it kicked into storms by a soft, warm wind. It had already formed a coating on his new flesh, and he ran a finger along it, seeing that it wasn't dust at all but ash. He spat, waving it away from his face, squinting at the buildings that crowded between the hills. They might have been skyscrapers at one point, but that point had to have been centuries ago because they were little more than skeletons now.

"I don't get it," Marlow said, climbing to his knees, then on to legs that felt too brittle to hold his weight. "Where are we?"

Pan coughed the dust from her lungs, shaking her head.

"Do you really want to know?" she said, that weird noise filling her throat again. There was a flutter of movement inside Marlow's stomach, something squirming down there.

Something was wrong.

He snorted a humorless laugh. *Everything* was wrong. He had died. He'd been ripped apart by demons. His soul—or whatever you could call this part of him—had been dragged to hell, where he'd grown a new body out of the remains of a million dead. It was insane. It was impossible. The thought of it was a rat trying to claw its way out of the overheating bucket of his brain and for a moment he was lost in a maelstrom of panic. The world rocked off its axis and he straightened his arms to try to keep his balance. Deep breaths, in through the nose, out through the mouth, like his mom had always shown him, the oxygen like water on the fire of his panic. He waited for the rattle, for the gunk to flood his lungs the way it always did after a panic attack, but whatever his new body was made of evidently didn't suffer from the same weakness as the old one.

You may be in hell, Marlow, he told himself. *But at least you can breathe.*

The right side of his face was burning and he turned to see Pan watching him, her head cocked, her eyes wide. There it was again, the tickle of movement right in the middle of him.

"What?" he said.

"You're laughing," she replied. "Why?"

He chewed his knuckle again, feeling his teeth grate against a shard of metal beneath the skin. He was glad of the pain—it meant that this body, however weird it was, was his.

"I'm not," he said. "It's just . . ."

"Just what?" Pan asked when he didn't continue. She took a

12

lurching step toward him, her loose skin fluttering, one eye drooping. "Don't you like it here?"

"Like it?" Marlow asked. Pan took another step in his direction and he'd staggered back before he even knew it. He was conscious of the fact that he wasn't wearing a scrap of clothing, felt as vulnerable here as a newborn baby. The loose ground beneath him crumbled and he glanced down, the cliff edge too close. "What are you talking about, Pan? Why would I like it?"

When he looked up again she was even closer, close enough to touch, and she lifted a hand and rested it on his elbow. Whatever his new heart was made of, it was hammering at his ribs like an old engine—and Marlow wanted to put his foot down, get the hell out of here, because there was still something wrong with her, not something there but something *missing*.

"Pan?" he said when she didn't answer. He tried to step to the side only for her to step with him, her grip on his arm tightening. Her uneven eyes were huge and unblinking and he could see himself in their wetness, he could see a version of him that was not really him.

"This place, it isn't what you think. It's not as bad as we thought it would be." She smiled, her teeth small and neat and dirty. "I can make you like it, Marlow. I can make you happy here."

She leaned in, still grinning, and the sudden smell of her made him reel. It was sweet, almost too sweet—like rotten fruit. And there was something else just behind it, something that could have been sulfur.

"Pan," he pleaded. She leaned in closer and he arced his back, feeling the drop behind him, feeling like it was yawning open. His foot slid again, old bone exploding into powder beneath his heel then falling into the abyss.

"Everything else was a lie, Marlow," she said, her breath

impossibly hot on his face. "All of that other stuff, it never really mattered. There is only here, and only now, and only us."

Her mouth opened wide, too wide, a split appearing down the middle of her nose and in her chin like somebody was peeling her open with an invisible scalpel. There were more teeth there, lining the two halves of her face, needle sharp. He thought he caught a glimpse of metal, tiny components whirring like gears.

"Pan?" he yelled, and she cocked her head again, her eyes burning holes in him.

"Marlow," she said, her voice distorted by her broken face. She laughed, and it was like a mourning cry, like a dozen sobs all echoing from her throat. When she spoke next she spoke with more than one voice. "Why do you keep calling me Pan?"

HERE WE GO AGAIN

Pan pushed herself up, her foot skidding in the loose ash. Marlow was fifty yards away with the *thing* that looked like her, and it had just pounced on him. By the look of things, it was eating his face. She gripped the club in her fist—a two-foot-long femur bone with a heavy joint at the end—and ran.

Up ahead, Marlow was in serious trouble. The *other* her had opened up its head like a snake and was trying to swallow him whole. It was making gagging noises that she could hear even over the pounding of her feet, and beneath them an endless, muffled, awful scream from inside. Marlow was throwing wild punches at its body but the doppelgänger didn't even seem to feel them.

Twenty yards and Pan swung the bone up over her head. The creature must have heard her coming because it tried to turn and she caught a glimpse of her own head, split in two. She almost hesitated, some part of her unwilling to fight something so familiar, so impossible. *That's my face*, she thought, and the anger boiled inside her, driving her forward. She swung the club as she moved, arcing it down toward the creature's back.

It hit like a demolition ball, a crack that echoed off the mountainside and out over the cliff. The other her folded awkwardly, collapsing, pulling Marlow down with it. His head was completely inside its gaping mouth and he obviously couldn't breathe in there because he was kicking like a drowning man.

"Hang on!" she yelled at him, lifting the club again. She never got the chance to swing, because suddenly the doppelgänger was moving, its arms and legs working like a spider's as it scuttled backward. Its tissue-thin skin was tearing, revealing something black beneath, as hard as a beetle's carapace. Black and metallic.

It moved fast, Marlow dragged behind it. It was still trying to swallow him, its whole body writhing with peristalsis as it forced him down. And all the time it kept those eyes—the same eyes she'd seen in the mirror every single day of her life—on her.

She bolted after it, chasing it up the slope. Even with Marlow gripped in its jaws it was too fast for her, cutting crablike to the side. Another few seconds and it would lose her in the contours of the mountainside. She dug deep, her lungs like bucking mules inside her chest.

Come on, come on.

The thing zigged one way, expecting her to follow, but she broke right, catching it as it changed direction. She swung wildly, the knuckled tip of the thigh bone catching its arm and causing it to collapse. One of Marlow's shoulders was lost in the cavern of its mouth, its throat bulging obscenely as it worked him down. He wasn't moving anymore.

"Marlow!"

She lifted the bone again and brought it down on the doppelgänger's back, the noise like she'd struck a fire hydrant. She heard its squeal even past the blockage and she hit it again, her arm muscles burning with the effort. It was choking now, panicking.

"Die!" she screamed at it, hitting it again, and again. "Just die, you mother—"

It retched, regurgitating Marlow from its throat.

He slid free—a lump of wet meat—and the thing scuttled away, its metal parts glinting. It took one last look at her, its mouth a grotesque open sack, its tongue hanging out like old rope. Then it pushed its face into the ground and tunneled like a digging dog, vanishing.

Somehow Pan found the strength to move, crawling to Marlow's side and placing a hand on his neck. His skin was streaked with layers of dark metal, *Engine* metal, but there was no sign of gears, no moving parts. She pressed her fingers there, searching for a pulse.

Nothing. Nothing. Nothing.

"Come on," she said, using her other hand to pound his chest.

Nothing. Nothing. Nothing.

"Come on!" she yelled. "You're not leaving me here alone again!"

Nothing. Nothing. Thump.

He sat up, a spray of black fluid erupting from his mouth. His hands grabbed her, fingers gouging her skin, and for a second she thought she'd been tricked, that this wasn't really Marlow at all but another doppelgänger.

His eyes, though. His eyes were copper pennies, glinting, but so full of terror that there could be no doubt. Those eyes were human.

"Hey, hey," she said, both hands clutching his shoulders. "Hey, Marlow, it's me."

She didn't exactly blame him for not believing her.

"It's me," she said again.

Marlow was hauling in breaths like he was having an asthma attack, shuffling backward. If he wasn't careful, he was going to end up retreating off the cliff.

"It's me," she said again. "Pan. Your name is Marlow Green,

17

uh, I met you on Staten Island, you lived with your mom, your brother's name was Danny."

Marlow slowed. His face was slick with gunk, his hair plastered to his scalp. Flecks of iron glinted darkly, his irises burning machine-bright. He gulped, then shook his head.

"I don't believe you," he said. "That . . . that whatever the hell it was, it knew stuff, too."

"It didn't know you snore like a warthog," she said. "It didn't know that you were jealous of a Frenchman called Taupe. It didn't know that the first time you tried to kiss me I kneed you in the family jewels. Hard."

He lifted a hand to his mouth, biting his knuckle like he hadn't eaten in a week. But she could see the way his body relaxed, she could hear the gentling of his breaths.

"Technically *you* kissed *me*," he said eventually, his voice shaking.

He managed a smile, and for an instant she thought about kicking him off the cliff herself. Instead, she did something that took her by surprise, something she didn't even know was happening until she'd thrown herself to her knees and wrapped her hands around him. He fought her for all of a second, then she felt his arms around her, squeezing, and suddenly her body was betraying her again. She buried her head into his neck, into the disgusting sulfur stench of him, and she began to cry.

"I didn't think you were coming," she said, or tried to say. The sobs were too powerful. "I thought I was going to be . . . I thought—"

"Hey," he said, and she realized that he was crying too. "Hey, Pan, it's okay."

She wasn't sure how long they stayed like that, bound to each other in hell. It could have been a minute, it could have been forever. It was Marlow that started to pull free, and she wasn't sure if she could let him go.

"Sorry," he said. "It's just that you're kneeling on my leg and it's really painful."

She was, she saw, her knee planted in his shin. She rolled away, pushing herself to her feet just to prove that she was still capable of standing. Marlow held out his hand and she hauled him up, both of them smudging tears from their faces. She tried not to notice the fact that he was naked.

"Better?" she asked when she could find her voice again. He spluttered a laugh.

"Oh, yeah, sure," he said. "Never been better, Pan."

"What happened back there," she said. "You did it, right? You destroyed the Engine."

"In the ten seconds after they took you?" he replied. "Even I'm not that good, Pan."

She frowned.

"What are you talking about? Ten seconds?"

"The demons came for you, Pan," Marlow said. "They tore you to pieces."

"Yeah," Pan said, "but that was, like, a day ago."

She had no way of knowing for sure, of course, because this place—wherever it was—seemed to flick from day to night in a heartbeat. But it had certainly felt like a day.

"What?" Marlow said, shaking his head. "No, Pan, it was just now. Minutes."

Pan blew out a long breath, staring over the edge of the cliff. It didn't make sense, but then nothing that had happened in the last few weeks—few years—made any sense. Marlow took a step toward her but she held out her hand to stop him.

"I thought you might have destroyed it," she said. "I thought that's why . . . I thought maybe it's why you . . ."

She couldn't bring herself to say it and the unspoken words hung in the air before her. *I thought that's why you hadn't come.*

Because she'd spent the last day thinking she was alone here. Thinking that she would be alone for the rest of time.

"Herc and Charlie are still there," Marlow said. "They might be able to end it."

"Without contracts?" Pan said, shaking her head. "You and I made the deal to travel between, to stop time. Without us I think they'd have been pulled back into the present, into the Engine. They'd have ended up right in his lap."

Ostheim. If that was true, then he'd have murdered them without a second thought. Marlow wiped his eyes again, staring out to the distant horizon.

"A day," he said. "You see anything?"

"Sure," she snapped back. "I read the guidebook. Checked out some sights, bought a snow globe with a demon in it." She took a shuddering breath as she looked out over the landscape of ruin. "Look, I appeared here, same way you did: the ground, I don't know, *making* me." She clenched her fists. The thought of it, of those little threads that had woven her from the dirt, from the black liquid inside those glass tubes, made her want to scream the world away. "I didn't do much. *Couldn't* do much. It was all too . . . I don't know. Then it got dark. I spent the night here, and the next day I started exploring. Didn't go far, I kept coming back, just in case . . ."

"In case what?" Marlow asked.

"In case you, somebody, *anybody*, showed up," she said. "Far as I can tell, this place is, I don't know, it's a city, long dead."

"A city?" asked Marlow. "So we're on Earth? Did you see any landmarks, anything we can use?"

She squinted at him through the dust. Then she turned to the horizon, to a distant smudge of darkness that polluted the sky like an oil slick.

"I saw . . . *something.*"

A noise broke the silence of the hillside, a rattle of gravel and bone. Pan flinched, scanning the rocky terrain, expecting to see another her or another Marlow walk toward them, smiling. She searched the ground, found the femur, and hefted it up.

"We should go," she said quietly. "This place, it's not nice. Not even close."

"You have any idea what this place even is?" he asked as she started walking, her bare feet crunching through bones, through skulls, tatters of skin caught between her toes. How many dead were here? How many corpses did it take to make a mountain? She thought of the creatures that squirmed down there, wearing stolen faces, ready to open their mouths and swallow her whole.

"Hell," she said. "How could it be anything but hell?"

PUT SOME DAMN CLOTHES ON

"Look, I don't want to lower the tone or anything, Marlow, but you do realize you're naked?"

Marlow ignored the question, staring at Pan, studying her properly for the first time. Like the imposter that had tried to eat him, she was made up of layers of flesh and metal, her skin streaked and striated like she'd been chipped from the wall of a copper mine. Her face was her face, but marbled by a diagonal streak of dark metal that stretched down her cheek and over her chin. In one hand she still held that leg bone, swinging it with every step. She was wearing a white tee and jeans that looked like they were held together by a hope and a prayer.

It was a good look.

He half thought about covering himself up but the honest truth was that it didn't seem to matter anymore. He was in hell. He was doomed to an eternity of suffering. Clothes didn't exactly seem like a priority. All the same, he angled himself away from Pan, asking, "So, where'd you get the T-shirt and jeans?"

She looked down at herself, brushing a cloud of dust from the shirt.

"Found them," she said. "Just lying there. There's stuff all over. Must have belonged—"

She cut herself off and Marlow finished the sentence in his head.

To the dead.

"Look, just put this on, yeah?" she said, tugging something free from the dirt and lobbing it at him. He snatched it, hard enough to release a halo of dust, shaking it out to reveal a section of gray cloth. It was filthy, and greasy to the touch, but he wrapped it around his middle like a beach towel just so that Pan would stop staring awkwardly at the horizon.

"Thanks," he said. "Where were you at Christmas? It's what I always wanted, a loincloth from a dead man."

He looked at the corpse Pan had pulled it from, nothing left of it but a knotted section of spine and half a pelvic bone. He rubbed his throat, grimacing. It hurt to move, hurt to swallow, hurt to breathe. He'd almost been one of the dead too, swallowed into that awful, airless, crushing dark. One of the *deader than dead*, really, because he wasn't sure how that really worked when you were in hell. He glanced at Pan, still wary. He had no idea if it was actually her but this one *seemed* right. And what choice did he have? Anything was better than the thought of being here alone.

She started walking again and Marlow followed. Every other step his bare foot would plunge ankle-deep into the bone dust, shards embedding themselves in his skin. He stood on those glass tubes, too, releasing gouts of black fluid that was as dark as ink. Pan was leading them along the edge of the cliff and now the path they were on—if you could call it a path, because it was just another section of crushed bone—sloped eagerly downward. He wasn't sure how long they'd been walking. Time was slow here, treacle thick. It felt a hundred degrees hotter. Marlow wiped his brow but it was bone-dry up there.

"I know," said Pan. "No sweat. Weird, right?"

"It'll save money on antiperspirant."

Pan stopped, planting her hands on her hips.

"Marlow, you seem pretty chill about this whole 'going to hell' thing."

He blew a laugh from his nose, but there wasn't much humor in it. Pan was right. He should have been rolling on the floor screaming away the last of his sanity. But the truth was his brain was doing a remarkable job of taking it in its stride. This was weird, yes. But he'd seen weirder. He'd seen *worse*.

"Hey," he said with a shrug. "This is bad, but it's gotta be better than the old 'hood back on Shaolin, right?"

Her frown deepened.

"You're nuts," she said.

"You don't have to be crazy to work here," he said with an insane giggle, "but it helps. Besides, you're not exactly losing it."

"I . . ." she started, then shook the words away. He didn't push it. He didn't need to. Pan had arrived here alone, nobody to talk her through the horror, nobody to hold her. He couldn't imagine what she must have gone through when she first opened her eyes. That was it, he realized, the reason he felt so calm: that no matter where they were, no matter what would happen next, Pan was here. She wiped a hand over her face, her whole body shaking. Then she looked up at the sky. It was bright, even though the sun was hidden behind the clouds of ash.

"It's going to get dark soon, I think," said Pan. "We shouldn't be outside."

"You got somewhere to go?" he asked.

She stuck out the femur bone, pointing at the city below. They were low enough now for Marlow to make out the streets, or what was left of them. Most were hidden by sweeping dunes of dark ash and buried in shadow from the ruined towers. Bands of black dissected the view, huge snakelike constructions that might have been pipes or conduits, stretching as far as he could see, converging on the horizon, ending beneath a distant, darker cloud. There was a hum in the air, he suddenly noticed, one that seemed to make his entire skull vibrate. He stuck a finger in his ear, wiggling, but the noise was coming from all around him.

There was a smell, too. The familiar, gagging stench of sulfur.

"There," Pan said, pointing to a cluster of skeletal shapes. There was something red fluttering between the white, reminding him of the scraps of meat in the teeth of the creature that had tried to eat him.

"What?" he said, then, understanding, "Wait, you want me to *wear* it?"

"Marlow, that towel is going to come off any minute. You either put some clothes on or watch me gouge my own eyes out."

"Nice," he said, blushing as he hopped across the path and pulled the cloth free. It was a pair of shorts, covered in stains from substances he had no desire to identify. "Really?" he said, holding them up to Pan.

"Really."

He stepped into them, tightening the drawstring. Trapped beneath the same collection of old bones was another scrap of cloth, this one harder to retrieve. It came free with a tear and he held it up like a tattered sail—a T-shirt, the logo faded beyond recognition. He was just pulling it on when there was a rattle behind them, toward the top of the slope. Pieces of bone pattered down around his feet. Pan held up a hand, holding them both in silence for a full minute.

"Come on," she whispered, stepping past him and walking swiftly down the hill. He ran after her and they made their way without speaking, both of them casting nervous glances back up the vast, shadowed bulk of the mountain. There was no sign of anything living up there, but the slope was pocked with craters and hills. His skin was crawling, too, like there were eyeballs pressed right up against his flesh.

25

He didn't know how much longer it was when he skidded down the last section of the hill, skulls and bones skittering out across a cracked and broken street. Pan had been right, it was getting darker, the shadows growing longer. The generator hum in the air was louder now, like he had a bumblebee inside his head.

"You feeling that?" he asked Pan.

She nodded, grimacing. "Was the same last night," she said. "It gets weirder."

"Got any idea where to go?"

She nodded toward the nearest building. It was an immense concrete corpse, its crumbling flesh pierced by huge shards of steel all the way up to where its top floors were shielded by the smoke.

"That place looks . . . *wrong*," he said.

Something screamed, the noise distant but still somehow deafening. Marlow pressed himself up against Pan before he even knew what he was doing. She didn't move away, and he could feel her tremble. The shriek came again, closer this time, then again from another direction, and only then did Marlow recognize what he was hearing.

"Demons," he said, and Pan nodded.

"They come out in the night," she said quietly. "There were hundreds of them."

"Great," he muttered.

Three more screams, and the streets were darkening at an alarming rate. He didn't know much about this place, but it didn't take a genius to work out that if they got stranded outside then bad things were going to happen. The building was a hundred yards away, behind one of the snaking pipelines that crossed the city. The pipe was as tall and as thick as a car, a knotted cord of metal rings and tubes and fleshy parts that looked almost like muscle. Marlow put his hand on an exposed section and the hum inside his head seemed to double in strength, pulsing. A supernova of darkness exploded in his vision, a darkness that coiled like snakes, that parted to reveal a figure there, as big as a mountain—one that watched him with a cluster of insect eyes.

It was like something was pulling him, or part of him at least—a magnet trying to tease out the shrapnel in his skin, in his muscles, in his organs. He snapped his hand free, staring at Pan. She had clamped her hand under her armpit, her body spasming like she'd had an electric shock.

"You see that?" she said.

"I *felt* it," he answered. "Is there another way around?"

A shriek answered him, coming from close behind. He searched the rubble, seeing nothing, turning back to see Pan lobbing the femur over the top of the pipe. She followed it, yelping as she dropped down the other side. He sucked in a lungful of air and climbed, ignoring the pain, ignoring the figure who thumped into his head. He jumped, landing on a pillow of ash. As soon as he let go of the conduit his skull stopped buzzing, but it felt like it had left a mark there, greasy fingerprints on his thoughts. He shook it away to see that he was at the base of a drift that covered the lower floors of the tower.

"Hurry," said Pan, already scaling the slope. He started after her, struggling with the effort.

It was almost dark by the time they scrabbled through the broken window and onto solid ground. Marlow leaned against the frame, seeing that they were in a large space that could once have been an open-plan office. It was completely empty.

"Where now?" he panted.

She didn't answer, but Marlow could see her shrug, her body an ink spill against the dark. He heard her shuffle closer, felt her press against him, and he fumbled through the night, found her hand. He squeezed, and she squeezed back.

"I'm glad," she whispered into his ear. "I'm glad you're here."

"Glad I got torn to pieces and sent to hell," he said. "Jeez, thanks, Pan."

Her other hand slapped him across the shoulder and he had to stifle a laugh, pinching his nose to hold it at bay. Even so, it still came out as a wet snort. It seemed crazy, that he was having to hold back laughter, but then how else were you supposed to fight? It was the only weapon he had here.

"I take it back," Pan said, letting go of his hand. He could still hear the fear in her voice but it was quieter now. It had lost some of its power. "I'm *not* glad."

A fresh round of screams had started up outside and he waited until they had died down before speaking again.

"What now?"

"Nothing," she said. "The dark, it's . . . it's like some kind of wild dream, Marlow. A nightmare. You can't see anything. But I don't think they can either. If we're quiet, they might not be able to find us."

"Sit still, be quiet," said Marlow. "That sounds like one of Herc's plans."

This time it was Pan who breathed a laugh, but it was short-lived. Marlow wondered where the old guy was now, whether he was still alive. Charlie, too, and Truck, abandoned in Venice. He half hoped they'd all show up here the way that he had—better to enter hell with an army by your side, right? But none of them had been under contract. If they had died, they'd have gone somewhere else, or nowhere at all.

Outside, a demon howled—the sound half pig squeal and half death rattle—too close.

"It won't be long," Pan said. "Night here isn't like back home. Just be quiet, just stay in the dark, and they won't find us."

And the words were still leaving her mouth when the sky began to burn.

THE WALL

It burst up from the horizon, a wave of flame that could have been an oil fire. The inferno burned across the sky, so low that it engulfed the tops of the skyscrapers in whirling, spitting vortexes. The heat was unbearable, like sitting underneath a grill, and Pan covered her head with her hands, curling up beneath its spitting, crackling fury, beneath its unending thunder.

It wasn't the noise and the heat that worried her, though.

It was the *light*.

The world was bathed in it, brighter than the day. It seared its way through the broken windows of the high-rise like a searchlight. The city was picked out in shades of orange and red, echoes of the fire rippling across its surface. Above, the sky burned like the surface of the sun, choked with smoke. Molten energy burst from the chaos, dripping down to earth and forming glowing pools on the asphalt, revealing the shapes that moved there.

Demons. The city crawled with them. Twisted forms of bone and muscle, some with two legs, some with three or four or five or more. From here she couldn't make out their faces, thankfully, but she could see enough to know that they had no eyes, just those cement-mixer mouths lined with shark teeth. They seemed to be reveling in the raging sky, bounding wildly across the scorched earth, screaming into the smoke. Whenever two demons crossed paths they would fight, pounding each other until one either collapsed or retreated. Pan could hear the thump and slap of their heavy paws even over the groaning skies.

"Did this happen last night?" Marlow asked. His face was a mask of light, the fire reflected in the metallic sheen of his eyes, in the ribs of metal that carved through his face. She shook her head.

No. This was something new.

He said something else, lost beneath the noise. But she got the drift.

We need to move.

She glanced through the window again, the demons teeming from the earth like ants—too many to even begin to count them. They had no eyes, but that didn't mean they couldn't hunt.

Marlow tugged at her and they crawled away from the window, into the interior of the building. Her muscles were cramping from the weight of the weapon she held, and she shifted it to her other hand. There was a concrete shaft up ahead for the elevator, and once she was clear she got to her feet and ran for it. To the side of the elevator was another door and she shouldered it open, seeing the stairwell. Light burned in from above, but the steps leading down were drenched in darkness, as if the night had crawled down there to hide.

"Down?" said Marlow, and she could hear the doubt in his voice.

She answered by leading the way, stepping cautiously onto the first step, her foot slipping on the layer of ash that covered it. Marlow walked by her side, closing the door gently behind him and plunging them into a muffled quiet. She held her breath, waiting for a scream, for any sign of life down there, and when there was only silence she carried on.

Now that her eyes had shaken off the afterglow of the outside she noticed that there was a little light in here, just a whisper on the walls and floor. When she turned the bend in the stairwell it was stronger, and she could make out the outline of the door that led into the floor below. Marlow pushed the bar but it was wedged tight, and he braced himself, shunting. She joined him, the door opening an inch, then two, ash pouring through the bottom of the widening crack. It had to be a foot thick on the other side, but together they managed to create a gap big enough to let them pass.

She let Marlow go first, her whole body tense, waiting for a shape to pounce from the shadows, to sink its teeth into him. But after a moment he beckoned her in.

"Seems safe," he said. "It's dark, anyway."

She pushed through the door into a space identical to the one above. The only difference was that this floor was beneath the dunes that had formed outside. Mounds of ash shielded all but the very tops of the windows, letting through fingers of firelight that reached maybe a dozen yards. They muted the screams, too. She took a step, her foot sinking into the soft ground.

"Pan," said Marlow.

"What?" she replied, working her way around the elevator shaft.

"What?" said Marlow.

She turned to him, just a smudge of shadow fringed by firelight.

"What?" she asked.

"Pan," he said again, and this time she froze, because the voice hadn't come from Marlow at all, but from another part of the room.

Somebody else was calling her name.

She half thought about running, but what was the point? If they stepped outside they were dead anyway. She gripped the bone, swinging it lightly from side to side. If it was one of the doppelgängers, then at least she knew she could stave its head in.

"Who's there?" she said.

"We are." The voice was a whisper—no, it was a *hundred* whispers, so quietly spoken that it was like a pulse of alien noise. "We have been hiding. We have been waiting for you."

She glanced at Marlow, just to make sure he was still there. She could see the whites of his eyes hovering in the gloom, wide and frightened. She nodded, willing him to go first.

"Hey, it's your party," he said. "You're the one they're waiting for."

"We have been waiting for you both," the voice said, then it shaped his name from a legion of rasping whispers. "Marlow."

"Great," he muttered.

"It is safe here," it said. "We are hidden. He cannot find us."

Pan stared into the dark, trying to work out who was speaking. But nothing was there, just the open space of the office and then the far wall, everything filthy with dirt and ash and buried in darkness.

"You can hide here, too," the voice said. "Come, join us."

No stampeding feet, no growls, no screams. Whatever was over there, she was pretty sure it would have attacked them by now if it had any plans to. She stumbled forward, her feet sinking into the ash, kicking up great clouds of it that filled her mouth, her lungs.

"Pan," said Marlow. She ignored him, squinting into the shadows, still no sign of who was there. Another step away from the elevator shaft. She felt like a boat that had pushed itself away from shore, drifting into the moonless night.

"Who are you?" she asked again. "What is this place?"

This time there was laughter, soft and yet deafening, like the drum of rain on a tin roof.

"You know what this place is," it said when the laughter had passed.

Another step, and the far wall was visible now. There was something growing there, like ivy. Pan could just about discern the contours of it, etched in the light from outside. It seemed to be rustling gently, as if there were a wind. The air here was perfectly still, though, and a creeping sense of unease began to burrow out from the center of her.

"This place is your home now, too," it said. "But he doesn't have to have you. You can hide here with us. It is safe here. It will always be safe here."

"Pan," Marlow said again, but she kept walking. She didn't think she could stop. The closer she got to the wall, the more movement she saw there, as if it were itching with spiders, thousands of them scuttling over and over and over one another. But they weren't spiders, because she could see something else in the faint glow from the windows—countless pale white circles.

It was only when she took one last step, the wall now a stone's throw away, that she realized they were eyes.

"Welcome," the voices said. "We are glad you are here."

It wasn't a wall of brick and plaster, of steel and stone. It was a wall of *flesh*. People hung from it like creepers, their bodies peeled open and woven together so that it was impossible to tell where one ended and another began. Internal organs drooped like heavy figs, ready to be plucked, glistening in the muted firelight. Limbs, withered into vines, twitched and swung with deranged excitement, fingers clasping feebly.

It was the faces, though, that made Pan's blood run river cold. There were a hundred of them, maybe twice that, most of them crushed beneath the vegetative weight of all those bodies. Cheeks bulged, cracked eye sockets leaked fluid, distended mouths hung open like shopping bags, some stuffed with arms and legs and intestines and whatever else had grown there. The eyes stared at her, unblinking, rimmed by dust so thick it might have been mascara.

"We are glad that you are here," it—*they*—said again, the mouths moving as one, the bodies trembling as one, the eyes staring as one. A shudder ran through Pan, one that made her feel as if her own body would start to unravel, as if her skin would slough right off her bones.

"Please," she said, because it was the only word she had. *Please tell me who you are. Please let me go. Please don't let me be in hell anymore. Please just put me out of my misery, let me die and stay dead.* She didn't even know which thing she wanted more.

"What happened to you?" Marlow said, speaking for her in a voice made of dust.

Another laugh, the faces choking on it, the eyes opening so wide they looked ready to roll right out, to patter onto the floor.

"We were like you, once," they said. "We used the Engine."

"No," said Pan, taking a step away from them.

"Our fate is your fate is our fate is your fate is our fate," they said, the words rolling over each other. "The demons came for us, they brought us to hell, and now we hide here."

"They're Engineers," said Marlow.

"But why?" Pan said, ignoring him. "I mean . . . it doesn't make sense. What happened to you?"

"For the first years we roamed," said the faces in a voice made of a thousand breaths. "We tried to find a way out, the way that you will try to find a way out. But you cannot leave this place. There is nothing else but this. So instead we hid."

"From who?" Pan asked, and at this the faces fell into motion, shaking themselves as if they meant to rip free of the wall. They all began to gibber—not as one, this time, but individually, the sound threatening to drown her. The voices shook and shuddered themselves back into one:

"From him. From him. From him."

A scream, from outside, and hundreds of eyeballs slid wetly that way in their sockets.

"They must not hear us," they said, more quietly this time.

"Pan, let's go," said Marlow. But there was so much she didn't understand, so much she needed to know.

"You're Engineers," she said, thinking of the *Book of Dead Engineers* that had once sat in the Bullpen, back home, back in another world. How many names had been inscribed inside that book, in those countless pages? Thousands of them, all men and women and children who had made a deal with the Engine and lost everything in the process.

"This place is hell," the wall said. "It is our punishment. Our souls were sent here, but a soul cannot exist without flesh, so the mountains grow us, over and over again. You cannot die here, Pan. Whatever you do, however you try to end it, you will come back. This place is a prison of souls, and yours will lie here forever."

The groan climbed her throat and spilled between her lips. She was shaking her head, as if it might scare away the madness that was already frothing there.

"How long?" she found herself asking. "How long have you been here?"

At this the wall broke into chaos again, each face screaming out its own answer. The noise was like a tide but she could still hear them, she could still hear those individual cries—*eight hundred years, a millennium, a hundred millennia*—before the cacophony collapsed into itself again.

"There is no time here," they said. "There is only now, there is only forever."

And the laugh that spilled from those bloodless lips almost pushed her over the edge. An eternity here. It couldn't be real, it couldn't be happening, not to her.

Please God please God please God please God.

"He will not help you here," they said, reading her thoughts. "Only we can help you. Come."

A hundred withered arms began to twitch away from the wall, stretching out toward her like iron filings to a magnet, fingers trembling with the effort.

"Come, Pan. Come, Marlow. We will keep you safe. In time you will not know enough to suffer."

Woven into this forest of the damned, hanging there in the dark, in that web of cold flesh. Pan felt as though her mind might boil itself into nothing.

"Come," the faces said. "He will not find you here."

A hand snaked up from the ash beneath her, sapling thin, just two fingers attached to the gnarled palm. It pinched the skin of her leg and she staggered away, the fingernails peeling off like they were dead leaves. One of them stuck to her and she brushed it away.

"No," she said.

More limbs were breaking free, feeling for her. She stepped in something beneath the ash, felt a toothless jaw gnawing at her heel, two milky eyes watching her. She'd stamped down before she even knew it, feeling the crack of brittle bone.

"No," she kept on saying, like the word might be powerful enough to wipe it all away.

"Yes," said the faces. "The answer is always yes, eventually. Because the alternative is *him*."

Another hand around her leg and this time she couldn't hold it in anymore. The scream was a living thing, one that climbed up inside her and clawed its way from her mouth, unleashed with the full force of her terror. It filled the room, it seemed loud enough to shake the building, and even when it dried up its echo chased itself from wall to wall to wall, growing louder, louder, as if it meant to find its way back to her.

No, it wasn't her scream she was hearing, not anymore. A shriek tore in through the window, followed by a blade of fire-light. Something was up there, a knotted lump of tooth and claw that pushed its ugly muzzle inside and sniffed. As one, all of the heads on the wall snatched in a breath, then broke into fits of panic.

"Oh no," said Marlow as the demon started to claw at the ash, widening the gap and revealing that burning sky above. Another demon appeared in the next window, howling, and before Pan could take another breath they were swarming inside on a wave of fire.

FEEDING TIME

The first demon lost its balance, rolling through the window in a cloud of ash, landing awkwardly. It kicked out with five stunted legs, scattering dust. By the time it was back on its feet the second creature had fallen in after it, this one bounding toward Marlow and Pan—its mouth big enough to swallow them whole.

"Go!" Pan yelled.

Marlow didn't need to be told twice, but when he turned to bolt his feet slipped on the ash and he crunched onto all fours. Something wormed up from the dune beneath him, a hand as thin as rope, fingers snatching at his T-shirt. He tried to shake it loose but its grip was surprisingly strong, ratcheting him down, down, until he was pressed against the dirt. There was another face there, half hidden, just a mouth that opened and closed like it wanted to kiss him. Marlow twisted his head away, breathed in a lungful of ash and rot. He pounded at the floor, at the arm, at anything he could reach. Behind him he could hear the drum of feet as the demons closed in, a scream razoring into his skull.

He braced himself, but it wasn't teeth he felt in his flesh, it was fingers—grabbing a fistful of his shirt and skin and hauling him back up. Pan, grunting with the effort of lifting him. She kicked the arm and it snapped in two, dropping limply.

There was another scream right behind them and Marlow

looked back to see a demon on their heels. It pounced, teeth glinting in the fire, and Marlow reacted before he could even think about what he was doing—shunting Pan to one side then diving to the other. The demon passed between them, landed, turned, then it was running back with Marlow in its sights.

"Hey!" Pan yelled, tossing him the bone she was carrying. Marlow reached for it, fumbled, the bone cracking off his fingertips and spinning away. The demon was distracted by Pan's call, reaching her in a heartbeat.

"No!" Marlow shouted, snatching up the femur and running.

He swung the bone, striking the demon on the back of its head just as it was lunging for her. He hit it again, the bone shattering as it made contact. The demon snarled, bucked its body to try to turn. Marlow jumped on it, a shard of bone clasped in his fingers. He jabbed the blade into the demon's neck, and again, a gout of black blood steaming into the room. By the time he'd stabbed it a third time its movements were starting to slow, its jaw flexing weakly.

He looked up, seeing that the second demon had thrown itself at the wall of people, tearing at the bodies there, at the faces. The air was thick with screams and they were drawing more guests to the party—two more demons clambering over the dunes and tumbling into the building.

"Marlow!"

Pan was still on the floor but there were limbs snaking up on either side of her, wrapping themselves around her chest and stomach like seaweed. They were trying to pull her into the ash, trying to drown her, and it was working, her body sinking fast. Marlow dropped to his knees and grabbed at them, tearing, wrenching, then he took Pan's hands and pulled. She screamed as one of the faces bit into her leg, teeth gouging through flesh until she kicked herself free.

"Can you make it?" he said.

"Yeah," she grunted.

He slung her hand over his shoulder and she limped beside him. They were halfway to the elevator, digging a trench through the ash. Behind them was nothing but noise—tearing flesh, gargled shrieks.

Marlow couldn't stop himself from looking back. There were six demons there now, more still pouring through. They were all attacking the wall, crunching heads, tearing off limbs, gouging stomachs and chests—a feeding frenzy of the dead and the damned. And all the while the room shook and shook and shook with the sound of their screams.

But at least, for now, the demons had forgotten them.

Marlow spilled against the wall of the elevator shaft, drew in a shaky breath of smoke and misted blood. Pan's face was as gray as old cloth, and for an instant, when she turned to him, her eyes started to roll up in their sockets. He slapped her cheek, bringing her back, carrying her to where the door still stood open.

He pushed her through, looked once more to the chaos behind him. Some of the demons had turned his way, nuzzling the air with their eyeless faces. He stepped into the stairwell, happy to leave the screams behind him, but then he glanced back again, suddenly making sense of what he was hearing.

The people on the wall, the Engineers, they weren't screaming at all.

They were *laughing*.

Marlow stumbled through the door, trying to close it behind him. There was too much ash in the way, though. Pan was sitting on the step clutching her leg, her face a rictus of agony. There was a jagged wound in her calf and it was bleeding badly, but nothing was spurting out—which had to be a good thing, right? Marlow pulled off his T-shirt, rolling it into a tourniquet. He ducked down, tying it as tight as he could beneath her knee.

"I hope . . ." Pan started, clearing her throat. "I hope that's sterile."

He doubled the knot, then helped her to her feet.

"We'd better hurry," she said.

"They're not interested in us," he replied, "they're eating those . . . whatever they were."

"Yeah?"

He checked back through the open door, his reply on the tip of his tongue, held there by the sight of three of the demons sniffing at the corpse of the one he had killed. One opened its mouth and howled, then turned to Marlow, its monstrous jaw flexing.

"Actually you're right," he said. "We should probably hurry."

Pan grabbed hold of the banister, looping her other arm tight around his neck as she hopped up the steps. They'd only just made it to the first bend when something threw itself against the door below. The demon had a paw through the gap but fortunately its bulk was in the way and it was too stupid to know that it needed to pull. Another demon hurled itself against the door and the first one squealed, pulling its paw free. Then they both charged, and the door slammed shut.

Thank you, said Marlow to no one, to everyone.

They reached the floor they'd entered through and Marlow pushed open the stairwell door. The fury of heat and movement from outside the windows was so sudden that he'd taken a step before he noticed there was something inside. He only caught a glimpse of it—a lumbering shape of muscle, too tall to be a demon, its face too human, dark eyes blinking wetly—before Pan pulled him back, gently closing the door.

"You saw that?" he whispered, and she nodded.

"It's nothing good."

They struggled up the steps to the next floor, every muscle in Marlow's body aching like he had hot coals stitched beneath his skin. The sound of hammering from below was growing more urgent—even with the steel plates in the fire doors he didn't think they'd last long against an onslaught like that.

"You got a plan?" he asked Pan as they rounded the bend. She was so pale she was almost invisible against the wall, and she left bloody footprints on every step.

"Just . . . keep . . . moving," she said, pulling in a desperate breath between each word.

He did just that, reaching the next level and pushing open the door. It was another huge room, only here the floor was free of all but a dusting of ash. The inferno burning in the sky seemed more intense than ever. Marlow hunkered low as he crossed the threshold, Pan peeling away from him and crashing down onto her ass.

"You think—" he started, cut off by a splintering crunch from below. "Oh crap, I think they're through."

"You realize," wheezed Pan, "that *oh crap* doesn't really capture the full gravity of this situation?"

"Sorry," he said, hearing the slap of feet. "*Crappity* crap."

"Better," she said, holding out her hand and letting him pull her up. Marlow closed the door, searching for something to wedge it shut. But there was literally nothing up here. Pan was making her way painfully to the nearest window, and Marlow jogged after her. They looked out onto an upside-down world— the sky like a roiling ocean, the buildings below choked in clouds of smoke. It took Marlow's breath away. It would have been beautiful, he thought, if it wasn't so terrifying.

"What now?" he asked.

"We jump."

"You're crazy," he said, "that's like, I don't know, forty feet. There's no way I'm—"

The door behind them exploded open, a frenzied shape of flesh and teeth bursting through. The demon sniffed at them, then unleashed a bellow of rage from the cavern of its mouth. Then it was running, its claws churning up the concrete floor.

Death by falling, or death by mauling. It wasn't exactly the best—

Pan's hands connected with his back and suddenly he was out the window. His stomach ejected from his mouth and he couldn't even pull in a breath to scream with. There was just the ground, then the burning sky, then the ground, rushing toward him like a freight train.

He thumped into the dune headfirst, plunging into a suffocating mattress of ash. There was an instant of relief before he tried to breathe and realized he couldn't, his lungs locking as they filled with dust. The panic was an atomic blast in the middle of his head and he scrabbled to free himself, pushing his way out of the dune and sucking air. There was a whumph as Pan landed next to him, blood spraying from her leg. She looked up, then began sweeping handfuls of dirt over herself until she was almost completely buried.

Marlow heard a scream from overhead, looked to see the demon halfway out the window. He swore, digging his way back into the dune, covering his body, his head, until there was just his mouth.

Silence, just the muffled thud of his thrashing heart.

Then the ground shook and the demon roared—just feet away. Marlow held his breath, praying, praying, praying, as the demon cried out again. It snorted, so close that Marlow could feel its breath on his stomach. Then, with another scream, it stepped over him—one clawed paw pinching the skin of his arm—and broke into a gallop.

For what felt like forever, Marlow lay there. It was almost peaceful, beneath the blanket of ash, beneath the warmth of the burning sky. He couldn't even hear the demons anymore. He couldn't hear much of anything.

He couldn't hear *Pan*.

He struggled against the weight of the dune, sitting up. There was no sign of her, and he suddenly knew that the demon had found her, had carried her off to the pack. Then he saw a lump, the ash on top of it crumbling as it rose and fell, rose and fell. He crawled to her, brushing dust from her face. She was alive, but she was out cold.

"Just hang in there, Pan," he whispered to her, scooping his arms through hers and dragging her down the slope. "I got you."

And slowly, inch by inch, he pulled her away from the carnage into the burning night.

WAKING THE DEAD

For a blissful moment, she thought it was death. Then she understood that if she was thinking, then she was still alive, and it all came back to her with the brutal force of a guillotine blade—the fire, the demons, the wall of rot and ruin.

I'm in hell, she said to herself, the last, blissful remnants of sleep scattering. Her throat was red raw, and she wondered if she'd been screaming.

"Easy," said Marlow, confirming it. "Easy, Pan. I thought you were going to wake the dead. And I'm not even joking about that here."

She finally let her eyes open, squinting against the light. Marlow was there, lifting a hand and waving. She didn't wave back, just sat up to check her leg. Her jeans were ripped to shreds and the skin beneath was almost as bad, layers of muscle visible in the mess. There was pain, she could feel it as a dull ache, but it didn't seem anywhere near as bad as it ought to be.

"Cleaned it as best I could," said Marlow. "Which wasn't easy given that there's no water here."

"Please tell me you didn't pee on it," she said, cupping a hand to her brow and looking at him.

The smile he gave her was almost as bright as the sun.

"It's day," she said. "How long was I out for?"

He shrugged, sitting down next to her. She looked past him and saw that they were under what might have been an overpass at one point, or a bridge. She was leaning against a vast brick pillar and fifty feet or more overhead grew a stunted arm of concrete and steel. The rest of it had broken off and lay in pieces on the ground around them, halfway to dust.

"It's hard to tell," he said. "You're right, time is weird here, the night comes and goes pretty quick. A few hours, though. You passed out when we hit the ground; I got you here."

"Here?"

He shrugged, looking out across the ash-strewn wasteland. She thought she could see a familiar shape through the haze, a high-rise.

"Yeah, we're only a couple hundred yards away," he said. "You're heavier than you look."

"They didn't follow?" she said, easing herself into a more comfortable position.

"The demons? No, they had plenty to keep them going. By the time I'd dragged you here—"

"*Dragged?*" she said. "You mean you didn't even carry me?"

"Like I said, you're heavy." He shook his head. "Anyway, by the time we were here the fire, up there, it was going out. The demons kinda just vanished with it. Then it was dark."

He frowned.

"What?"

"There was something else out there, though. Something big. It was calling your name."

She bit her bottom lip, trying to make sense of it all.

"The Engineers," she said. "Marlow, they were hung up there like . . . Like I don't even know. What happened to them?"

"This place happened to them," he said. "Did you hear them, when we were running?"

"Screaming? Yeah, sure, but—"

"Laughing, Pan," Marlow said, rubbing his eyes with dirty fingers. "They were laughing, like it was some huge joke."

She tried to swallow, her throat sandpaper dry. The sound of it was still in her head and she understood that Marlow had been right—those had been shrieks of lunatic delight, something right out of bedlam.

But then who could blame them?

"A hundred thousand years," she said.

"Huh?"

"A hundred millennia. That's what I heard, when they were talking about how long they'd been here, that's what one of them said."

"That's impossible," Marlow said, but he was wrong, wasn't he? Pan thought about Meridiana, trapped inside time, building an Engine out of her own cloned body. Time had no meaning there, and why would this place be any different? This was hell, after all, and Ostheim had always told her that hell was eternal.

She pressed a hand to her face, pushed into that darkness as if she could hide there. An engine of panic roared inside her, filling her head with noise, and she tightened her grip, pinching her cheeks, the pain grounding her.

"It can't be," she said. "It can't be like this."

"It isn't," said Marlow. "I mean, there has to be a way out, a way *back*. Meridiana said it herself, she said people have come back."

Pan looked at him, at that expression of goofy optimism on his stupid face.

"She said that?"

"Yeah," he said. "I mean, not like actually said it, but her ghost did, or whatever was in our blood right before we died. You know, that voice thing."

He tried to convince her with another smile but she just

scowled at him. Meridiana had been a crazy old witch who'd known enough to get them killed, and get them sent to hell. And it dawned on her, right there, that maybe that had been Ostheim's plan after all. He'd been one step ahead of them since all this began, he'd known exactly what they were going to do. It was almost *more* than that, though. It was like they were puppets who'd carried out every last piece of his plan. Why wouldn't this be exactly what he had wanted? He'd sent them to Meridiana's lair so that they would destroy her and end themselves in the process.

"Bastard," she said, wanting to spit but finding no scrap of moisture to do it with.

"Hey, I'm just saying what I heard," Marlow said, hands held up in defense.

"Not you," she said. "Not you."

They sat in silence for a moment, the air perfectly still. It was hot, like NYC summer hot, and it was almost *peaceful*.

"You see anything else?" she asked after a moment. "When you were *dragging* me here?"

Marlow shook his head.

"It's like you said, this place was a city, once upon a time. There's nothing left, though, apart from the bones. Even the metal is crumbling in places. I mean, how long does it take steel to decay?"

Years, she thought. *Thousands and thousands and thousands of years.*

"So where, though?" she asked, prodding the wound in her leg and wondering why she could barely feel it. "I mean *where* is this place?"

Marlow shrugged again.

"Look, it doesn't matter," she said, almost choking on the words. "Forget the Engineers, forget everything. We've got to try to find our way home, right?"

He shrugged a third time and she almost punched him for it. He must have seen the emotion there because he nodded.

"Yeah, we have to try."

"So let's try. Here."

She held out her hand and he took it, hauling her to her feet. There was still no real pain in her leg but it was stiff, and weak, and for a moment she wasn't even sure it would hold her. She took a step—the loose skin flapping—then another, lurching like she was drunk. She wouldn't be running any marathons, but at least she could move.

Marlow kept his hand hovering there, ready to catch her. She slapped it away.

"Don't worry yourself, Marlow, you won't have to drag me."

She walked out of the shadow of the column, squinting into the day. Her mind was a rowboat on an ocean of terror, she could feel the force of it beneath her, the depth of it, and its power, roiling on the very edge of every thought. It wouldn't take much, she knew, for her to sink and never recover. It was only the thought of those Engineers, beaten by time into quivering shadows of their former selves, that kept her afloat.

She wouldn't be like them.

She *would not* be like them.

"Which way?" she asked, feeling the warm, sandy ash between her toes.

Marlow scratched his bare chest.

"I don't even know what we're looking for," he said. "But there's that."

He nodded to the horizon, to the pocket of darkness that sat there, like somebody had taken a pair of scissors and cut a slice out of the day. Pan looked at it for as long as she could, until it felt like her eyes were in a nutcracker.

"Him," she said.

"Who?" Marlow asked, one knuckle between his teeth.

49

"The Engineers. They were talking about somebody else. *Him*."

He will not find you here.

She had no idea who *he* was, and what he'd do to them if he found them. But what if they *wanted* to be found? What if that was the only way to get answers? It had to be worth the risk. It had to be better than the alternative.

Right?

"Let's go," she said to Marlow before she could answer herself. "We'll find him, whoever he is, sooner or later. We'll figure this out."

That was the one good thing about hell, she realized.

They were never going to run out of time.

OLD FRIENDS

They started to walk. It wasn't like they could do anything else.

Pan stumbled away from the broken bridge, down a slope that might have once been a riverbed but which was now just another scar on the face of this forgotten city. It, too, was inches deep with dust and they kicked up peacock tails of it as they walked. It landed in her eyes, impossibly fine, in her mouth, in her nose. She wore it like a second skin, and after a few minutes she stopped trying to wipe it away.

She stopped trying to think about what it might be, as well, because it wasn't sand, it was ash. It made her think of a crematorium, and that in turn made her picture the mountain of bones where she had been born here, all those bodies. Was that what she was breathing in? The dust of a billion dead?

They followed the desiccated river as it wove its way in loose curves. Its banks were too high for them to see over and that was fine with her, because the less they saw of this place, the better. They just kept that impossible piece of missing skyline in sight. Time here was syrup-thick and cloying. That sun beat down on her like a fist, not hot exactly, just *there*.

Another of those weird mechanical conduits ran parallel to the river, forged of bronze and copper and what might have been obsidian. It was bigger than the one they'd crossed back in the city, maybe twenty feet tall, stretching as far as she could see to each side. It seemed to flex, reminding her of a snake gulping down its prey. It was made of metal, sure, but there was something horribly organic about it as well. And it was kicking out a maddening hum, a deep, throbbing pulse that was amplified every time she looked up at it.

The vibration was echoed in her, in the metal pieces of her new flesh. Even though she tried not to, she couldn't help studying them—those layers of copper and bronze fused to her skin, to her bones, to her organs as well, because she could feel them there, rubbing. She scratched at her arms, her neck, until her nails bled, then she scratched some more.

"Don't," said Marlow, after what might have been ten minutes or ten hours of walking. He held her hand, tight enough to stop her pulling away. He had blood beneath his nails too and his skin was ragged. "Don't."

"I hate it," she said, her skin crawling like she had chicken pox. She needed oven mitts if she was going to survive down here. "I hate that it's inside me."

It was more than just inside her, it *was* her. She was forged from hell.

"I know," he said. "It sucks. But you're not, I mean it's not you. All this, Pan, it's not you." He prodded her in the side of the head, a little too hard. "That's you, yeah? Your brain, your heart. How many times did the Engine make you whole again, after a mission?"

She pushed a hand against her heart, against the mangled lump of gristle that had somehow kept beating even after a demon had put its bladed tail through it. Marlow was right, the Engine had repaired her back on Earth, and she'd never felt less human for it.

"You might have a little bit of hell in you," said Marlow, finally letting her pull her hand free, "but you're still a hundred percent Pan. Ain't nothing brave enough to try to take that away."

It still itched like a bastard, though.

They walked for a while again in silence, Pan's throat as dry as the riverbed. She was about to mention it to Marlow when she caught him looking back the way they'd come, dust caught in the furrows of his brow.

"Something's following us."

The ash erased everything they'd walked through, turning the world behind them into a blank page. But Marlow was right, there was something there. She squinted, seeing a mass of darkness swimming in the haze, like the body of a shark beneath its exposed fin. Whatever it was, it was *big*.

"You think we should wait for it?" Marlow asked. "Might be on our side."

"No," she said, scratching at her arm again. Nothing here was on their side.

She started walking, faster this time, the sun grinding a path across the sky. There were times when it seemed to pause, where it seemed to do nothing but stare. She could feel it boring into her and twice she lifted her head ready to scream at it. Then it would lurch into motion again—too subtle for her to see but enough for her to feel, like she was on a fairground wheel that had started to turn. The motion sickness churned in her gut, and she almost longed for night, until she remembered what the dark would bring.

It seemed like every other step she looked back, staring into that formless nothing, and every single time that lumbering shape would peel its way from the ash, matching them step for step. It might have been her imagination, but she swore she could hear it, too, a distant cry.

"Can you make that out?" she asked.

"You can't hear it?" Marlow said, and when she shook her

head he breathed out a sigh, wiping his chapped lips. "Your name, Pan. It's calling your name."

It was this that made her stop, cocking her head and finally hearing it, a cry like a distant gunshot fired again and again and again.

"Pan."

She tried to turn away, tried to start walking again, but she couldn't. She had to know what it was that called to her, what it was that hounded her through hell.

And sure enough, just minutes later, it peeled its way from the ash. A man—a *huge* man—rolls of fat spilling out from him like a candle melting in the sun. He looked like he'd been fed through a wood chipper, a dozen scraps of skin barely held together and yellow stuff oozing out of the wounds. He pushed a smell before him the way a boat pushes a wave, a stench of old meat and sewage.

He moved relentlessly forward, struggling with his own weight. Pan saw that there was something slung around his neck, but she couldn't make out what it was. Only when the man lowered his head to it and Pan heard something rip did she understand it was food. He was chewing something; she could see his cheeks bulge, could see his throat flex as he swallowed.

Her stomach growled before she understood what it was he was eating.

"No," she groaned. But there was no denying it. The man had halved the distance between them now and Pan could make out a grotesque figure strapped around his neck like a horse's feeding bag—a hairless scalp, ridged with scars, a pair of eyes blinking up at the darkening sky. The figure was half eaten already, but she was *still alive*. There was no pain in her expression, just something defiant, something made of steel.

And that's what did it. Pan knew that expression, she knew that face.

"Brianna?" she said, the word like a startled bird, leaving her mouth before she could stop it.

The man kept walking, fixing Pan with two eyes as dark as pitch. His face was loose, hanging off him like a cheap Halloween mask, gaping holes worn through his cheeks and nose. But there was no mistaking that look of hate, a look worn not by a man but by a boy.

"Patrick," said Pan. "Oh God, it's Patrick."

It was them, the twins who had worked with Mammon, whom she'd faced in countless battles—whom she'd sent to hell. The world was reeling and Pan realized it was because she was shaking her head, desperate to deny it. The last she'd seen of them was back in New York, the demons dragging Patrick and his wormbag sister into the molten earth. How had she not even considered the thought of meeting them here?

Patrick's face split open into a smile, his blunt teeth slick with blood. Then a noise spilled out of him, a wet, lurching groan. Brianna was looking, too, the stumps of her arms swiveling. She was giggling so hard her eyes had rolled back in their sockets.

"Pan," said Patrick. "Pan. Pan. Pan."

"Listen," said Pan, trying to find the words in the chaos of her thoughts. "I know, I know we were wrong. I should have listened to you, I'm . . . I'm sorry. It was Ostheim, he—"

"We didn't know," added Marlow.

"I told you," said Patrick, close enough now that Pan could see his spine, his ribs, in the pockets of his flesh. He was too tall—eight, nine, ten feet—and swayed like a snake in its basket, the movements hypnotic. "I told you we'd see you in hell."

"Please," said Pan, barely able to speak past the lump in her throat, past the horror of what she had done to them. "Patrick, we need each other. We can help each other get out."

"You want out?" he said, spitting a blood-drenched laugh. "So did we. So did my sister. And we found a way."

Pan wanted nothing more than to turn and run but she held her ground, she had to hear what he was going to say.

"We found a way," he said again. "Because this place can't hold us here forever. It can't. How many times now, Brianna? How many times is it? Fifty? Sixty?"

"What?" said Marlow, and Pan felt his hand on her arm. "Sixty what?"

"How many times have I eaten you?" he said to Brianna. "Skin, bone, brain, eyes, every last scrap of you. You keep coming back, sister, but one day you won't. You'll be free."

Brianna screamed her lunatic laughter into his throat. He swung his head toward Pan and she could see his bared teeth through his flapping cheeks, she could see the hatred in his clenched jaw, the insanity that boiled in his eyes.

"It's only been a few days," she said, thinking back to New York. But she knew that was a lie. It had been days on Earth, but this place was cruel. It might have been centuries since Patrick and Brianna had crawled up from the dirt. "Please," she said. "We're on the same side, I know that now."

He took a step toward her, using a filthy nail to fish a scrap of meat from between his bloodied molars. Then he laughed, hissing it through his nose.

"I've been waiting for you for such a long time, Pan," he said, taking another step. "I've had so many years to think about what I'll do to you."

Another step, his arms reaching for her.

"Why wait any longer?"

NIGHTRISE

He moved fast, faster than he had any right to with a body that huge.

Pan was bolting, scrambling up the riverbank, but the monster was chasing, dwarfing her. He reached her before Marlow could even remember how to move, wrapping an immense hand around her throat. She hung there, punching, kicking, but Patrick was impossibly strong.

"Hey!" Marlow yelled, breaking into a run. He bunched his fists, ready to knock Patrick down into the next level of hell.

He never got the chance.

Patrick didn't hesitate. He didn't gloat. He gripped Pan under one arm, grabbed her head with his hand, and pulled.

"No!" Marlow screamed.

Pan had time for a muffled cry, a final, unspoken plea for mercy.

Then her head came off, blood misting over Patrick's broken face. The boy's bucket jaw stretched obscenely wide and he pushed Pan's head into it, gagging with the effort. He cast her twitching body away, using both hands to shovel her head inside him until his cheeks bulged.

Marlow's legs gave up on him and he fell to his knees.

"Nonono," he said, not a scream but a whimper.

Patrick turned to Marlow, those black eyes dripping glee. His jaw flexed and he crunched on Pan's skull like he was chewing ice. It was the worst sound Marlow had ever heard and the horror of it pulled him up again, drove him across the dust. He roared, his fury like a furnace as he threw himself at Patrick.

The impact knocked them both over, Patrick hitting the ground hard enough to make his gigantic body tremble. He grunted, spitting scraps of skull and hair—*her skull, her hair*—and Marlow clambered up him, grabbing handfuls of blubber. He drove his fist into the side of the monster's head, feeling the old bone crumble. He hit him again, and again, then Patrick grunted like a bear, rolling to the side and bucking Marlow off.

Marlow panicked, the dust in his eyes blinding him. Fingers wrapped themselves around his neck and clamped hard, hauling him up into the air. He could feel the strength there, knew that Patrick would rip his head off as easily as he had Pan's. He kicked back, trying to find him, only to feel Patrick's lips against his ear. The boy blew out a breath that stank of a butcher's garbage bag.

"Your turn," he said, spraying him with pieces of half-chewed Pan.

Marlow angled his head, saw that vast jaw open wide, saw the blunt teeth inside.

"Haven't you eaten enough, *gordo de mierda*?"

The voice came out of nowhere, and so did the spear—piercing Patrick's bloated flank, punching right through him. He grunted, his grip on Marlow's throat loosening.

A figure burst from the dust. It was a woman, short and lithe and wrapped from head to toe in brown rags. Only a pair of eyes were visible, dark and fierce. She was holding another spear in her free hand and she launched it. This one javelined into Patrick's throat and he staggered back. Marlow squirmed out of his grip, dropping to the ground. The stranger grabbed the handle of the spear and ran *up* Patrick's side, pushing herself away and ripping the blade free. She flipped gracefully in the air, landed, then thrust the weapon into Patrick's eye.

Patrick stumbled back another couple of steps, his whole body shaking. His mouth was still full of Pan but he was muttering choked words. "Not over, not over, not over."

Then he hit the ground in a tidal wave of dust, spasmed, and fell still.

The woman grabbed the spear and wrenched it free, then she rammed it into Brianna's head, cutting off her inhuman laughter. She tucked the weapon beneath her arm then turned to Marlow, gesturing.

"Huh?" Marlow said. He wasn't sure if he could remember how to speak real words.

The figure gestured again—*come on*—then moved swiftly along the riverbed. Marlow hesitated, looking to where Pan's body lay still, an ocean of dark blood growing from the delta of her neck. His sense of loss was vast, overwhelming. He'd had to watch her die twice, and both times something inside him had died as well.

"Hey!" the girl yelled. "*Chu* waiting for?"

He stumbled after her, running until his body decided it had had enough. Then he just lay there, staring up at the ice-white sky, at that sun that couldn't decide whether it was coming or going. He lay there and thought of Pan, and waited for the dust to drift down and bury him.

Something moved in front of him, throwing him into shade, and he looked to see the woman there. Her face was still concealed by rags but there was something familiar about the way she held herself, the way she bounced on the balls of her feet. He didn't trust it and he stood, waiting for the girl's head to split open, for her to try to eat him. But there was something nagging at him, something about what she'd said. His thoughts

were heavy with ash. He couldn't work out what they were trying to show him.

"Marlow?" the girl said, and he realized it wasn't what she'd
said but *how* she'd said it—the accent.

"Who are you?" he asked.

"I . . . I don't know," she replied. "I don't remember my
name."

She grabbed the rags that hid her face and began to unwind
them, revealing her chin, her lips, her nose, and only then did
those dark eyes make sense.

"Holy sh— *Night*?"

Nightingale pulled the hood free and stood there, frowning
at Marlow.

"Night?" she repeated.

Marlow took a step toward her but she retreated, holding the
blade of the spear to his throat. He raised his hands, stepping
back.

"It's me," he said. "It's Marlow. Night, I can't believe it's you.
I thought you'd . . . I mean, you died, but I never thought—"

He saw it now, Night tumbling from the bridge with the
Magpie, swallowed by the molten river. She'd been under contract when she'd died, dragged to hell. How had he not even
thought about that?

Night just stared at him, barely blinking. The point of her
spear wavered, then dropped into the dust.

"Night," she said, chewing on the word.

"It wasn't your real name," Marlow said. "It was your Engineer name. Your real name was Catalina—"

"It was my real name," she interrupted. "I didn't have another."

She stabbed the spear into the dirt and sat down cross-
legged. He sat, too, close enough that he could see the flecks of
dark metal in her skin, woven into the fabric of her flesh, a dozen

scars threaded through her face and neck. Other than that, she looked the same as she always had, the same face, the same hair. Her eyes, though, told a different story. Her eyes told of endless suffering.

"Night, how long have you been here?" he asked.

She looked at him as if she might be able to find an answer there, then she stared down the length of the barren river.

"I lost count," she said. "After five hundred days I lost count."

Marlow wanted to hold her, but instead he wrapped his arms around himself. Night had died yesterday, but this place had imprisoned her in time. Five hundred days—*more*—trapped here alone. Marlow knew that if he thought about it too much then he would ram the tip of that spear into his own head.

"It won't do you any good," she said, like she was reading his thoughts. "Don't you think I didn't try it? I tried it, I tried it so many times."

"And you came back?" he said, and it hit him like a rising sun. "*Pan* is coming back?"

He saw her shape Pan's name with her lips as if she had just remembered it. She turned back to him, breathed out a sigh that was almost a sob.

"She's coming back. They always come back."

"And you know where?"

She nodded, then glanced at the sky.

"I do," she said. "But we've got to hurry."

INFINITE LIVES ACTIVATED

It was different this time.

Pan heard that familiar hiss of static, felt the pins-and-needles tingle of it. She lifted a hand—an arm, really, because she had no hand there. There was just the blunt stump of her wrist, trailing those same threads of color from the ground below, and trails of black liquid so dark they looked like cracks in the air. It was knitting her from the dead, once more, weaving her from the bones that lay there, from the dark metal that sat deeper, from that weird glass-tubed fluid that veined the hill.

I came back, she said to herself, knowing from the numbness that her face was only half formed. The memories slotted in like punch cards, one at a time and ridiculously clumsy. And they ended with Patrick's hands on her, that awful tension in her neck, agony . . . and then nothing. *I came back.* And she could do nothing but groan inwardly because the enormity of it felt like it was about to swallow her whole. *I came back.*

"Easy," said a voice. It was Marlow, or at least it sounded like him.

She opened her mouth, tried to speak, and released only dust. But he must have known what she needed.

"Uh . . . your real name is Amelia, we met when I saved your ass in an underground parking lot, and your greatest desire is for me to fall in love with you. See, it's me."

Go screw yourself, she tried to say. The pins and needles had moved to her feet and she wiggled her toes, feeling them form, feeling the dust suddenly gather between them. She tried to sit up but her body wasn't strong enough.

"I've got somebody else here," said Marlow. His voice sounded a million miles away and when she managed to blink him into focus she saw he was looking the other way.

"Who?" she asked. "What's wrong?"

"Nothing," he said. "I'll show you, but you gotta put some clothes on first."

She rolled over, seeing that he'd dropped a couple of pieces of sackcloth beside her. She managed to sit up this time, draping one around her shoulders. It was as she was fumbling with the second piece that somebody stepped into her field of vision. Her face was so scarred that it took Pan a while to recognize it, and when she did she didn't know whether to laugh or cry.

"Night?" she asked.

Night crouched down beside her and Pan flinched.

"It's me," said the other girl. "It's me. First time I met you I was terrified, wouldn't peek out from behind Herc's back."

"Don't worry," said Marlow. "She hasn't tried to eat me."

Night's eyes caught the dying light, looked like they'd been cast in a blacksmith's forge.

"I'm sorry," Night said. "I'm sorry I didn't get to you in time."

"With Patrick?" Pan shuddered as a phantom pain shot through her neck. She rubbed it, feeling a scar there. "What *is* that?"

"A memory," Night said, scratching at the scars on her own neck. "Your body remembers. Every time, your body remembers."

"Every time?" she asked.

"Every time hell kills you."

She looked at Night, at her ravaged skin.

"How many times has it happened to you?" she asked. In the pause that followed Pan felt her heart grind into a rhythm.

"Too many," said Night eventually.

"You decent yet?" asked Marlow. Pan wrapped the second piece of cloth around her waist, knotting it. Her skin felt the same as it had the last time she'd woken here, but the patterns of metal there were different. She studied them, tracing a finger along the marbled striations and feeling the ridge of them. When she'd finished she looked past Marlow, past Night, to see that she was back on the bone mountain where she'd first arrived.

No, it was similar, she realized, but this, too, was different. She couldn't see the city beneath them, just a desert of dust lined with those black conduits. Night followed her gaze, nodding. She started to say something, then swallowed painfully.

"Sorry, it has been a long time since . . . since I spoke."

"Five hundred days," Marlow said before she had a chance to ask.

"More," said Night. "Much more than that. But I know this place. I have seen it work. These places, these graveyards, they are like . . . like petri dishes."

"Like *what*?" said Marlow.

"Or, I don't know, grow bags. For tomatoes."

"Right . . ." said Marlow, raising a copper-brushed eyebrow.

"These are mountains of the dead," said Night. "Bones and flesh, hair, DNA, I guess. Everything you need to make a person. Plus this stuff," she dug into the dirt with her toes, revealing a glass tube filled with black. "No idea what it is."

It sounded crazy, but it made perfect sense. What had Meridiana told them, back in her lair? That the human body contained elements, metals, stardust. Why wouldn't you be able to grow something from the dead?

"Your soul cannot die here," Night said, and again that

supernova of panic erupted in Pan's stomach. "Every time your body is killed, your soul gets, I don't know, rebooted. It travels to the nearest mountain, where it's remade."

"Like an infinite-lives hack," muttered Marlow.

Night nodded.

"What else do you know?" Pan asked.

"I know that the more it happens, the less you are you," she said. "How's your head? Full of fluff?"

Pan nodded, feeling her thoughts slosh around inside.

"You are remade, but each time you become a little less like yourself. You forget things, like your name, like where you came from. Patrick and Brianna, they were lost."

"He was eating her," said Marlow, sifting the ash through his fingers.

"He has been eating her for years," she said. "Over and over and over. I have crossed paths with them already, many times, but from a distance. There are others here that are far, far worse."

"We saw," said Pan. "People, back in the city. They were strung up like plants. They were insane."

"We are all insane here," said Night. "You will be, too."

"No," said Marlow, chewing his knuckles. "Not me."

"But what are they?" Pan said. "They said they were Engineers."

Night nodded.

"Hell is full of them. I don't know how many people used the Engine, how many made a deal. It must have been thousands, tens of thousands. You remember the book, right, the book with their names? How many centuries did it go back?"

"I think the first entry was like nine hundred years ago," said Pan.

"And you said I've been here, what? A day? A day for you is years here. So what is nine hundred years?"

65

An eternity, Pan thought.

"And it's not even that simple," said Night. "The longer you're here, the slower time goes. I think after a while, it just stops altogether."

Pan rubbed her eyes, launching fireworks across the dark.

"So we've got Engineers," she heard Marlow say. "They're dangerous, right? I got attacked by one when I first arrived. I thought it was Pan."

When Pan opened her eyes Night was shaking her head.

"I don't know what they are," she said. "But they're not Engineers. They're ghosts. They come and go, and they always look like people you know, but under their skin they're mechanical, like insects made of pieces of Engine. I don't know where they come from, but they sure want to keep killing you."

Night hissed a laugh.

"I've been killed by five of the *hijos de puta* already. One of them looked like my mom. One of them looked like you, Marlow."

"Sorry," he said.

"Luckily you see them coming," she said. "They home in on you. It's why I took so long getting to you when Patrick attacked; I was waiting to see if it was really you."

Night glanced up at the darkening sky.

"So we've got Engineers that want to kill us," said Marlow. "Plus those . . . things, ghosts. Not to mention the demons. Anything else in the way of us and the exit?"

"Exit?" Night whispered, shaking her head. "No, everything here, it's been here forever. Nothing escapes."

"Yeah?" said Marlow. "Well, hell hasn't met me yet."

Pan sputtered a laugh, but Night held up a hand in caution.

"Careful what you say, Marlow. This place, it feeds on hope. It feeds on it, and devours it. And it's always hungry."

"Hope?" said Marlow.

"*Sí*," she said. "That's what hell is, *claro*? The end of hope."

"So we just wait here to die, again and again?" asked Pan, a wave of darkness swelling up inside her.

The silence that followed smothered her, made her feel ocean-deep.

"No," said Marlow. "You must have seen something else, something we can use." He scanned the sky and Pan followed his gaze, finding a deeper darkness in the dusk. "That," he said. "What's over there?"

Night shook her head, a little too quickly.

"What?" asked Pan.

"No," she said.

"You have to say," said Marlow. "Please, Night. What is it?"

"I cannot," she said.

She pushed herself up, began pacing. Trails of dust defied gravity, stretching like rockets toward the sky. She waved them away, her face a mask of concern.

"When I got here, I tried to explore, tried to find a way out. There isn't one, and even if there were, there are too many dangers here. Even if we found a door, the demons wouldn't let us leave. They'd kill us and we'd end up right back here, or on another one of these damn mountains."

"But—" said Marlow.

"I saw it too," she interrupted. "The darkness. God knows why I thought it would help. I tried to get close but . . . The things you have already seen, they are nothing compared with this. They are *sane* compared with what I found down there."

"But you think it might be a way out?" asked Pan.

"No, not a way out," said Night. "Something else." Her mouth flexed, her throat gulping as if she physically couldn't get the words up.

Pan saw her glance to the edge of the world, to where that spiral of not-quite-darkness leaked into the sky.

"Night, please," said Pan. She stood, swaying until her new legs found their strength. She walked to the girl and put her hands on her shoulders, squeezing.

Night shuddered, falling against Pan and letting her hold her. The noises she was making weren't exactly sobs, they were almost mechanical, like she'd forgotten how to cry.

"*Please*," Pan said again. "What did you see?"

"I saw *him*," said Night, breathing the words into Pan's ears, looking once more at the horizon. "I saw the Devil."

HUNGER

They sat on the mountain and watched the night burn.

It happened almost without warning. The sun seemed to give up. There was a sudden, vertiginous sweep of light as it tumbled toward the horizon, struggling there for a moment before spilling over the edge. For a while, the dark was absolute, as if the sun hadn't just moved to the other side of the planet but been extinguished altogether.

Then came the screams, feral and full of fury.

"Demons," Pan whispered.

"Means it's about to happen," said Night. "The fire."

It responded to her call, a distant plume of flame searing up, so bright that it left sparkler trails on Pan's vision. It filled the sky with orange and blue, a blazing pool that rippled outward. A second volcanic eruption surged skyward, this one much closer. Pan squinted against the force of it, seeing that it was coming from one of the black pipelines that crossed the land. A third joined in, then a fourth, until the heavens burned and the night was lit up like the day. Their roar made the earth tremble.

"It's not safe to stay put for long," Night said, getting to her feet. "They have a way of finding you."

Past the glare Pan could see movement down below as the demons crawled up from the baked earth. Their screams filled the night but they were far enough away for now. Night had picked up her spear and was walking down the slope. Pan had to heft herself up like her body was made of solid iron. It took her reformed brain a moment to work out how to take a step. At least she had clothes, though. Night had skipped off a while back and found her a threadbare shirt. It was gray and riddled with holes, and it made her skin feel like it wanted to crawl right off her bones, but it was better than an old sack. She'd found her some sweatpants in the dirt, too, which had to have been a thousand years old.

"None of this makes any sense," Pan said, and she could hear the desperation in her voice. "This place, it's just *wrong*."

"What did you expect?" asked Night, leading the way down. "You make a deal with the Devil then you won't exactly find yourself in the Intercontinental. This place is two-star at best."

"Two-star?" said Marlow.

"An extra star for the view," she said, and her laugh drew a smile from him.

"You kept your sense of humor in hell," he said. "That's pretty impressive."

"I didn't," said Night, studying the insect shapes that scurried across the land, treading carefully as the ground grew steeper. "I lost hope, I lost my name, I thought I'd lost myself. But you guys, you gave it back." She cleared her throat. "I'll lose it all again, and so will you, but for now, right here, it's not so bad."

"Speak for yourself," muttered Pan. "You didn't get your head ripped off."

"Actually, I did," said Night, jutting her chin in the air to reveal a jagged scar around her throat. "Not by Patrick, but by a ghost. It hurt. Didn't even come off all the way, took forever to bleed out."

"All right, Nearly Headless Night," said Pan. "You win."

"Don't suppose there's a Famous Ray's New York Pizza

70

around here?" Marlow asked. Pan's own hunger was an aching void inside her, her thirst unreal. Night just laughed again, but this time it was bitter.

"No food," she said. "No water. You want to eat, then . . . Then there's flesh, plenty of it. But you don't want to go there. No faster way to lose yourself than to end up like Patrick."

"Don't we need food?" said Marlow. "Don't we, like, die without it?"

Night nodded, scrubbing her face with her filthy hand.

"Those are the worst deaths," she said. The metal in her skin caught the firelight, glowed like the filament in a lightbulb. "They take weeks, and you grow weaker and weaker and weaker until you can't even move. Those are the very worst. But you get used to them."

"You really saw the Devil?" Pan asked, trying to change the subject and instantly wishing she'd picked something else.

Night waited until she'd skipped off the foot of the mountain into the desert of ash, checking left and right before walking again. She was heading for another of those conduits, this one looking like a massive oil pipeline.

"I don't know what he was. Don't ask me to describe it, because I cannot. I saw the end of the world, the end of everything. And *he* was there."

"How do you know?" Pan asked.

"Because I have seen him before," she said. "In the black pool. I saw him there every time I made a deal. You saw him, too, he is unmistakable."

Pan had seen it countless times, when she'd climbed into that pool of death to forge a contract with the Engine—a madness of eyes and teeth, as big as the world, who had asked her, *"This is what you desire?"*

"You saw *him*?" she asked. "Here?"

Night nodded.

71

"Great," muttered Marlow.

They walked in silence for a while, trailing the giant pipeline. Pan reached out, grabbed the conduit for support, only to feel that sensation again, so much stronger this time—like the metal pieces that made up her flesh were trying to pull their way out of her. There was an explosion of dark light at the front of her skull and she let go, blinking away spots of shadow. Her whole body thrummed like a plucked guitar string.

"What?" Marlow asked.

"You don't feel that?" Pan said, nodding at the conduit. It wasn't really much of a pipe, more a snaking piece of machinery. This section must have been thirty feet tall, sculpted from a thousand pieces of iron. Black, fleshy veins as big as her arm ran the length of it, weaving in and out of the mechanical components, pulsing gently. She watched as Marlow put his hand to it, as what little blood was left in his face drained away.

"What is that?" he asked.

"Remind you of anything?" said Night. She stood there, spear gripped in her hand.

Millions of cogs, springs, filaments. Yeah, they reminded Pan of something.

"The Engine," she said.

Marlow nodded.

"Yeah, the Devil's Engine," said Night. "I don't know what they are, but I know this: if you follow them, you find *him*."

And Pan suddenly understood what she was feeling when she touched the metal, that magnetic pull.

The Devil was calling them.

"We have to go to him," said Marlow, reaching the same understanding.

Pan spat out a dry laugh.

"No way. No way in hell."

"You think we have a choice?" he asked.

Pan looked at Night and the girl shrugged, digging her spear into the ash.

"You felt it call you," Marlow added. "What else can we do?"

Whatever these pipes were, wherever they led, Pan wanted no part of them.

"Come on, Night," said Marlow. "Where else are we going to find answers?"

"Even if it is the Devil," said Pan. "What makes you think we'll get answers?"

He chewed his shrapneled knuckles for a moment, frowning.

"Because this place has to mean something," he said. "It can't just be . . . *this*."

Pan stopped walking, flexing her toes in the cloud-soft ash. Her thoughts were boxed away, pushed into storage. Uncovering them felt ridiculously slow. She tried not to think about the fact that she had died, that her brain had literally grown again from the earth, each and every synapse formed from the stuff of the dead. Going down that road would lead her to madness and nothing else.

But she could still feel that awful pressure, the moment her head had come off. And she'd heard it, that crunch of bone, as Patrick chewed on her skull. She'd still been conscious for that first, awful bite.

I deserve it, she told herself, thinking of what she'd done to Patrick, to his sister, to everyone she'd ever hurt. Her procession of the dead would stretch a long, long way, starting all those years ago with Christoph. *I deserve all of it.*

And maybe she should just lie down, wait for the demons to take her. She could lie there and die and die and die, over and over and over. After a while, surely, she wouldn't even notice it. She rubbed the scar that ringed her neck, swallowed dust into a stomach as dry as sandpaper.

"This place doesn't mean anything," she said. "All it wants is for us to suffer."

"But—"

Marlow stopped speaking, stopped walking, ducked down. Pan froze, too, her borrowed heart clamoring. Night had taken a couple more steps before she realized she was alone, crouching, all of them listening to a voice ghosting out of the night.

"Marlow? Marlow? Marlow?" It was thin and reedy, just a whisper over the roar. It grew louder, louder, muffled by the pipe that lay between them. Then it faded.

For a while, nobody moved, then Night pushed on, leaving tiptoe prints in the ash. Marlow hesitated, and Pan could read his thoughts as they flashed across his face—*What if it wasn't a ghost? What if it was somebody real?*—before he gave up and kept walking.

"Your but," said Pan.

"My *what*?" he asked.

"You said but."

"Oh, yeah, this place. I can't . . ." He chomped on a knuckle and she could see the blood there where he'd broken the skin. "Oh, right. But *why* are we here? I mean, I know about the contract and everything, but why? You ever stop to ask why you'd lose your soul if you couldn't break your contract? Why the Devil would even want your soul?"

She had, she'd thought about it so many times, but the answer had always been the same: *It doesn't matter, because it will never happen to you.*

"He eats them," says Night. "That's what we always got told. Went to Catholic school back in Mexico, before they kicked me out for drinking the sacramental wine. You should have seen *that* Eucharist, we replaced it with *antifreeze*." She laughed softly, the sound like sunlight. "Anyway, we always got told if we sinned, the Devil would feast on our souls."

"Like barbecue?" said Marlow.

74

"*Sí,* like he wanted to drain something from us, our energy or something. *Ay dios mío,* Sister Margarita would freak knowing that she'd actually been right about me. She always said I would burn."

"Sounds like a nice lady," said Marlow.

"Don't even get me started on *la chancla.*"

"So you're saying we're here because the Devil wants to eat our souls," said Pan. "Which means I'm right, we shouldn't go anywhere near him."

"But you're still walking," Marlow said. And he was right, she was.

Pan sniffed, staring out into the desert. A wind had blown up, forming ripples in the ash and pulling it up into the air. It was so thick it looked like mist and she was glad of it because it meant they were harder to find.

"I'm just saying," Marlow said. "We don't know anything about this . . . this whatever you want to call it. We all saw him inside the Engine, yes. He gave us the powers, granted our wishes, yes. He took our souls and dragged them into this craphole, yes."

"Yes?" said Pan when he didn't continue.

"What if there's something else he wants?" Marlow said with a half-assed shrug. "What if there's something we can give him?"

"In return for what?" Pan asked. "Special treatment? He might serve us for the main course instead of dessert."

"I'm just trying to think of ideas," Marlow snapped back. "I'm just trying to do some—"

"Whoa!"

Marlow thumped into the back of Night, Pan almost walking into Marlow. She craned her head over Marlow's shoulder but all she could see up ahead was the same desert, the same cloud of ash bathed in firelight.

"What's up?" she said.

"What's *down*," said Night, standing to the side to make room for her.

Pan took a couple of steps forward and was about to take another one when Marlow grabbed her arm. She retreated, finally seeing the slope, the ledge just beneath it, and then nothing.

"Oh," she said, kicking at the ash and watching it slide into oblivion. Only the conduit carried on, stretching out into the haze like the Brooklyn Bridge in the fog. She looked to the side, seeing the vague line of the cliff, and beyond that what could have been the edge of the world. "You think it's deep?"

"Could just be a couple of feet," said Marlow. "Dibs not checking."

"Dibs," said Night.

"Yeah, I'm pretty sure dibs doesn't work down here," Pan said. She ducked, rooting her hand in the ash, staring into the swirling abyss. Every now and then the clouds would thin and she was certain she could see something churning far below, an ocean. A fist of vertigo struck her in the gut and she moved back on her hands and knees until she felt steady enough to stand.

"Well, that answers that, then," said Pan.

"Huh?" Marlow and Night said together.

"Our field trip to see the Devil. We can't go any farther."

Marlow was looking at the pipe, chewing his knuckles, and Pan shook her head.

"Don't even think it," she said.

"It's huge. It will be like walking along a footbridge."

Yeah, a footbridge that filled your head with shadows, that blinded you.

He put a hand up to the metal, not quite touching it. His expression belonged to a man who was about to jam a fork into an electrical outlet.

"I'm not going," Pan said.

76

"Then wait here," he replied, wincing as he put his hand to the pipe. She heard a noise—or not quite a noise, more a cross between a generator hum and the buzz of a bluebottle trapped inside the pipes of her sinuses, tickling them so much she had to pinch the bridge of her nose. Marlow had pulled his hand away and was flexing it madly. His face was like parchment, like it had been drawn onto a paper bag.

"Come on. Whatever is over there, it can't be worse than what we've already seen."

She glanced back into the swirling wall of dust. Demons, ghosts, and Patrick the Monster, too, probably. He'd have regenerated by now and she had a funny feeling he wasn't done with her.

Could the Devil be worse than that?

Yeah, she thought. *He could.*

But however awful it was, nothing could be more awful than being alone here. And it was that thought—watching Night and Marlow vanish into the dust, leaving her behind—that made her nod her head.

"Fine," she grunted. "After you."

CROSSING

It was like standing on a washing machine at full spin—a pulse of discomfort rising through Marlow's feet.

But it was more than that, too. He felt like he was standing on the sidewalk back in New York, the subway rumbling beneath him as trains smashed their way through the tunnels. He could feel the force of it, something vast and dark and unstoppable tearing through the mechanism that lay beneath his feet. There was an electric pulse vibrating inside his skull, relentless, hard enough to shatter it, and he pushed his hands against his temples to hold his mind in place. The roar of vertigo was overpowering, it was the sensation of feeling a train hurtle toward you, seeing it loom over you, the awful, inevitable rush of death.

He gritted his teeth against it, loosed a roar of his own that was lost in the storm. It was hot up here, the burning sky roasting the top of his head, making his hair shrivel. Glowing flakes of plasma dripped from the inferno, like it was snowing fire, and he crouched, resting a hand on the pipe.

It was as though he'd been pulled inside it, a rush of roller-coaster movement that wrung his aching stomach. He reeled into the sudden quiet, into the unexpected dark, feeling the power that flowed through the machine beneath him—feeling it and *following* it, seeing the land pass by beneath him, seeing it grow more and more fractured, more and more broken until even gravity seemed to have given up.

And there, a black hole on the horizon, leaking darkness.

For an instant he feared his asthma had come back, because he couldn't get a breath. It was just a phantom in the dust, a mirage, but there was no denying what he was looking at. And even though there was no way it could have seen him, Marlow just wanted the strands of himself to unravel and return to the ground, he wanted to unwind—because he could feel that thing, whatever it was, he could feel it in every single cell of his being.

He could feel it watching him.

What is it you desire?

He grunted.

"The trick is to keep saying it to yourself," said Night as she clambered up.

"Huh?"

"Your name, your age, your family. This place swallows your mind, it tries to take everything you got. Keep looking back, keep remembering who you are. Say it."

"Marlow," he said. "Marlow . . ." And his whole body seemed to lurch as he reached for his surname and found nothing, just a void. Then it was back, sliding into his skull. "Green. Uh, I'm fifteen, my mom's name is Audrey, my dog's name is Donovan, my brother's name is . . ." And there it was again, like stepping off the end of the world. "D-Danny," he stuttered, finding it.

"Told you," said Night. "Try to remember further back. It doesn't seem to be able to get those memories."

He did, the gears of his mind grinding, stalling. He could remember being five, maybe six—walking across his bedroom, his mom running through the door and hugging him tight. Was that when Danny had died, maybe? Was that the moment she told him? He couldn't be sure. There was nothing before that, just an abyss where his past had once sat.

But the conversation had power, it had cleared the fog from his head. Gradually the world swam into focus—the pipe beneath him, ridged with metal plates and wires and cogs and springs, all moving frantically, veined with tubes that might have been fat, black arteries. The only good news was that it was easily five feet across, wide enough to walk.

"Dude, this is horrible," he said, wiping the saliva from his chin and offering Pan the same hand as she neared the top. She waved it away, crouching while she rode out that nightmare vision.

Night took the lead, skipping across the uneven surface of the giant conduit. Marlow followed, the metal digging into the bruised flesh of his feet. Beneath him the pipeline hummed and thundered as though there were a million working pieces inside, all pumping an icy darkness into his thoughts.

It took only twelve steps before the edge of the cliff passed beneath them and the void took its place. Fingers of dust whirled around his feet, trying to flick him off, and past them he could see movement, something far, far below. It might have been water, the churning of some great ocean. The thought of it seemed to infinitely multiply his thirst. He felt as if he were made of ash, every drop of moisture evaporated and burned away. Was this going to be his first death? Gasping like a landed fish, every organ failing?

He was tempted to hurl himself off the pipe and into the water. Drowning seemed like a better way to go.

The pipe pierced the ash, a straight black line that seemed to go on forever. Every time Marlow put his foot down he'd sense the metallic parts of him drawn earthward. He felt like an iron filing next to a magnet, wondered if he'd be able to stop himself moving this way even if he wanted to. Each step brought with it a flower bloom of night, a concussive strobing, and twice he had to stop to find his equilibrium. The second time Pan was there, grimacing against her own pain as she took hold of his hand. He squeezed, and for a while they walked like lovers. And still the pipe stretched on, erased in both directions by the dust, now, so that it seemed like it was floating in the air.

"Getting dark," said Pan. She was right, the inferno above them was losing some of its strength. There were no plumes of fire here, nothing to feed the conflagration, and with every step they took the darkness gathered around them a little more confidently. "Watch your step."

Marlow did, the ridges of the conduit growing harder to make out. He looked down again, and with less firelight diffusing through the ash he got a clearer picture of what lay under them.

And he was so, so glad that he hadn't jumped.

There was an ocean down there, but it was an ocean of people. He could see thousands of them, hundreds of thousands, every single scrap of the ground covered by crawling, fighting, biting, chewing figures. They were far enough below that he couldn't make out their individual cries but the collective noise of them was like a booming tide. He was aware of the smell now, too, a rolling wave of rot that swelled up and settled in his nose.

The sight was overwhelming, and he had to crouch before the dizziness pulled him into the festering pit. He forced himself to count to three, taking as deep a breath of putrid air as he was able each time. Then he walked, trying not to look down, failing, watching the hordes as they teemed over one another, a crushing mass of misery and pain. It was almost too dark to see, and when he glanced back he could make out the line of fire in the sky above the land. They'd come farther than he'd thought.

When he turned the other way he thought he saw something in the darkness, as welcome as the shore of a desert island to a shipwrecked sailor.

The end of the line.

He moved as fast as he dared. Night was quick and graceful, already rendered half invisible by the churning ash. Behind him was Pan, navigating the uneven surface with care, her arms held out to her sides like a tightrope walker. It felt like they were on a conveyor belt, a treadmill. Maybe they'd walk this thing forever.

"We've got company," Night said.

Marlow twisted his head around, saw something walking toward them from the end of the conduit. Night planted her feet, aiming the blade of her spear at whoever was coming. It was hard to tell but it looked like a person rather than a demon. "Another ghost, I bet," she said. "They just don't know when to quit."

The figure took on substance as it approached, like it was forming from the clouds. A guy, dark hair, kind of handsome. A smile carved his face in two as he walked, and he held out his hand to them.

"Amelia," he said in a voice made out of a hundred whispers.

"No," whispered Pan.

"I've missed you."

"No."

"Pan, who is that?" asked Marlow.

"You killed me, Amelia," the man said. "Now's your chance to make it right."

"No," Pan repeated.

"Make it right," he said. "It can all end here. Just one step, and it's over."

Pan's face fell, like something had been pulled right out of her. Marlow saw her look down, over the edge of the conduit. The thought was right there, etched in every line of her frown— *she's going to jump.* And Marlow had reached for her before her expression hardened. This time, her reply wasn't a whisper, it was a roar.

"No!"

The man shrugged, using a finger to scratch at his nose. His smile widened further, too big to be human. Marlow could almost see the mechanisms beneath.

"That's what he said you'd say," came another voice, this one behind them. Marlow looked to see another man stepping out of the swirling dust, and this one crushed his lungs in a fist of grief.

Danny, he tried to say. His brother was wearing his desert combat fatigues, a helmet angled on his head. He strode confidently, wearing a smile that Marlow had never seen before—not that he remembered anything of his brother other than the photos that his mom kept.

"Marlow," the thing that wasn't Danny said. "I wondered when you'd show up."

"You're not real," said Marlow, closing ranks with Pan, standing back-to-back with her. He felt her fingers worm into his and he held her tight.

"*I'm* not real?" the ghost said, not slowing. "You got some cheek, Marlow. You're the one who isn't real. You're the intruder here, the imposter."

"No place here for you," said the other man, walking faster now. "Any of you. You're not welcome."

Marlow steeled himself, waiting for their heads to crack open, for those black limbs to slice free of their stolen skin. *It's not Danny*, he kept saying. *It's not real, it's not real.*

"Just keep your heads," said Night, spear at the ready.

"You're not welcome!" cried Danny, a hollow sound from his distending mouth. He roared, and as he did so the inferno on the horizon began to gutter.

"Oh no," said Pan.

With a rumble that Marlow could feel in his bones the final gasp of sky fire burned out, and in the darkness that followed came a pounding of feet and a howl of rage.

GHOSTS

The dark was absolute, like her eyes had been ripped from their sockets.

Pan was a spinning top, her mind reeling, and she collapsed onto the conduit. The sound of drumming footsteps was almost on her, the ghosts howling as they moved in for the kill. She knew it wasn't Christoph, the rapist who'd assaulted her years ago in Queens, the man whose murder she would have been imprisoned for if it weren't for Herc, coming to her rescue, stealing her away to join the Fist.

It *couldn't* be him, but it had looked so real, so real.

"Incoming!" yelled Night. She grunted, something growling. Pan heard the whump of her spear as she swung it, the crack of metal on metal. Then something laughed in Pan's ear and a pair of arms wrapped themselves around her from behind. They tugged hard, almost lifted her off the ground, but she managed to wrap her fingers around a piece of the pipe, rooting herself.

"Don't fight it," said Christoph. It wasn't his voice but they were his words. She'd know them anywhere. "You're mine, Amelia."

He pulled again, and she clung to the pipe with both hands, feeling like her fingers might snap. Above his laughter, above the loud cries of whatever lay beneath them, Pan could hear a sound like tearing flesh. The ghost was changing, shedding its disguise.

It was going to eat her.

She kicked back, hitting air. Christoph laughed, tightening his grip around her waist. She could feel his body pressed against her and it was changing, something fracturing beneath his skin. She kicked again, her heel connecting with something that shattered like glass. Christoph made a choking sound that bubbled back into laughter.

"That all you got?" he whispered.

She smashed her head back into the ghost's nose and his hold on her loosened. Christoph's laughter was liquid thick, gurgled through blood. She could feel his fingers pushing into her waist, trying to claw into her skin.

"Come to me, Amelia," he said. "You know you want to."

She kicked out, squirmed loose, managed to turn onto her back. She could see nothing, but she imagined him there—shirtless, grinning, expectant—and she kicked up with everything she had.

The heel of her foot hit with a wet crunch, a jarring pain shooting up her leg. The ghost whined like a beaten dog and she kicked again, fumbled her way to her knees—too frightened to stand.

"Marlow?" she said, her voice trembling. She could hear somebody fighting but she didn't know who it was. "Night?"

Something whipped up to her side—just a whirl of sound—and punched into her flank. It slid free with a lightning show of pain and she collapsed. When she put a hand to the wound she felt her own blood, as hot as spilled coffee.

"Pan!" came Marlow's voice. "Watch out! I think it's—"

Something barged into her and she rolled over the edge, the world dropping out from beneath her. She reached for the pipe, grabbing a part of it with blood-slicked fingers. Her legs scuffed the side, seeking purchase, but the agony in her ribs was too much, it felt like her body was about to tear in two. Beneath her the ocean screamed and screamed.

Not an ocean, then, she thought, and she finally made sense of the motion she'd seen there.

"Pan?" Night this time. "Where are you?"

She grunted, the only sound she could make. Her hand was slipping and she tried to adjust her grip. Her fingers might have had razors for bones, the pain unbearable.

"Pan?"

Night sounded closer this time, and her fingers brushed the top of Pan's head.

"Marlow, she's here. Pan, grab my hand."

Footsteps, panted breaths, then Marlow: "Quick, I don't know where Danny went."

She let go of the pipe with one hand, reached up. It seemed like an eternity before somebody grabbed her, fingers locking tight around her wrist.

"Come on!" said Marlow.

Pan reached for Marlow with her other hand. Then she planted a foot in a divot, the iron biting into her sole.

Marlow and Night hauled, reeling her up.

Then something even darker than the night loomed up above Marlow and his grip on her vanished. She fell, slipping through Night's fingers, reaching for the conduit and finding nothing but air. She tumbled into the void, her stomach looping, her cry locked in her throat. Beneath her the chorus of screams rose into a nightmare crescendo, as if the ground knew she was coming. She fell, and she fell, and—

She landed on something soft, something wet, something *moving*. Her breath was snatched from her and she had no time to claim it back because she was rolling, gaining speed as she thumped her way deeper into the earth. Nails scratched at her, fingers grabbed her hair, she could hear teeth snapping, and all the time that bone-shaking chorus of screams and shouts drummed at her ears.

She grabbed hold of something that felt like flesh, managed to stop herself. Whatever she was holding struggled against her and she let go, trying to stand on ground that lurched and swayed. Jaws flexed beneath her, teeth chewing. A million figures pressed in around her in that blinding dark and the noise of them was deafening. Her senses had been robbed—all apart from the agony in her side, the wounds that were being opened up in her feet and legs.

They were going to crush her, she knew. They were going to crush her, and devour her, and when hell remade her down here they'd do it again, and again, and again.

No.

She pushed into the crowds, into those endless moans and cries. Bodies thumped against her, tried to wrap their hands around her, tried to press their lips against hers. She pushed them away, grunting through their embraces. The smell of them was unreal, like she was swimming in rot. Each breath held a thimbleful of air and her whole body howled with the effort of it. Blood still gushed between her fingers, dripping to a floor that was already drenched with it, like she was wading through marshland. Each step she took sank ankle-deep and she felt the people who lay beneath the water try to claim it.

No.

She tried to focus, tried to get her bearings. They'd seen the edge of the canyon, seen the wall of rock. All she needed to do was get to it, but which way was it? She looked up; nothing there but the night, coffin dark. Somebody took hold of her hand, spoke to her in a language she didn't recognize, her voice laced with desperation and madness. She tried to pull loose but it wouldn't let her go and she lashed out with her fist, punching wildly until she was free. She'd only taken two steps before somebody else took hold of her, this one uttering frantic gasps of English that rose above the pulsing wave of sound.

". . . told her, I told her, I . . . are you her? Mary? Mary?"

She shunted her way past, thumping into another walking corpse and ducking around it. But somebody hit her before she could straighten and she fell, splashing into the pool of liquid rot. A foot stood on her head, pushing her deeper, a finger sliding into her mouth from below, scraping her tongue and making her gag. The pressure on her disappeared and she arched her head out of the blood, managing half a breath before somebody else stepped on her, crushing her into the mess. She twisted her head to the side, trying to keep her mouth above water. There were too many people there, all of them shambling and stumbling, trampling her.

"Help!" she screamed, not sure who she was screaming at, knowing it would do no good. "Pl—"

Somebody tripped on her, fell, their hand slamming into her nose. She tried to push them free but they were too heavy, pushing her into the mud of blood and flesh. Somebody else landed, squeezing the last drop of air from her. They were all sinking, the water bubbling up over her mouth, her nose. Her arms were too weak to free her, the pain in her side too great. She took a breath but there was nothing in her lungs but old blood. More and more people fell, tumbling onto her, pressing her, crushing her.

No, she said—to everyone, to no one.

She tried again to breathe, and the dark night grew darker.

GONE

"Pan!"

Marlow lunged for her, almost fell. Only Night's grip on his arm held him back.

"She's gone," Night said. "Come on, we're not safe y—"

Marlow felt it coming this time, a subtle shift in the air pressure as something big swooped toward him. He ducked, rolling into the dark, no idea which way was which.

"Marlow," said Danny—a voice that couldn't have been his brother's even if Marlow had remembered what his brother sounded like. "You took my place. You made her forget about me."

"Who, Mom?" Marlow grunted, pushing himself onto his knees. He knew he shouldn't be talking with it, knew it was just trying to distract him, but he couldn't stop himself. It was just too *real*.

"It should have been me," Danny said. "I should have been the one who lived. You messed it all up, Marlow. You wasted your life. You drove Mom to drink."

"And you got a big mouth, asshole," said Night.

Marlow sensed her leaping past him toward Danny, heard the wet slice of her blade against its flesh.

There was another noise, too, something low and deep—a growl. Was it the ghost? He listened for it, every muscle tense.

Something whispered past him, something big, and he heard the snap of teeth, a wet crunch.

Marlow found his feet, teetered. He stepped along what he thought was the length of the pipe only to feel the edge, the abyss screaming up at him. He angled toward the sounds of Night laying into the ghost with everything she had. She was screaming in Spanish but the ghost was just laughing.

"Kill yourself," it said, the words chewed into lumps. "Kill yourself, Marlow. End it, just like Pan did."

"Shut up," Marlow growled, feeling his way forward. "Shut your face, Danny, or I swear I'll—"

"You'll what?" More laughter, punctuated by the sound of Night stabbing the blade into the ghost's body. "You did that already, Marlow. You did that and took my place."

"Go screw yourself," he said. That growl again, the drumming of feet, a soft thud—and then the ghost howled as it tumbled over the edge. There was a soft snort right by Marlow's ear, then something as big and as wet as a cow's tongue slid over his face, leaving a trail of slime. He gagged, rolling back, hearing the thunder of footsteps fading.

"Night?" Marlow said, wiping away whatever had been plastered to his face.

"Yeah, I'm here."

"What's going on?"

He crouched there, waiting for the ghost to renew its attack. Ten seconds passed, then thirty, and by the time he'd counted out a minute he let himself breathe. He felt Night's fingers on his head, then she sat down next to him. Beneath them a million dead screamed into the night, and he knew that one of those screams belonged to Pan. He covered his ears, wincing as the wound in his back flared.

"What happened?" he asked. "What were those things?"

He felt her body tense as she leaned over the edge.

"Whatever—they're gone," she said. "Pan, too. Come on, we should keep moving."

"We can go after her," he said, but the words were just breaths, because he knew that however much he loved Pan—and he did love her, he knew, he loved her with every piece of himself—nothing could make him stand on the edge of this pipe and throw himself into death. Nothing, not even her.

"Come on," said Night, taking his hand, urging him up. "She'll come back; hell will make her again. We have to keep moving, we have to get off this bridge."

She walked, leading him along behind her. Marlow was happy to follow, navigating the uneven surface without thinking. They'd seen the far end of the canyon, it couldn't have been more than thirty yards away from where they'd been attacked, but all the same Night led him for what had to have been three times that distance before she stopped. The noise of the ocean was far behind them, just a dull rumble on the edge of his hearing.

"Wait here," Night said. He listened to the sound of her climbing down the edge of the conduit, then she spoke again from below. "It's safe." She snorted a laugh. "Well, maybe not safe, but solid."

He wasn't sure he could make it, but he eased himself over the edge and started to descend. His back felt like one big slab of pain, everything soaked with blood, but he made his way slowly, surely, downward. When his foot hit warm ash he almost cheered. He wasn't quite ready to trust it, though, dropping to his knees and using his fingers to feel for any sudden drops. But there was only ash. This whole place was made of ash.

"We should wait here," said Night. "Wait for the light."

"Best idea I've heard yet," said Marlow, leaning back against the conduit and yelping at a sudden bloom of cold shadow inside his head. He lay on his side instead, on a pillow of dust, exhaustion making the night even darker than it already was. He closed his eyes, but all he could see there was Pan—Pan fighting, Pan screaming, Pan calling his name, Pan dying.

Pain pulsed in his back, in his muscles, in his head. He wondered how bad the wound was, whether he'd bleed out in his sleep, wake in the pit with teeth in his throat. "I don't know how much longer I can do this, Night."

"You quitting already?" she said with a soft laugh. *"No mames."*

"Huh?" he slurred. He thought he could actually feel the life draining from him, or was it just sleep pulling him in? Death and sleep, he wasn't sure he could tell the difference anymore.

"No mames," she said again. "You've been here, what, two days? Try hundreds. Try almost a thousand. That's nearly three *years*. You stay here that long, *then* you can start whining."

"Sorry," he said.

"Back there?" said Night. "Who was that? Ghosts always take the form of somebody you know."

"My brother," he said.

"Didn't even know you had one."

"I don't." Marlow tried to remember his brother the way he'd known him. "I mean, not anymore. He died when I was five. I never really . . ."

Marlow had been so young that he could barely remember Danny. He was just a photograph on the kitchen wall, desert camo, Oakley shades, big smile. Marlow couldn't even think about what his mother had been like back then. He reached into his head, searching for one memory, for *any* memory, but there was just a cushion-soft void, one he felt like falling into and never coming out of.

"Leave them alone," he said, speaking to hell, knowing it was trying to wipe his mind clear, trying to drive him insane. "They're mine."

"*Qué?*" asked Night.

"Nothing," he said.

"Was it true?" she asked. "The things he was saying?"

"Why?"

"I don't know how they do it," she said. "How they know things. Your brother isn't actually in hell, right?"

"No, of course not," said Marlow. "He never used the Engine, died in Afghanistan."

"So how does it know that stuff about your mom, about her drinking?"

Because hell seeped into your head, Marlow thought. Because it cracked open your skull with icy fingers and peered inside.

"It got it wrong, about me and Danny. We did know each other, when I was a kid."

Again he reached for those memories, and again he found nothing.

"We should sleep," he said. "When it's light we need to go back, we need to look for Pan."

"Yeah, sure," said Night.

But there was nothing in her voice that made him think she was telling the truth.

He lay there, visions playing against the backdrop of the night—Danny charging at him, Pan falling, as clear as day even though he hadn't seen it. He thought he would see those things until the end of his life.

Lives.

Yeah, lives. Hell would torment him with these visions until the end of time.

A soft growl, the same one he'd heard before. But whatever it was, it could have him. Sleep was smothering him. He couldn't have sat up if he'd wanted to.

"Good night, Pan," he said.

"It's Night. Not Pan."

"Yeah," he slurred. "That's what I meant."

But it was Pan he spoke to, and it wasn't so much good night as goodbye. Because he was afraid there were some deaths you couldn't come back from, not even in hell.

ASCENSION

They were burying her alive, entombing her in flesh and blood.

Another weight thumped down onto the pile, pressing her deeper. She lay on her stomach, a mask of rot choking her, her vision a mess of static.

And still they came, shambling onto her like the walking dead, like they were seeking out her life, her warmth. Hands grabbed at her, fingers like iron rods pinching her skin, jagged nails tearing. The weight of them was impossible, surely enough to snap her spine, to turn her organs to jelly.

They came from below, too. It was too dark to see, but weren't those eyeballs in the wet ground beneath her? She could feel the motion of them blinking against her cheek. Lips sought her, the jagged edge of a tooth catching the bridge of her nose. A word bubbled up, or a noise that might have been a word— lost in the mindless panic of her thoughts.

She stopped fighting. It was too much, too much. *Just let it happen*, she told herself. *Just let it be over.* Maybe this time she wouldn't come back. Maybe this time hell would let her go home.

And she heard laughter, deep inside the cavern of her thoughts. She heard *his* laughter.

I knew you'd come, Christoph had said.

It was a hallucination, a memory, but her fury was real. It burned its way through her, its force nuclear.

"Never," she told him, spitting the word into the gulping face beneath her.

She planted her hands in rot, pushed hard. The dead Engineers above her pressed back but she was stronger than them. She was stronger than the dead. She felt them give, felt one of them slide away. Screaming, she braced her foot and shoved, driving herself forward. The blood beneath her helped and she slid through it, her hands clawing at the pit, dragging herself out. A hand looped around the side of her head, a finger hooked in her cheek, and she bit hard, chewing on the corpse-cold flesh until it tore free.

Never, she said, pulling, kicking, finding a gap in the chaos and sucking in a lungful of air. It was like nitro thrown into the engine of her rage and she screamed again, a feral cry that seemed to carry a power of its own, that seemed to shake the world to pieces. She grabbed hold of faces, skulls, arms, whatever she could find, ratcheting herself out inch by inch by inch until she could get onto her knees, then onto her feet.

She stood there, every bit of her sticky with blood, her breaths ragged. The dead brushed past and as she heard them collapse onto the pile, she imagined them folding onto one another, a living, breathing, shrieking sculpture that grew and grew and grew.

No time to wait for them to notice she was free. She moved, her feet crunching old bones, blood bubbling through her toes. Somebody walked into her and she punched them, as hard as she could, her fist disappearing into the festering shell of a skull. She shook free the gore, stepping over the twitching corpse, shoving another dead man to the side.

A growl rose above the screams, and she felt something big move past her. There was a savage howl, a tearing of flesh. There were more noises ahead, a shriek that might have been a demon. Pan waited for the sting of teeth, for oblivion, but it didn't come. The path seemed to clear, those feeding-time noises following her as she broke into a run, slipping, tripping through a swamp of remains.

Please please please, she prayed, and she wasn't even sure what she was asking for until she slammed into something too hard to be human. She staggered back, stars exploding against the night. Then she reached out, finding it again—a wall, beautifully solid.

There was a moment of panic when she slid her palm along it and there was only a smooth, unbroken plane. Then she found a jagged edge, enough to grab with her fingers. She levered herself up, her bare feet finding purchase. The noise behind her was a solid force and it seemed to buoy her up, allowing her to stretch and find another handhold. The wound in her side sloshed, but the adrenaline was numbing the pain.

How long to go? She hung on to the rock, the ridges eating into her palms, tearing her feet. It was still so dark that she might as well be hanging on to the edge of a black hole. One slip and she'd be back in the pit—and she knew she didn't have it in her to fight her way out again.

So she climbed, resting when she could, pushing upward even when it seemed like there was nothing left of her. Even when it seemed like she was a husk, drifting on the wind. She climbed until she reached for the rock and it wasn't there, just a big nothing that she hauled herself into. Crawling away from the edge, she couldn't even be sure if she was laughing or crying or screaming. Whatever it was, it carried that same word up from inside her, spewing it out into the ash.

"Never. Never. Never."

And she kept saying it, a heartbeat that carried her out of the nightmare and into the blissful reality of sleep.

* * *

"Open your eyes."

The voice drew her from an abyss, one that didn't want to let her go. She pushed up like a swimmer who has dived too deep, seeing the glorious glow of sunlight just beyond the surface.

"Pan."

She peeled open her eyes, light flooding into her skull like water. The pain was quick to move in, too, every part of her blasting a siren of agony. She curled onto her side, blinking until the world spun into shape—the desert, the sky, and a face with a goofy grin leering down at her.

"Hi," said Marlow.

It seemed to take an age for her to work up a word, and when it came free it was made of dust.

"Hi."

"You're definitely Pan, right?" Marlow said.

She fought the pain long enough to raise her hand, extending her middle finger. He laughed.

"You made it out. *How?*"

She kept her hand there and Marlow grabbed it, easing her up. She felt like a baby learning to sit, her body too weak to hold itself. For a second she thought she was about to fall flat on her face but then Night was there, arms wrapped around her.

"Easy, *hermana*," she said. "I got you."

"How?" Marlow said again. "I mean . . . I didn't think you were coming back from this one."

"You always come back," she managed, the sunlight still running into her, chasing away the last of the shadows. She looked at her hands, stained red and black, flecked with scraps of . . . meat? Her entire body was crimson. When she tried to

98

lift her T-shirt it was stuck to her, and Night had to help her peel it loose. The wound there was a mouth, something as fat and red as a tongue sticking out. She shook her head, pushed the T-shirt back in place so she didn't have to look at it anymore.

How *had* she gotten out?

"I don't know," she said. "There were demons down there, too, I think."

"Yeah," said Marlow. "About that."

He looked to the side, and she followed, a brutal rush of adrenaline twisting her insides, making her groan.

A demon stood there, maybe thirty yards away. It had three legs, and a fourth that looked half chewed, swiveling uselessly in its socket. Its gray skin was a patchwork of scars. Its face was the same as every other demon's—just a ragged hole lined with teeth.

A second demon lumbered across from it, treading circles in the ash. This one had six legs, and all of them ended in what could have been human hands. It looked hungry, huge gobs of saliva dripping from its jaws. But after growling softly at Pan it crunched onto its haunches, making a noise that could have been a sigh.

"What . . . in the hell . . ." said Pan. Both demons looked her way when she spoke—not that they had eyes to see with. The first one whined, walking in circles before lying down. Then, incredibly, it yawned.

"Yeah," said Marlow, shrugging. "Weird, right?"

"Why haven't they, you know, eaten us?"

Marlow spluttered out a sigh. "Have you seen the state of us, Pan?" he said, nodding at her gore-encrusted skin. "I wouldn't touch us either."

"It's more than that," said Night. "I think they might have saved us. I think they killed the ghosts."

Pan frowned, remembering the growls in the canyon, the snap of jaws. Had those demons been down there with her? Had they chewed a path through the dead? It seemed impossible, but then what in this place *didn't* seem impossible?

"Why?" she said.

"My guess," said Marlow, "is because of that."

He moved, the sky behind him a churning vortex of darkness. It was hard to look at. *Painful* to look at. The more she stared at it, the more it felt like somebody was squeezing her eyes, trying to pop them like grapes. She looked away and carried some of that darkness with her, great big spots of it hanging in her vision. They faded after a while, but she thought she could see a shape in them, something that looked like an immense black mountain.

She looked again but Marlow held a hand up in front of her face.

"Don't stare," he said. "I think it's like looking at the sun."

"It'll burn your eyes right out," said Night.

"Help me up," Pan said, holding out a hand to Night.

Marlow helped, both of them hauling Pan to her feet. The world spun, like it was trying to knock her back down, but she stood her ground. The pain was a dull pulse inside her. She could bear it. As soon as she was standing the demons pushed themselves up. They made no move to attack. The first one just stood there, snorting, the second walking awkwardly, heading toward the distant storm.

"You thinking what I'm thinking?" said Night.

"They want us to follow them," said Pan.

"I think this might be our escort," said Marlow, nodding in wonder.

"But that's crazy, right?" Pan said. "We're not actually going to go?"

A throbbing growl rose up in the first demon's throat. It pawed at the ground with razor-tipped claws.

"I don't think we have a choice," said Marlow.

He was right. They didn't have a choice. They didn't need one, either. Pan closed her eyes, saw Christoph's grin, his dark eyes burning.

I knew you'd come.

Hell had taken the worst of her life and made it real again. And that *seriously* pissed her off.

"So we go find this asshole," she said. "We go find him and show him."

"Show him?" said Marlow.

"Show him that we've got nothing to lose," she said.

She took one step, then another, clenching her fists. The first demon bounded alongside them, keeping its distance. The second howled into the day.

"Show him that he may be the Devil," Pan said. "But he should never have messed with the Hellraisers."

SAFE PASSAGE

He was right, it was an escort.

The demons padded along slowly, like horses at the head of a funeral procession. They followed the conduit, heading for the ruptured sky. The pipe grew taller and wider the farther along it they walked, becoming more grotesque with every half mile. The mechanical parts clicked and whirred, those black veins bulging like they were trying to make contact. The surface was slick and greasy, and Marlow was so thirsty he had to resist the urge to lick it. He wasn't sure how long you could last without a drink, but they were going on three days now and his organs were as dry as raisins. His kidneys, especially, ached like he'd been kicked by a mule.

The farther they walked, the more conduits they saw. Another large one snaked toward them from the right, just as big and just as ugly. Eventually, after what felt like an eternity, they reached the point where the two conduits met. There was no join, as such, they just seemed to grow into each other, like the limb of a tree meeting the trunk. They were forty feet tall at this point, made up of thousands of metal components that spun like atoms. It was mesmerizing, hypnotic.

With nowhere else to go, the demons bounded off the ground and onto the conduit. Marlow gritted his teeth against the nightmare visions as he climbed after them. Night was already there, and her face was as ashen as the ground they'd just left.

It wasn't hard to see why.

Ahead, for as far as he could see, the world was a machine. Hundreds of those weird conduits merged into one another over the next half mile, looking like some deranged labyrinth. The noise they were kicking out was enough to make Marlow's teeth chatter, almost enough to mute that world-shaking pulse.

All of the conduits led the same way.

All of them led to *him*, Marlow guessed.

He stared at the sky and it was as if a charge had been detonated in the side of his skull. He screwed his eyes shut against a sudden torrent of horror that passed through his thoughts, like he was sitting next to a slaughterhouse conveyor belt.

"And I thought the Red Door was bad," Pan said, talking about the infernal portal they'd had to pass through every time they entered the Engine. Incredibly, she was smiling. Marlow smiled back, and as he did, some of the horror flowed out of him. He rubbed his eyes, glanced back at the dark horizon.

It was a mountain, but a mountain made of moving parts— of cogs and gears and pipes, of pistons and chimneys, of springs and levers and counterweights, of organic veins that wove in and out of the mechanism, pumping black. The entire Engine— because that's exactly what it was, even bigger than the one back in the Nest—moved with a fury that threatened to overwhelm him, as if the whole of the earth had shattered into squirming parts.

Marlow felt something drip into his mouth, tasted copper. When he put his fingers to his nose they came away red. Pan's ears were bleeding hard, great red drops pattering down onto her shoulders. Night had her fists pressed to her temples like she meant to cave in her own head.

He glanced back, wondering whether he could go, just put his head down and run. But he was pretty sure the demons weren't going to let them go. Every now and again they'd sniff Marlow or Pan or Night, as if to remind themselves who they were escorting, but they never showed any sign of aggression. It was like the creatures back in Meridiana's cavern, he thought. They'd been gundogs, perfectly obedient.

The only difference was these dogs had the Devil as their master.

That mountain of madness up ahead grew bigger with every step, the conduits sloping toward it like foothills. The going was getting tough, Marlow's whole body trembling with the effort of the climb. The storm dominated the skyline. It was vast, huge clouds of smoke and debris churning around it like dirty water down a drain. It looked like it was moving in slow motion but he knew it was just an illusion caused by the sheer size of it. He couldn't work out if they were one mile away or a hundred; the fractured landscape of hell made a mockery of time and space. The constant, beating sound of it was like the world ending.

"We should probably work out what we're going to say," Pan said, looking to the top of the mountain. "When we get there."

"Hey there," said Marlow. "We know you're the Devil, Lord of All That Is Evil. But we think it's time for a major reboot on your public image. Think of us as your new PR team. Let us go and we promise we'll tell everyone you're awesome."

"Riiiight," said Pan.

Night coughed out a laugh.

"Sorry. It's the nerves talking. I mean, you know, the abject terror. And the hunger. Anyone else looking at those demons spraying saliva everywhere and thinking they might want to suck it up?"

"Ew," said Pan, licking her own chapped, desiccated lips.

"But yeah," said Marlow. "What do we say?"

He clambered over a section of metal that grew from the conduit, hopping down the other side and continuing the upward slog.

"Who says it will even give us a chance to speak?" Pan said.

"I don't know," said Marlow. "It might not. But there's got to be a reason these demons are keeping us alive, right? It's got to be curious, if nothing else."

"But you said you'd seen them attack Engineers," said Pan, looking at Night. "We saw it, too, back in the first building we took shelter in."

It seemed like a million years ago, that wall of screaming faces, the men and women and children who had rooted themselves there for a hundred thousand years. Marlow saw the demons clawing at them, peeling them loose, and suddenly understood.

"Because it *frees* them," he said. "They were bound to one another, wrapped around one another like . . . like some rat king. The demons killed them so they could be reborn on one of those mountains, so they could be free again."

"Free in hell," said Pan. "What good does that do them?"

"Them? Maybe nothing," said Marlow, nodding ahead. "But *him*. What if, I mean, maybe he needs them to be free. Maybe he *wants* them to come to him."

And the thought that they were walking into a trap, walking into the vast, open maw of the Devil, made his heart hurt.

"It doesn't matter," said Marlow. "We've lost our lives, we lost our souls, too. We've got nothing left to lose."

But he wasn't so sure about that.

Up ahead, the monstrous Engine formed a solid cliff face, the churning storm directly above it. It was made of the same stuff as the conduit, what must have been a million pieces of machinery ticking and whirring and moving in perfect harmony.

Through those mechanisms of dark metal he could see enormous veins, thousands of them, each black and moist and flexing as something pumped through them. The mesmerizing mass of movement was broken up by several openings, as dark as tombs, and the demons led them straight to one of them.

Marlow craned his head up, the storm overhead now, those huge clouds spiraling like vultures. Every time that infernal pulse thundered out across the world he saw the Devil imprinted on his retinas, a disease that crept ever deeper into the flesh of his brain. He could see its expression, stuffed with glee.

He could see it *smiling*.

All around him pieces of the world were fighting against gravity, rising up toward the chaotic sky. He could feel that pull, too, invisible fingers on his skin ready to lift him up and devour him. Whipcracks of negative lightning sliced through the clouds, so dark that it was like the world being sheared into pieces. He couldn't tear his eyes away from it.

"In or out?" said Pan, looking into the fissure in the Engine, at a flicker of light there. "Door number one or door number two."

Choices.

Press on and face whatever awaited them inside, or surrender themselves to the never-ending nightmare of hell. Both ways led to death—and death, and death, and death—but only one would lead to answers.

"Door number one," he said. "It's always door number one."

He walked up the final stretch of slope, entering the tomb. It was like falling into a grave, the sudden quiet as suffocating as dirt. He had to ball his fists, clench his jaw, to stop the explosion of cold fear inside him. It was a passage like you might find in an old church, only the walls were made of machinery instead of stone. The floor was trenched by a million footsteps.

He glanced back. Behind them the world was almost dark

again, although he didn't see how there was any way another day could have passed. It wouldn't be long before the sky started burning, but they didn't need the light in here. There was a weak glow leaking from the far end of the passage.

There were noises, too, something too faint to identify.

"Maybe it's the band," he said, walking to Pan's side. "All parties should have a band, right?"

"Party?" said Night.

"Welcome party," Marlow replied. "Something's waiting for us."

"Hope it's mariachi," said Night. She leaned her forehead against Marlow's back, muttering, "I'm so tired."

He was, too, his body running on fumes, running on *fear*.

"So tired," Night said again.

The passage angled to the right, then to the left, worming its path up into the heart of the mountain and getting steeper with every turn. The noises ahead were growing louder but he still couldn't identify them. They echoed off the walls, off one another, becoming some twisted chorus of half sounds that grated on his every nerve.

"Yeah," said Marlow, his voice just a whisper. "That's definitely a mariachi."

"Shut it," said Night, thumping Marlow on the arm.

He yelped, but his mouth snapped shut around it as they turned a corner in the corridor and it suddenly opened up into a bigger space.

A *much* bigger space.

It was like a football stadium, like MetLife or somewhere, the far end almost invisible. One vast circular wall enclosed the space—or not so much a wall as an engine, its mechanisms churning. Struts arced skyward like the ribs of some enormous animal, meeting in the middle where the tornado of darkness still roiled. Beneath it sat what could have been a pyramid, its walls

107

made of machinery and its top lost in the clouds. The ground around it was a wasteland of rock and gleaming metal.

Hundreds of those fat black arterial pipelines crossed the space, draped over one another like a nest of snakes. They must have been leaking, because there were pools of dark liquid everywhere. The pools seemed as if they were rippling, or at least that's what he thought until he looked closer and saw that there were things moving on the edge of them, shapes that could almost be human.

There was noise in here, that thumping pulse reverberating around the space, but it was quieter than it had been outside—quiet enough for him to hear the screams from the people there, screams and songs and laughter and incessant chatter and howls of glee and sorrow. It was the lullaby of a madhouse, of bedlam, and he felt the tattered threads of his own sanity pull loose a little more.

"What now?" he said, chewing his knuckles to pieces.

He turned to the center of the giant room, where the mechanical pyramid rose toward the clouds above, its tip invisible in the maelstrom. Everything led to it—the pipes, the finger-like stretches of Engine, the black pools. Everything led right here.

Including us, he thought. Because what was the point in coming all this way just to turn back now?

He hopped down from the end of the passage, slipping on the damp stone. He could feel the moisture seeping into the wounds in his feet—not painful, just weird, like it was probing them. There was a puddle of it ahead and he ducked down, trying to make sense of what he saw, and why it looked so familiar. Dozens of silver flecks swirled in the darkness like miniature shoals of fish, and when he leaned over to get a better look there was no sign of his reflection there.

"Like the Black Pool," he said aloud, thinking of their Engine and the pool that sat by it—that grotesque body of water you had to throw yourself in to make a deal. He looked up to see Pan pulling a face. She looked gaunt, half dead. He guessed he probably looked worse.

"Always hated that thing," she said.

He helped her up and they kept moving, their footsteps falling into time with that bone-shaking pulse from the Engine. The piles of rock made it difficult to see where they were going, but so long as they kept that pyramid in sight he knew they wouldn't stray too far. The sound of the other people in here was alternately muted and amplified by the metal walls, making it so that when he rounded one cairn the sudden rush of noise and movement took his breath away.

There was a black lake ahead, almost as big as an Olympic swimming pool. Positioned around the rough edges were cages—the bars formed from pieces of Engine, all brass and obsidian. They were all empty save for the last one, which held a creature that he could make no sense of. It was almost human—two arms, two legs partially submerged in the pool— but it looked like it had been skinned, and there was something wrong with its head. There was no face there anymore, just a sucking hole right in the middle of it.

Marlow splashed across the uneven ground. He didn't exactly want to get a better look but he couldn't turn away, seeing the tubes fastened into this creature's limbs, seeing the veins that bulged black beneath its muscle, seeing the baby teeth that were pushing through the circumference of its mouth, small and sharp. The demon—because there was no doubt in his mind that that's what he was looking at—must have sensed them, because it angled its head their way, sniffing. Its mouth drooped open, great gobs of black gunk dripping from it, and it started to laugh—*uhuhuhuhuhuh*—the sound unbearably real, and unbearably human.

It smashed two clublike hands against the bars, rattling the cage, and Marlow quick-marched past it, walking up a small rise and past another mound of fractured stone. The lake he saw here had no cages, just four figures crouched at the edge of it, people who were completely naked and wire thin, apart from their distended stomachs. They were scooping up the black liquid and drinking it, over and over, barely even stopping for breath. It sprayed back out of their lips and dripped from their noses, their eyes, their ears, but still they drank, their dark eyes wide with mindless joy.

Except for one who had no eyes at all.

"Oh no," Marlow said, the sudden recognition like a gunshot going off between his ears.

"No," echoed Pan.

It couldn't be, could it? It couldn't be who Marlow thought it was. The worst guy imaginable, yes, the guy who made his time in the Fist unbearable. But not even he had deserved this.

"Hanson?" said Night. "It's him, Pan."

"Hanson!" Pan called out, taking a step toward him.

He flinched, turned his head her way to reveal those gaping sockets where his eyes had never been. His body was covered in scars, riddled with them, and Marlow understood that he'd fought it, he'd fought hell. He must have died here a hundred times to have scars like those, a *thousand*. But then how long had it been since he died, since Mammon had killed him? And how long was that on this side of the void?

Hanson licked his lips with a tongue that was too long, too black. Then he ducked down and scooped another handful of water into his mouth, swallowing, gagging, bursting with it.

Pan was crying, sobs punching their way up from somewhere deep inside her. She covered her mouth, as if it were possible to be embarrassed in this place, hurrying past the drinkers and following the path ever deeper.

It was the same at the next pool, where a young woman stood neck-deep in the black fluid and sang what could have been a keening song, her eyes as dark as pitch and drenched in sadness. They were all Engineers, Marlow knew, people who had died under contract, whose minds had been corrupted into rot by the black fluid, by the presence of the Devil. By the time they'd passed by, all three of them were crying their way toward the rotten heart of this cathedral.

Only a distant voice held them back.

"Hang on," said Marlow, reaching out and stopping Pan. He stared back the way they'd come, back past the pools, past those ruins of flesh.

"Wh—"

"Just hang on," he said again.

He cocked his head, listened as a voice rose up, shrill and wicked. It spoke only one word, over and over, but it was a word that speared its way right through him.

"Pan."

"It's Patrick!" Pan proclaimed. But it didn't matter. They were here. A spiral staircase wound its way up the outside of the central pyramid, leading into the vortex. Marlow could make out a shape in the storm, a coiling mass of shadow and madness whose nightmare pulse seemed to have become something else, something full of humor.

The bastard was *laughing* at them.

Something shuddered inside his head, a tectonic shift of emotion—fear, confusion, sorrow, guilt, and anger. It was a rage he'd never felt before, a fury that burned up from the deepest part of him, that threatened to split his throat in two, that escaped from his lips as a roar.

No more, he thought, unable to shape the words. *No more.*

And he was running, running without even knowing how, or why. The stairs were tall, surely carved for a giant, but he pulled himself up them, one at a time, one after the other, the world turning around him in slow, relentless circles. His legs burned, but the pain wasn't real. *He* wasn't real. How could he be? He'd been woven from the dead, he was a little piece of hell, as big a freak as anything here.

"Marlow, wait," Pan called out from below. But he didn't listen to her, because she wasn't real either. There was nothing real in this place, nothing but *him*. Whatever lay above them, in that tornado of movement and noise, it was the only real thing here.

He climbed, the cavern vanishing into smoke and thunder, the maelstrom all around him. But the top of the pyramid couldn't be far, he could almost see it, a ledge, and beyond it only darkness. He was on his knees now, his legs too weak to carry him. But still he moved forward, turning the final corner, scaling the last dozen steps, and finally seeing what lay there, at the very summit of hell.

HOME

He should have known that hell would save the very worst till last.

He should have been ready for it.

But nothing could have prepared him for this, not the demons, not the ghosts, not the horrors they'd been through since materializing here.

The summit of this engineered mountain was the size of a basketball court, almost perfectly flat. Right in the middle of it was another pool of black water, the same size as the one back in the Fist's original Engine. There was only one building here, and the sight of it was enough to make him want to throw himself off the ledge and end it all—not that jumping would have ended anything, of course.

It was a house. A wooden house, the slats of the siding so old that there was only a haze of blue paint left. A set of steps led up to a front door that was shut tight, the filthy windows all closed, too. The curtains were drawn, the porch coming loose. Dozens of those black tubes fed into the house, along with sections of Engine that ticked and whirred like clockworks. The roof was missing, replaced by a bulging mass of black flesh that looked tumorous, diseased, one that stretched up into the seething gyre of the sky.

It was a house, the kind you'd see on any street, the kind

that a young family might live in, an old couple maybe. Only he knew this wasn't home to either. He knew exactly who lived in this house: a woman, a teenage boy, and the ghost of a dead brother.

It was a house.

It was *his* house.

"It's . . ." he tried, but he couldn't find the words. It was like the storm had plucked them right out of him. *It's a trick*, he told himself. It had to be, another of hell's games—the same thing that had forced them to see their mothers, fathers, brothers.

"You are seeing that, right?" Marlow asked, the words fluttering like sails in the wind.

"A house," said Pan.

"You'd think the Devil would upgrade," said Night, her laugh hollow. "Pick somewhere with a good color scheme, maybe fewer rats. Must be a recession down here."

"You see a house?" he asked Pan, ignoring Night. "Blue, kinda, brown door, steps? A Staten Island kind of house?"

"Yeah," said Pan. Then she frowned. "Wait, you *know* it?"

Marlow nodded. Something big had crawled out from his stomach, was clawing its way up his throat.

"I *live* there."

"What?"

His mind was reeling, like a bird thrashing inside a cage—it was only a matter of time before it broke free, before it got caught in the storm. He put his hands to his face, grabbed hold of it like he meant to pull it loose. His nails dug into the skin, the pain unbearable but still more bearable than this. He closed his eyes and wished it all away—*pleasepleaseplease*—but when he looked through his fingers again there was the black pool, the raging storm, and that house, that awful, impossible house.

And as he stared at it, tears streaming down his face, the door clicked open.

Pan took hold of his hands, pulled them away from his face. Then she threw herself at him, her arms locked tight around his shoulders, her head buried in his neck. She was speaking, the words hot against his skin.

"We'll do it together. Whatever is in there, you won't be on your own."

He pressed his face into her hair, wondering how despite the fact she had been born again here, despite the fact she'd waded through the countless dead, despite the fact that none of them had washed for days, she still smelled just like Pan. He gripped her, held her like she was a part of him, like she was keeping him alive.

Which was true, wasn't it? It had been true since that day back in the parking garage, a million years ago.

He held her, and breathed her, until she pulled away—awkwardly, because he couldn't remember how to relax his arms.

"You really live there?"

"Yeah," Marlow said. "Like, forever."

He thought back as far as he could, which had never been far. He had spent his childhood here, but his memory of the place began from when he was about five. He couldn't remember a thing before that, except the death of his brother—more nightmare than memory, dulled by age but sharpened by imagination. He'd always just assumed that when Danny had died his brain had done some emergency surgery on itself, packed everything away in Styrofoam and bubble wrap. It wasn't like there had been anything much of his childhood worth keeping.

"But why?" Night said. "I don't get it."

"You think it's a trap?" asked Pan.

"I don't know," he said. "What else could it be?"

And for some reason, his head answered him: *the truth*.

"There's one way to find out," he said, forcing his reluctant legs to start moving. He reached out and felt Pan take his hand,

Night grabbing hold of the other one. He had the sudden, insane desire to start skipping, like a kid between his parents, and before he could stop it a giggle escaped his lips.

The house replied. Or something in the house. A voice seemed to spill out of it, just a whisper, the words somehow wrong like they were being played backward. Then another sound, a cry of grief, like somebody in there had just discovered the cold body of a loved one.

A blade of pain pushed its way inside Marlow's head, just above his left ear, and he had to let go of Night to rub at his scalp. His skin was crawling as if there were maggots feasting beneath it. The house was twenty yards away now and the door had opened further, revealing a shadowed hallway that looked just as he remembered it.

"You think the Devil's in there?" Night asked.

"Yeah," said Marlow. Then, for a reason he wasn't quite sure of, he said, "Or something worse."

Fifteen yards, and Marlow had to look behind him because he thought he heard that voice, rising up over the storm. There it was again, faint but close enough to make out Pan's name, called over and over.

Ten yards, he could see the windows shaking in their frames, could hear the squeal of glass about to break. The whole building looked like it was about to collapse, only those pipes and mechanisms holding it together.

Five yards, and through the open door Marlow saw the wooden floorboards, scuffed by Donovan's claws when the dog went crazy at the sound of somebody knocking. He saw the mirror on the floor, resting against the wall because it had fallen off months ago and Marlow had always told his mom he'd put it back up one day. He saw the fan of letters stuffed behind the radiator, bills he knew his mom would never read. But the darkness was too heavy, too thick, to see beyond those first few feet. It looked like a throat, and Marlow couldn't help but think of anglerfish, those glowing lures. The house looked like it could swallow him whole.

"We go in together," said Pan.

"Yeah," he said. "Just give me a—"

"Pan?" That voice again, behind them, louder now. "Pan? Pan?"

She looked back, her face creased with anxiety.

Marlow.

Another voice. He snapped his head back because *this* voice had come from inside the house—thin and reedy, a thousand years old. There was a desperate gasp for air, then it called his name again—not a sound but something else, something that seemed to come from inside him.

"Your nose is bleeding again," said Pan, smudging it away with her thumb.

His head pounded in time with that relentless pulse, the force of it surely enough to liquefy his brain. It was impossible to think straight and he wondered how long it would be before he, too, was wandering the cavern, drinking from those black pools, tearing off his own face.

"You sure you want to—"

"Yeah," he said, trying to stare inside the house, trying to make sense of the darkness there. Whatever it was, it was moving, swaying, beckoning. "Yeah, I'm sure."

Because he had to know why his house was here. He had to know who was inside.

He stepped up to the threshold, opened his mouth to speak.

Hello? Who's in there? Whoever it is, I'm gonna crush your ass.

Nothing came out, though.

"Whatever it is," Pan said. "We deal with it together. All of us." And he could hear her whisper *together* again and again beneath her breath as she stood behind him, as she waited for him to take that step.

He took a deep breath, the air full of the scent of machine oil, of blood, of copper, and of something else, something *sweet*. Then he walked inside.

That sweetness hit him again, the unmistakable smell of rum, his mother's drink of choice. It dragged a memory from his head, something he hadn't thought about in years: him, running through the house chasing the puppy that would later be named Donovan, skidding into the kitchen and swiping a full bottle from the kitchen counter. It had smashed, soaked in through the floor, through the chipboard of the cabinets, through the wallpaper. The house had reeked for weeks, but his mom hadn't been mad. She'd hugged him, told him it was okay, checked his feet for broken glass.

Because everything had been new. Everything had been new.

He had no idea what that meant, something itching at the back of his head, some long-forgotten truth, something that felt *wrong*.

Movement up ahead, something big, something that seemed to fill up that ocean of darkness at the end of the corridor. It writhed like a nest of leeches, dozens of them coiling, sliding wetly over one another.

"See anything?" said Pan.

Marlow turned to her, and that's when he saw them, on the far side of the pyramid—a lumbering beast whose bloated belly dragged on the ground like the skirt of a wedding dress. Knotted around his neck was a woman, a girl, her tiny body twisted and knotted and scarred like it had been fed through a wood chipper.

"Not this asshole again," said Marlow.

Pan spun around, fists bunched, in time to see Patrick throw his sister to the ground and start running, the ground actually trembling with the force of his footsteps.

"Go!" yelled Night. "I got this."

Patrick roared, halfway to them. His giant hands flexed, ready to rip Pan's head off a second time.

"Go!" Marlow echoed, running out of the house. "Just—"

Something coiled around his waist, ripping him inside so hard he thought his spine would snap. He grunted, seeing Patrick's catcher's-mitt hand wrap around Pan's face.

Marlow just had time to mouth her name.

Then the door slammed shut, and there was nothing but the boundless dark.

UNFINISHED BUSINESS

Patrick came at Pan like a freight train, too quick for her to react, his giant hand snapping shut around her face and starting to squeeze.

"No!" she screamed into his filthy palm. She was lifted off the ground, Patrick's other hand around her arm and pulling hard. She could feel the immense power there, feel the fabric of her start to tear.

And over it all she could hear him laughing like a two-year-old pulling the wings from a fly. He was going to kill her, and when she came back he was going to find her and do it again, and again, and again.

"No!" she yelled, and this time she opened her mouth and clamped her teeth around Patrick's palm. She bit, and she kicked, kicked, kicked until she hit bone and the laughter stopped.

Patrick ripped his hand away, leaving a piece of it in her mouth. He still had her arm, though, and he slammed her into the ground. Her head hit rock and her thoughts kept going, sinking into darkness. Only for an instant, then she was back, hoisted into the air, Patrick's sagging clown face grinning down at her.

"Why don't you stay dead?" yelled Night, jumping onto Patrick's back. He grunted, letting go of Pan, too slow to grab

Night as she hopped onto the ground. Pan scrabbled around the side of the pool, watching Patrick's obese body jiggle as he chased Night. It was only then that she saw that the front door of the house was closed.

Where was Marlow?

Night screamed as Patrick managed to grab her hair. She ducked, almost scalping herself as she twisted around him, breaking free. She drove her foot into the back of his leg and he juddered onto his knee. Pan ran to them. She had no weapon but she drove her fist hard into the back of his head. Patrick groaned, toppling like a felled tree.

"Patrick!" screamed Brianna. She was scuttling across the pyramid like a spider, her knotted limbs clumsy and out of sync with one another, but surprisingly effective.

"You take her," said Night.

No problem. Brianna was faltering already, her stunted arms collapsing beneath her. She face-planted just as Pan reached her, struggling to recover. She looked up, her face a patchwork doll's, even her eyes ridged with scars. But Pan could still see the girl she'd once been.

"I'm sorry," Pan said. "I'm so sorry."

Behind her Night was laying into Patrick with a vengeance. He was trying to get up but his bulk was stopping him. His face was turned to her, infinitely monstrous but still his. Past the madness, past the rage, there was just Patrick Rebarre, a boy who'd loved his sister so much he'd followed her to hell.

"I never wanted—"

Pain lanced through Pan's ankle before she could finish. She yelped, seeing Brianna there, yellow teeth sunk deep into her skin. Tugging free, Pan staggered back, but Brianna followed, a lunatic hunger in her eyes. Pan's foot struck something and she fell, landing on her back. Brianna didn't hesitate, climbing awkwardly up Pan's legs, across her stomach, biting her hard in the chest. Pan screamed, trying to push the girl away, but Brianna's claws were under her skin, hooked there like ticks.

"He never lets me eat," she was screeching, spraying the words out along with Pan's blood. "He never lets me eat."

Pan hit her, the strike driven by terror. Brianna's head snapped to the side but she lunged forward again, her blood-stained teeth going for Pan's throat. Pan hit her again, then opened her own mouth and lunged for Brianna's face. They bit as one, agony riding a burning path up Pan's neck, her teeth scraping against Brianna's skull. The girl bubbled out a scream, scampered back. Blood as black as ink dripped over her terrified face.

Pan felt like she had the weight of the underworld on top of her but she managed to get to her feet. She pressed a hand to her throat, stemming the blood, then she kicked Brianna hard in the head. Pan reached down and picked Brianna up by her waist. The girl was a husk, so easy to lift that it took Pan by surprise. She lifted her above her head and skirted around the black pool. Patrick was still taking a beating but he wasn't planning on staying down, his huge arms quivering with the effort.

"Here, boy!" Pan yelled.

Night jumped off Patrick's back, and he lumbered slowly to his feet. His head was a mess, and it took him a moment to notice what Pan had in her arms. When he saw Brianna there, he roared—a sound of pure fury. He dropped onto all fours, running at her like a bear.

"Oh shi—"

Pan ran, too, racing for the edge of the pyramid. She skidded to a halt, nearly tumbling over herself. The ground was only just visible below, masked by clouds.

"Brianna!" Patrick yelled. He was almost on her, kicking up a great plume of dust in his wake.

She didn't stop to think, just turned and threw Brianna as

hard as she could. The girl tried to grab Pan, tried to stop herself, and for an instant her momentum nearly pulled Pan over the edge. Then her finger-claws popped free and she was falling, tumbling into the clouds. Pan ducked, Patrick a blur of blubber as he barreled over her.

Pan watched him fall, his descent almost graceful. But she turned away before he hit the ground.

"Nicely done," said Night, limping over and rubbing her knuckles.

"They'll be back," said Pan.

"He'll have to regenerate," Night said. "It will take time."

"You see Marlow?" Pan asked.

Night glanced behind her, as if only just noticing he was gone. She shrugged.

"Not like him to miss a fight."

"It's *exactly* like him," Pan said. "I think he went into the house."

"Then I guess we should go help him," Night said.

She was already walking, and Pan followed.

Everything ached, her heart felt on the verge of stalling, but she had the feeling that if they walked through that front door then everything would end, one way or another. At least this way she might be able to rest.

And the thought of it, of not having to fight anymore, was so comforting that she didn't feel the tremor beneath her until it almost knocked her over. The entire pyramid was shaking, and there was a noise beneath her, an industrial growl growing louder and louder and louder until the air shook with the force of it.

"Get down!" Night yelled, throwing herself to the ground. And it was good advice, because a supernova of black light detonated from the middle of the pyramid, and with a final, catastrophic roar the house exploded.

STRANGER

The house was eating him.

It was eating him whole, its black tongue wrapped around his torso and reeling him toward a throat of absolute darkness. Marlow fought, drummed his fists against it, but it was dragging him too quickly, hard enough to knock him against the wall, then against the ceiling. Plaster dust rained down on him as the house wrenched him deeper, past the living room, heading for the kitchen. He tried to call Pan's name but he was moving too fast, he couldn't get the word out.

He smacked his head on the top of the kitchen doorway and his thoughts scattered like crows. Then he was slowing, the pressure on his ribs growing weaker, then disappearing altogether. He fell to his knees, fireworks exploding in his vision, the pain like a demolition ball swinging between the two sides of his skull.

Marlow.

The voice was a whisper, so close that it might have come from inside his own head. He blinked away the tears, tried to make sense of what he was seeing.

He was kneeling inside his kitchen, a room he'd known his whole life. But where there had once been counters, units, an oven, a sink, there was now just a seething mass of shadow. It covered the floor, the walls, and where the ceiling was supposed to be it ballooned upward like a circus tent. The shadows moved like leeches, squirming against one another, the motion making Marlow's stomach squirm. Two of those strands of liquid night approached him, coiling around his face like the fingers of a blind man, as if they were trying to work out who he was.

Only they knew, because that voice came again, breathing his name. He noticed how quiet it was here, the sonic boom from outside reduced to a uterine heartbeat. There was only the soft whir and click of the Engine, that and the wet, sliding madness of the moving shadows.

Marlow.

The voice was pushing into his right ear, insect sharp. He shook the pain away, angling his head to the side.

Somebody was standing there.

At least, he thought it was somebody. It was too dark to be sure, and those shadows danced and played in front of the figure, around it, so that it seemed to flit in and out of existence. It was a man, he could tell that much. A man so worn by time and ravaged by age that he looked like a corpse. He hung in the corner of the room—*literally* hung, as if he had met his fate on the gallows there—and looked down at Marlow with a face forged from sadness. He opened his mouth, more of those whispers scuttling out and climbing inside Marlow's head.

You came.

The man groaned, his lips stretching too far, his tongue lolling out. His voice carried such a sense of grief that Marlow felt it explode inside his chest, the tears a hurricane that battered against him. But he wouldn't show weakness, not here. He *couldn't*.

The hanged man twitched, jerking like a puppet on a string. He was making a noise that might have been laughter, might have been sobs. The coils of shadow that held him seemed to tighten, an anaconda strangling its prey. Marlow thought he heard the word *careful* in the confusion, spoken in a hundred different whispers.

I can't, said the man, and the shadows knotted themselves even tighter, making him groan again. *He was waiting for you, Marlow. He has been waiting for you for so long. You should not have come.*

Who was waiting? Was there somebody else there, hidden by the night? Marlow squinted, making out the top of the hanged man's head and something resting on it. It looked like a hand, too big, too many joints, the fingers actually penetrating his skull, *fused* there. Marlow followed it up, seeing a wrist, then an arm, and sure enough there was a shadow above the man, deeper and darker than the rest. He had to look away after a second because whatever stood there radiated something evil, something that made Marlow feel like his heart had been crushed.

I tried, said the hanged man, and he was weeping now. *I tried.*

Something replied to him, a sound that was almost too low for Marlow to hear—like a church organ playing a subsonic note. It thrummed through him, making his stomach flutter into a cramp.

No, said the man, his voice growing weaker by the second. *No.*

"What's going on?" Marlow asked.

That noise again, and the shadow behind the hanged man moved, bending forward into the room. Marlow could make no sense of it, there was no face there, no body, just a shape—and a cluster of eyes that burned like inverse suns, which dripped negative light.

"You," Marlow managed to say, recognizing it from the pool, from the way it had watched him with those spider eyes as he forged a contract. "The Devil."

He's not the Devil, the hanged man said. *He is a Stranger.* He thrashed against the darkness that held him, tendrils of shadow sliding into his mouth until he choked on them. The figure behind him loomed even closer, the room growing so dark that Marlow wondered if he'd been blinded by it. Two more fingers of shadow wrapped themselves around him, seemed to crawl inside his skin and coil around his ribs, his spine. The same subsonic noise rolled across the room, as powerful as thunder, and Marlow understood that this thing, whatever it was, was trying to speak to him.

He didn't understand the words, but he knew what it was saying. It rang like a clarion where his soul had once sat, loud enough to shake the world to dust.

WHAT IS IT YOU DESIRE?

The hanged man loosed a muffled groan, began to twitch and shake again. He was chewing on the shadows, spitting out gobs of black fluid.

Do not listen! he wailed. *Do not listen to him!*

WHAT IS IT YOU DESIRE?

If you listen then it's all over, please!

Marlow slammed his hands to his ears but it didn't do any good, the voices battling inside his head like artillery fire. He tried to move but the shadows wormed their way even deeper inside him, wrapping themselves around his organs and turning them to ice. He was shivering so hard he thought his teeth would shatter.

He has to see, said the hanged man. He was tearing at the darkness that held him, his stick-thin arms pulling chunks from it. The shadows inside the room were moving toward the man, a flood of them, like they meant to drown him, and the hand that held his head like a bowling ball tightened even further, his skull making a sound like a glacier shearing in two. But his determination was relentless. He looked at Marlow, growling, *You must see. You must see.*

"See *what?*" Marlow said.

The man ripped free of the last scrap of shadow, tried to take a step across the room only to be pulled back. He tried again, the crown of his skull actually coming loose, peeling away like the top of a boiled egg. The Stranger uttered its foghorn cry as it attempted to restrain the man, bind him in darkness. And it was working, there were just too many shadows. The hanged man stopped fighting, held out a hand to Marlow.

You have to see the truth, he said. *It's the only way.*

Somehow Marlow found the strength to move. He pushed himself up, the ground writhing beneath his feet. He was almost lost now, submerged in darkness, but that hand was still there, held up like a drowned man reaching for the boat.

It's the only way to beat him, the hanged man said, his voice just a gurgle now. He stretched forward, something dripping from the bowl of his skull. His eyes began to roll up in their sockets, like they were trying to see what had been done to him, but that hand still reached forth, still reached for Marlow.

Marlow threw himself across the kitchen, swiping shadows out of the way. He ran, he reached, and he grabbed hold of the hanged man's hand.

ONE LAST BREATH

The change was instantaneous—one moment he was in the stomach of his old house, battered by night, the next he was standing in a sun-drenched woodland, pigeons cooing in his ear and a gentle breeze blowing through his hair. He couldn't breathe, the shock of it paralyzing him until he literally smashed a fist against his chest. He sucked in air that smelled of blossoms, turning in circles and feeling the grass beneath his feet, sharp and warm.

"Where am I?" he asked, his voice older, grainier. It startled a pigeon and it broke from the canopy, its wings clapping. "Looks like heaven."

Not heaven, said the hanged man. *The beginning of hell.*

Something inside his head shifted, and he felt somebody else take control, steering him out of the woods and onto a dirt track that ran between hedges. He could feel an urgency that didn't sit with the rest of the illusion, a panic that came from nowhere. Then there was a distant scream and he started to run.

Smoke was rising from behind the bushes, clawing its way into Marlow's nose. He skidded around the corner to see a house—a cottage, really, small and thatched. It was on fire, the heat searing Marlow's eyebrows even though he stood thirty yards away, the inferno so fierce that it took him a moment to see the children in the flames.

There were five of them, four boys and one girl, the youngest maybe eight, the oldest no more than fourteen. There was something familiar about three of them, something *really* familiar. Marlow *knew* them, but he couldn't think from where. They hung from the windows, screaming.

Panic raged inside Marlow, one he knew didn't belong to him but which he felt with every iota of his being. He opened his mouth and howled, breaking into a run. But he was too slow. The cottage was old, made of thatch and stick, and it took only seconds for the flames to swallow it whole. One by one those faces vanished into the smoke, until the last scream was lost in the roar.

Marlow could hear himself shouting, words spilling from him that he'd never heard before. He was himself, but he had also become somebody else, the father of these children, the hanged man. He felt his body shudder and tremble, felt the weakness there, the disbelief, the unbearable sense of loss. He was running again, pushing himself into that wall of heat. He could feel the force of it against his skin, but he couldn't stop, barreling through the open door of the cottage. He called out, his children's names boiling into nothing inside his throat.

He was waiting for me, the man said.

"Who?" Marlow asked. "Why are you showing me this?"

Because it explains everything, the man said. *Hurry, we do not have long.*

Marlow could feel something pulling at him, something cold and dark trying to tug him free of the head he was inhabiting. It was gone in an instant, burned away by the fire. He stumbled into the inferno, his tears hissing. There was no air at all, just a fist of smoke rammed into his throat.

"Please," said Marlow.

There is nothing I can do, said the man. *This is just a memory. Don't you think I would have changed it if I could?*

A jagged bolt of lightning tore across Marlow's eyes. He tried to take a breath but couldn't—couldn't even bring in a scrap of oxygen. It was worse than any asthma attack, it was merciless, brutal, and he clawed at his neck, his chest.

And then he saw it, even through the flames, even past the tears. He saw the ground beneath him begin to crumble into dust and ash. There was something down there, a face buried in the fire.

A face that opened its eyes and looked right at him.

Death was flooding in, collecting in the corners of his vision, in the cradle of his brain. He was making a sound like a hiccup, over and over, but the fire was doing its job well. It was killing him.

The thing in the dirt was angling itself upright so that it could study him, its face unfolding like origami. Its body was too long, arms with too many joints curled tightly to its chest like a praying mantis. It seemed impervious to the fire, its beetle-black skin glowing. It never took those dark eyes off him and he screamed *hurry hurry hurry* with his breathless lungs. Because he knew this thing, this Stranger, was worse than the loss of his family.

He knew it was worse than death.

It rose up before him, a creature that belonged only in nightmares. Its face was an engine of parts, layers upon layers that fumbled and switched around each other like it was trying to work out how to look human. Only those eyes remained unchanged, eyes that seemed like holes cut in the fabric of the universe, revealing the impossible darkness of what lay beyond. They watched him with what might have been curiosity, or hunger, or glee, or love.

He collapsed, and knew it would be the last time. All he wanted—all the hanged man had wanted—was to rest here, to be reborn in paradise with his children. But the Stranger unfurled one of those too-long arms, uncurled a finger that had four or five joints, all of them crackling in the heat like fireworks. It rested a long, filthy nail on Marlow's forehead. Its face folded and unfolded until a mouth opened in the very center of it.

THEIR DEATH DOES NOT HAVE TO BE THE END, it said in a voice of quiet thunder, a voice that pushed back the power of the inferno.

Marlow's brain was shutting down, section by section. Death could only be seconds away, a void that loomed up before him, impossibly big and unfathomably empty. He felt the creature run its nail almost tenderly down his face, along his cheek, tracing the edge of his gulping mouth.

IT IS NOT TOO LATE FOR YOU.

It was, though. It was too late.

IT IS NOT TOO LATE FOR THEM.

And even though Marlow had no breath left to give, those words took his breath away. He felt it, the smallest flicker of hope in the churning ocean of pain.

ALL YOU HAVE TO DO IS ACCEPT MY GIFT. ALL YOU HAVE TO DO IS SAY YES.

All he had to do was say no.

All he had to do was say *no*.

But he didn't. His vision was a tunnel and he was being sucked inside it. The creature was growing more distant, shrinking from him, but he watched as it drew its nail along the putrid flesh of its throat, releasing a sludge of black blood that instantly started to bubble and boil. It dipped the nail into the wound, shuddering with what could only be pleasure. Then it extended its arm again, held that dripping finger before him.

LET US MAKE A DEAL, YOU AND I. ONE DEAL, SEALED IN BLOOD. WHAT IS IT YOU DESIRE?

He saw them, the faces of the children. And Marlow suddenly knew three of them—Mammon, Meridiana, Ostheim.

The panic was ocean-deep, drowning him even though he knew this was just another man's memory. Right now he would give anything for another breath. He would give everything he had and everything he was for just one more breath.

ALL YOU HAVE TO DO IS SAY YES.

Marlow should have said no—the hanged man should have said no—but death was on him and despite the fire it was cold, so cold.

He should have said no, but he saw their faces. He saw the faces of his children.

He should have said no, but instead he opened his mouth and used his very last breath, the very last of himself, to speak one final word.

"Yes."

THE WATCHMAKER

The Stranger's face rippled like a machine, the black pit of its mouth widening into a smile, its eyes dripping darkness. Then it slid its nail into Marlow's mouth, the blood dripping onto his tongue, sliding down his throat, tasting of rot.

IT IS DONE.

A supernova of inverse light detonated inside his skull, and suddenly the scene changed, the house, the fire, the Stranger exploding into dust. Marlow reeled inside a tornado, pieces of scenery clicking into place like a stage set until he saw a workshop, stone walls lit by torchlight. He turned his head left, then right, taking in workbenches littered with tools and mechanical parts.

I was a watchmaker, said the hanged man. *Maybe that's why he chose me.*

"Who?" said Marlow, but he knew the answer to that because he saw the Stranger in the corner of the room, cloaked in shadow, its face click-click-clicking like an insect as it watched him. He felt that strange sensation of being pulled, like he was a fish on a hook, half remembered some other world where his real body lay surrounded by coiling shadows.

Just pay attention, said the watchmaker. *I cannot hold you in this memory much longer.*

Marlow saw his hands starting to work, sliding an axle

through a cog and fixing it to a metal frame. He carried it across the room, into that pool of shadow where the Stranger stood. Marlow noticed that the creature was surrounded by mechanisms, glass pipes protruding from its body. The skin of its chest had been pulled away, its ribs cracked open and emptied. Beside it, pinned like a butterfly, rigged with tubes, was a shriveled heart that beat weakly. Marlow slotted the clockwork piece into the apparatus, his hands shaking. The Stranger made a noise like a cat purring, its body flexing, shuddering, rippling.

It was dying, said the man. *Its heart was too old to keep beating. It needed a way to stay alive.*

"A machine?" said Marlow.

An Engine.

A door opened at the other end of the room and a child ran in, one of the boys Marlow had just seen in the burning house, one of the children that had died. He laughed, trying to close the door against the young girl who was chasing him. Then they were all bursting through, shouting at one another, giggling. The joy in Marlow's heart belonged to the man, he knew, but it was still as welcome as dawn, filling him with sunlight. He found himself laughing, too, even when the children turned to him and he saw that their eyes were as black as pitch, as empty as unfinished dolls. They fell silent together, seemed to sag and deflate for a moment before remembering themselves, running from the room.

I should have known they weren't real—not the way they had been. They were something foul, something he dragged up from the darkest part of the world, or made from the foulest part of himself. He tricked me.

Marlow felt a cold hand wrap itself around his spine, pulling hard. The edges of this place, of this memory, started to fray and he clung on with everything he had. The scene began to speed up, his hands working tirelessly, the Engine growing and growing and growing, filling the room, expanding out into a cave, and then a cavern filled with bone—a graveyard, Marlow realized, remembering Paris—becoming a cancerous mass of parts that was relentless. For millennia, those five children watched, and played—climbing, hiding, sheltered by the Engine, drinking the blood that flowed through it—their humanity belied only by those inhuman eyes.

And all the while the Stranger stood there, its disembodied heart pumping, filling the Engine with contaminated blood.

"What is it?" Marlow asked.

Evil, said the man. *It is evil, and ancient, and wrong. Something that never should have been here, which slipped through the cracks. It has roamed the Earth for centuries making deals with humankind.*

"But how?"

Its blood is rotten, but powerful. Drink it and you do not die. Drink it and you are no longer human. Drink it, and anything is possible.

Speed, invisibility, mind control, anything you wished for, Marlow thought. The Engine had granted every desire and it had all come from this.

But it was old, so old. It was losing itself, and it needed my help. It tricked me into building the Engine, it showed me what to do, how to put the pieces together, and it held time at bay. A hundred thousand years is nothing to it, it became nothing to me.

Marlow watched as the Engine grew, as the watchmaker put a million pieces in place, and then a million more, as he chiseled out a pool from the stone and filled it with the Stranger's blood. The scale of it was infinite, unthinkable. He wouldn't have believed it if he hadn't already seen it.

And I came to love them, those things that were not my children. How can you not love something that you spend infinity with? I came to love them as I had loved my own flesh and blood, and they loved me, too. They changed, they remembered themselves. But I did not forget. In all that time I did not forget that it had deceived me.

"What did you do?" Marlow asked.

I deceived it.

A roar of outrage shook the memory, so hard that the vision began to dissolve. Marlow could still see through the watchmaker's eyes, though, as he ran frantically through the Engine, as he ducked beneath mechanisms, as he tried to cover his tracks. The Engine surrounded him like an ocean in a storm, every piece of it moving, every piece of it furious. There was something in his hand—something that might have been an old-fashioned lantern, a canister ribbed with metal parts, with glass tubes. This thing didn't give off light, though, it seemed to pulse with darkness, and when Marlow looked more closely he saw the Stranger's heart there—the Devil's heart—pumping.

In all those years, it never expected me to know enough to change its design.

Marlow looked on as the watchmaker pulled a knife from his pocket, ran it across his palm. He rested the wound against the canister and its mechanisms began to twist and coil around themselves, sealing it.

But I did know enough.

The Engine crashed to a halt, every piece of it freezing and plunging the cavern into silence.

I knew enough to change it.

Then it began to turn again, backward this time, everything working in reverse.

I knew enough to turn it against him.

Another howl filled Marlow's head, turning his brain to jelly. His stomach lurched like he was inside an elevator. He could feel himself moving—not him, but the whole cavern, the whole Engine, slowing to a halt again after a handful of seconds.

The Stranger came to trust me, over time. It trusted me with the very essence of itself—its heart.

"Heart?" Marlow asked.

Not a heart like you and I would understand it. It is the darkest part of it, the core that birthed the star. Without its heart, it is just a devil.

"And with it?" Marlow asked.

The watchmaker sighed.

With it, it is a god.

"Why didn't you just destroy it? Kill it?"

The Stranger cannot be killed. It is too old, too closely connected to the foundation of the universe. Neither can its heart be destroyed, as far as I know. But I locked it away, inside a mechanism that cannot be opened by infernal forces, or by human ones. And I used the Stranger's power, his blood, and split the Engine into incarnations of itself, each one trapped inside time. I trapped him here, inside this one. My children hid his heart inside another, somewhere he could never find it, some place he could never reach.

"What happened then?" Marlow said, craving the truth like he was craving water.

Then he turned one of them against me.

The scene juddered to a halt, four of the five children standing around their father—around Marlow. They were in a corridor, the stone walls damp, the air cold. One of the boys twisted the handle of a red door and opened it, night flooding inside.

"Hurry," said Marlow, the word spilling out of his mouth in another language, its meaning perfectly clear. "He's coming."

A shout from the other direction, full of rage. The three boys fled through the door, leaving just the girl. She ran forward, threw her arms around Marlow, sobbing into him, and he pried her away. Past the tears, her eyes were a brilliant shade of green, as human as anything Marlow had ever seen.

"You have to go, Meridiana. You have to leave me."

"I won't," she screamed. "I won't."

One of the boys ducked back in, and Marlow knew it was Mammon. He was holding the canister, the heart pumping so furiously it sounded like it was calling for help. He took hold of his sister with his free hand and dragged her through the door. Behind them came an animal cry and Marlow looked to see the missing brother there, his face warped into a carnival mask of anger, his eyes blazing black light.

"Father!"

"Come with us," pleaded Meridiana, but the watchmaker turned to her and shook his head.

"I have to lock the door," he said. "Go. And remember that I love you. Always."

He smiled at her, smiled at all of them, then grabbed the door and slammed it shut against their cries. He muttered a series of words and the corridor shook almost imperceptibly, that weird elevator lurch rising up in Marlow's guts again. The last brother—Ostheim, Marlow knew, how could it be anyone else?—ran the rest of the way, barging past his father and opening the door. Marlow had to hold up a hand against the tide of daylight, saw a field of snow, and beyond that a mountain. The children were nowhere to be seen.

"No!" Ostheim said, turning to his father. "What have you done?"

"It doesn't matter," he replied. "It's over. It cannot be undone."

Ostheim pulled a knife from his belt, a shard of Engine, and rammed it into Marlow's stomach. He doubled up, feeling the boy hoist him onto his shoulder as if he were a sack of feathers. Then they were running, back through the Engine, ducking beneath the mechanisms, climbing the cogs, leaving a trail of steaming blood in their wake. They ran deeper into the machine like they were running through a forest, until they stopped at the feet of the Stranger.

WHERE IS IT? The creature boomed.

"You will never have it," he replied, locking the truth of the hidden canister away inside his head. "You will never find it, I have made it impossible. You are trapped here, you will never leave."

IT DOES NOT MATTER. I WILL HAVE IT. I CAN WAIT HERE UNTIL THE END OF TIME. AND YOU WILL WAIT WITH ME.

The Stranger reached for him with those impossible arms, grabbed the top of his head, and squeezed. The pain was molten, those fingers drilling into his skull, pulling him close.

YOU WILL WAIT WITH ME.

More shadows closed over him, sliding into his mouth, down his throat. He felt the flow of cold blood, felt its evil spill into him.

YOU WILL WAIT WITH ME AND KNOW THAT YOUR CHILDREN WILL DIE AGAIN. THEY WILL DIE SLOWLY, AND THEIR PAIN WILL LAST FOREVER.

Inside the memory, Marlow gagged, trying to scream past the blockage in his throat, trying to fight it. But he was too weak, blood still gushing from the wound in his stomach, his strength deserting him. Slowly, slowly he sank into that squirming nest of shadow, the Stranger's hand pushing him deeper, deeper into darkness.

YOU WILL WAIT WITH ME UNTIL WE ARE FREE.

"I'm sorry," Marlow said in the voice of the watchmaker, not even sure who he was speaking to. "I'm sorry. God forgive me."

Then there was nothing, ink thick and choking. He felt that tugging sensation again, pulling him out of the memory—and he was glad to go, because he couldn't bear to be here, couldn't bear to see any more.

Do you understand why I showed you? asked the watchmaker

as the edges of the dark started to crumble. *Do you understand? I tried to keep you away.*

He had, Marlow saw—the watchmaker had a power all of his own. He saw him forging the ghosts, giving them their stolen faces and sending them out into the wastes of hell. He saw them slaughter Engineers one after the other, again and again, until they lost their minds.

I could not risk anyone finding us, he said. *All it will take is a deal—a deal between infernal forces, between things that should not be—and everything is lost. A deal will unite the Engines, and in doing so will bring this world and yours crashing together. Do not listen to him, do not bargain with him, do not set him free. You can end this, Marlow. You can end everything.*

"But I don't understand," Marlow said, the information breaking up into molten fragments as it burned into his head. "Why me? Why are you in my house?"

Because it is you who—

The memory let go and Marlow was catapulted across the void, back into his body, back into the fury of hell. He gasped, seeing his kitchen, seeing the shadows that writhed and squirmed, that coiled around the hanged man, drowning him. The Stranger was there, its face folding and unfolding just like it had in the memory, its eyes dripping. It extended its free hand—coiling its fingers around Marlow's throat and lifting him up, drawing him to it. It gave off a stench of rot, of unimaginable age and unquestionable power. There was a cavity where its heart should have been, stuffed with straw, as empty as a nest. Pipes and tubes and cogs formed an apparatus inside and around it, making it half monster and half machine.

LIES, it said.

No, replied the hanged man, and the shadows contracted like a fist around his head, unleashing a crack like a cannon shot.

The man dropped to the ground and the Stranger ripped its hand free, shaking loose pieces of skull and bone.

LIES, it said again. IT KNOWS HOW I CAN HELP YOU.

"Never," croaked Marlow.

IT KNOWS HOW I CAN HELP *HER*.

It waved its other hand and the kitchen blew apart, the walls exploding outward in a hail of shrapnel. Suddenly the cavern was around him, the raging storm overhead, pieces of house bouncing and sliding over the top of the pyramid. Pan was there, Night, too, with no sign of Patrick and his sister.

The Stranger stood straight, its mechanical parts whirring and grinding, linking it to the vastness of the Engine. Tubes and pipes ran into it from every direction, pumping black blood. It hoisted Marlow, its hand as tight as a hangman's noose.

"Marlow!" shouted Pan, running for him then stopping, throwing a hand to her face against the energy that radiated from the Stranger. Marlow hung there, his feet kicking pathetically at the air.

I CAN HELP HER, it said. I CAN SET HER FREE. I CAN SEND HER HOME.

"Run," grunted Marlow, the word too quiet for anyone to hear. He tried again, shouting it louder only to feel those fingers tighten even further. Pan held up her hands, her face full of terror.

"Let him go," she said. "Please."

COME TO ME, CHILD.

The Stranger's other hand unreeled, as long as a tree branch. It caught Pan, lifting her effortlessly so that she was hanging next to Marlow. She pulled desperately at its fingers, choking, her eyes bulging.

TELL ME WHAT YOU DESIRE, the Stranger said, its hand squeezing. Pan was choking, her eyes rolling up, her body convulsing.

TELL ME THAT YOU WANT TO LEAVE THIS PLACE. TELL ME, AND IT IS DONE.

Marlow reached out for Pan, found her hand. She gripped him and he held her, watching as she fought for her last breath. She shook her head and he knew what she was saying, he knew she was telling him not to make a deal. Because she was stronger than him. She had always been stronger than him.

All he had to do was say no. Pan would die, but she would come back. He might die, and he, too, would be reborn. Hell was bad, yes, but they could survive it together.

All he had to do was say no, but Pan was shaking hard, foaming at the mouth. How many times would he have to watch her die here? A hundred? A thousand? It would never get easier. He would never grow used to it. A thousand deaths, and he knew each one would be worse than the last.

TELL ME WHAT YOU DESIRE, MARLOW, AND IT IS DONE.

All he had to do was say no, but he opened his mouth and said "Yes."

The stranger laughed, a noise like thunder. Marlow fought against the chaos in his head, tried to remember what he'd been told the first time he'd been thrown into the Black Pool, the first time he'd made a deal. He could almost see Seth, the old man who'd shown him the ropes, as he said it: "It is the man who wants everything, and he who does not know what he wants, who lands himself in trouble."

And what had Pan told him? To be sure of what you're dealing for. "The Engine, it will try to trick you, it will try to fool you into making an unbreakable deal."

"I want to go home," Marlow said, dredging the words up past the fingers around his throat. "I want to go home, I want Pan to go home, I want Night to go home. I want us all to go home."

He could hear the hanged man moan in despair, and Marlow knew that he was making a mistake. All he had to do was say no, but he was cleverer than that, wasn't he? He could make this work.

"But only us three," Marlow said. "Once we're through, the passage closes, nobody else gets out. *You* don't get out."

That would work, wouldn't it? If the watchmaker was worried about setting the Devil free then surely this would work? He swung from the Stranger's grip, his thoughts sloshing back and forth, too messy to make sense of. It wasn't enough. He needed more.

"No, the gateway is destroyed," he grunted. "When we're through, all of us, me and Pan and Night, the gateway to hell is destroyed and it can never open again."

AND THAT IS ALL?

"Just us," Marlow said. "That's what I want, I want us to go home."

The Stranger laughed again, loud enough to shake the whole of hell.

IT IS DONE.

PART II
WHO HOLDS
THE DEVIL

THE FAST TRAIN HOME

IT IS DONE.

Even though she had no oxygen left in her lungs, even though her head fizzed with static, Pan heard those words and knew instantly what they meant.

Marlow had made a deal with the Devil.

You idiot, she tried to say, but she never got the chance because the creature that held her—a giant that radiated so much darkness she couldn't make sense of it—was striding forward, heading for the pool of black liquid that sat in the center of the pyramid. It held her above it and then let go, let both of them go.

She hit the water hard, and it was eager for her, sucking her deep beneath the surface. She burst out of the top, managed half a breath before the pool caught her again. She reached for the edge, finding cold stone. This time she managed to stay afloat, Marlow paddling furiously behind her. The Devil loomed above them, a phantom dressed in darkness, its face a mess of parts that opened and closed like machinery.

IT IS DONE, it said again, the words echoing around the cavern, kick-starting a hurricane of sound as the Engine began its work.

"What did you do?" she asked, looking at Marlow.

He disappeared beneath the surface, bobbing up again almost

instantly and spitting oily black blood. "I made a deal. It's okay, it's going to b—"

And he was gone again.

"What the hell, guys?" said Night, skidding onto her knees at the edge of the pool. She looked at the Devil, then back at Marlow as he emerged, gargling.

IT IS DONE.

This time, when the Devil spoke, the pool began to tremble— ripples spreading out across its surface. The whole cavern seemed to be shaking, chunks of rock dropping from those weird, riblike props above them.

YOU ARE FREE.

"*Free?*" said Pan, and despite everything she felt something shift inside her, an immense weight lifting.

"We're going home," said Marlow, treading water.

"But what did you give it?" Pan said. "What was the deal for?"

She saw Marlow frown, saw him shake his head.

"I didn't ask."

"Idiot!" she said, trying to pull herself out of the pool. Everything was happening too quickly, she didn't have time to think.

"What do we do?" Night asked.

"Come on!" Marlow yelled, caught in the unsettled water. "Pan, please, we can go home!"

Pan looked up at Night, fumbling for the girl's hand.

"What do we do?" Night asked again.

"I don't know," Pan said. "We take our chances in there." She nodded at the pool, then at the creature of nightmare who stood and watched them. "Or with *that*."

"In there," said Night without hesitation, ready to jump. Too late Pan saw movement behind the girl, a balloon of burst flesh, its skin split, great lumps of yellow fat and pink intestine hanging

148

from the open wounds. Patrick—the bastard had somehow survived the fall. He turned his mangled head to Pan, one eye hanging loose, swinging like a yo-yo. The other burned with hate.

"Watch—"

Patrick's bear-trap hands snapped shut around Night's chest with a firecracker pop of breaking ribs.

"No!" Pan screamed, trying to pull herself free. There was a current now, pulling her toward the center where Marlow floundered. She clung to the rock for as long as she could, then her fingers cramped and she let herself go. The water dragged her under but she fought it, breaking free long enough to see Patrick's jaw split open, to see his teeth clamp down over Night's face even as she fought him.

"Night!"

The current was too strong. She bumped against Marlow and they held each other, fighting to keep their heads out of the water, spinning in the vortex. Then Marlow disappeared, his hands grabbing Pan's legs and pulling her under too.

She sucked in black water that tasted like machine oil and decay, feeling herself wrenched deeper. The pool seemed to tip on its head and suddenly she was tearing upward like a torpedo, screaming against the force of it. Silver specks illuminated the dark, like distant solar systems, and still she was accelerating, the water around her glowing, bubbling, like she was a ship returning from orbit, burning through the atmosphere. The sound of it deafened her, but she could hear the cry of the Devil, echoing through the void.

YOU ARE FREE. YOU ARE HOME. AND THE GATE WILL BE DESTROYED AFTER THE LAST OF YOU.

She couldn't make sense of it, she just thought of Night, Patrick chewing through her face.

"I'll come back for you," she said, her stomach ripped out

through the soles of her feet as she was pulled faster still. "I'll come back."

Then the world flipped again and she was falling, falling through water into more water, like there was a pool of denser liquid beneath her. She slowed, stopped, then began to paddle up—or at least what she thought was up, because there was no light here.

She stuck her hands out, blind, fumbling for anything and finding stone. She pulled herself to it, trying to remember how to breathe, smudging the black water from her eyes. Something erupted from the pool behind her and she turned to see Marlow there, his face alive with panic as he sucked in air. He dropped and she grabbed him, pulling him close, both of them clinging like coral to the wall of the pool.

She didn't let go. She didn't dare. They both rested there, too exhausted to do anything else, too scared to look beyond the steep-sided walls. She just kept glancing back, waiting for Night to burst from the water, to grin that grin of hers as she splashed toward them.

But the surface of the pool fell still.

The air was heavy with noise, a mechanical pulse that shook her to the core. It was the same noise they'd left behind them, the soundtrack of hell.

We're still here, she thought.

"Help me," she said, her voice a witch's croak.

She grabbed the edge of the pool above her, planting a foot on Marlow's shoulder, hearing him yelp as she dunked him. She pushed herself up and over the edge, prepared for hell, prepared for anything—anything except *this*. Because when she made sense of the chaos in front of her it was a smile that found its way onto her face.

"No way."

"What?" said Marlow, coughing. "Where are we?"

Pan scrabbled around, offering him a hand and helping him onto solid ground. They were on a platform, tilted at an angle and cracked in a dozen places. The pool beside them was half drained. A control panel sat there, wires torn out and hanging limply.

She was almost too scared to look the other way, the noise still pummeling her ears. But she couldn't hide from it forever. She turned, seeing the Engine there, *her* Engine, stirred into a frenzy. Every single piece of it was in motion, great plumes of fire erupting, engulfing the ceiling. To her side was the staircase, partially melted but still intact. It led up to the vault door and she knew what lay beyond that—stairs, the Red Door, and freedom. Its call was birdsong inside her head, impossibly sweet. Twenty minutes of climbing and she could feel the wind on her skin. No more monsters, no more demons, just the glorious day and the rest of her life etched out in sunshine.

"It can't be," she said.

"It is," Marlow replied, struggling onto his knees. "We're home."

"When, though?" Pan asked. "*When* are we?"

Because when she'd last been here the Engine had been silent and still, straining against broken time.

"What did you deal for?" she asked. She rolled onto her side, then somehow managed to get to her feet. The flecks of metal in her skin caught the firelight, like she, too, was burning. She patted her side, feeling the wound there—gummed shut by blood, stitched by those ribs of metal.

"I . . . I don't know," he said. "It was all so quick. I just asked to go home."

"Home," she said, chewing on the word. "That's it?"

"Yeah," he said. "That's it."

Something didn't sit right, something niggling at the back of her brain.

"She'll come," said Marlow, staring at the pool, chewing his knuckles, his teeth clacking against the metal there. "She has to."

Pan wasn't so sure, wondering if she should throw herself back into the water and try to return for Night. But nothing, not one single thing, could draw her back to hell—to that creature who had watched her with eyes like burning coals.

"What happened in there?" she asked. "Who was that?"

Marlow grabbed her elbow and hefted himself up, standing there stooped and broken. He was about to reply when something crunched out in the Engine, an industrial roar.

"Ostheim," she said. The only reason they hadn't seen him before was because Meridiana had given them the power to step out of time, had locked them here in an infinite moment. When they'd died, when they'd been sent to hell, time had reclaimed this place with a vengeance, and it had freed Ostheim in the process.

The only good thing was that he couldn't know they were there.

She started to walk, her body too heavy, as if the gravity in hell had been weaker than here. She found her rhythm soon enough, running for the stairs. Clambering onto the lowest step, she saw Ostheim at the far end of the cavern, his bulk rolling cautiously over the Engine beneath it. He looked as far from human as it was possible to be, his body bloated to the size of a whale, a dozen or more tentacles writhing. He held something in one of them, something that gave off a metallic glint, but which pulsed darkly, too, an inverse lighthouse beam. Whatever it was, he was slamming it repeatedly against the floor like he was trying to break it.

"Asshole," she whispered, then continued to climb. She heard

Marlow clatter up behind her, making so much noise that she was amazed they made it to the top undetected. She ducked through the vault door into the security room. It was empty, but the door to the stairwell was open and she thought she could hear voices spilling out of it. Jabbing a finger in her ear to clear it, she tried again.

Yeah, they were definitely voices.

She looked at Marlow, his smile the brightest thing in the room. Then she burst through the door, craning her head up the stairwell. She could just about see them, figures illuminated by the emergency lights, three or four flights up and running. From the sound of it they were arguing as they went.

"Hey!" she yelled. Nothing, just the thump of footsteps and those voices, muted but still full of emotion. She tried again, yelling as loud as she could. "Hey!"

It was a gamble, of course, because she had no idea who it was. She didn't even truly know if they were back on Earth. This might have been the next level of hell, just a new way of breaking their hearts, ready to peel away in an instant, revealing a world of ash and bone. It was a gamble, but it paid off, because whoever was up there stopped running and a face peeked over the edge of the banister—old and grizzled and ugly as hell.

But kind, and wide-eyed, and the most beautiful thing Pan had ever seen.

"Herc!" she yelled, and she was running, tripping up the stairs in her haste. She heard him call her name, heard the rumble of his feet as he came to meet her. She turned a corner and he was suddenly there, a mess of sobs and scars and Old Spice who swept her up in his arms and hugged her so hard she heard her spine pop. She held him just as hard, pushing her face into him, practically screaming into his neck, "Ohgodohgodthank-youthankyouthankyou."

"What the . . . *Pan*?" said another voice, and she peeled her wet face from Herc to see Charlie with his eyeballs in danger of popping out and rolling down the stairs. *"Marlow?"*

"Hey," said Marlow, and then he was sobbing, too, breaking down right there, hands plastered to his face. She could hear him muttering, "It's real, please let it be real."

Herc took Pan's head between his palms, looked her right in the eye.

"What happened?" he asked. "I saw you die."

And he must have noticed the metal striations embedded in her face, the sheen of copper in her eye, because he was suddenly wary.

"You sure you're real?" he said. "You sure you're her?"

"Of course it's me, you miserable ass," she said, smudging the tears away.

"I don't get it," said Charlie. "You died. They tore you to pieces, like *minutes* ago."

"Four days," she said. "Four days, Charlie. I've been in hell."

Charlie and Herc shared a look.

"And you didn't even get me a T-shirt," Charlie said, his smile so big that she almost burst into tears again. He opened his arms. "Come here."

She did, but he pulled free almost immediately.

"Jesus, Pan," he said, putting a hand to his face. "You smell like you just crawled out of the Devil's armpit."

"You don't know how right you are," she said. "What happened out there?"

"In the five minutes between you dying and coming back?" said Herc. "A lot. The moment you went," he shot this comment at Marlow, although Pan wasn't sure why he was scowling, "the whole Engine started coming to life. Nearly ground us into mincemeat on the way out. Lucky we weren't too far in."

"And Ostheim came back," said Charlie. "Popped right out

of nowhere. Don't think he knew we were there, don't think he'd even noticed time stopping. He's uniting the Engines, won't be long before . . ." He frowned. "Wait, you said you were in hell, right? How'd you get back?"

"Long story," said Marlow.

Something was still tugging at Pan's mind, something important.

"No, wait," she said. "Marlow did a deal with the Devil. The *real* Devil."

"He *what*?" said Charlie.

"What kind of deal?" Herc asked.

"A deal to come home," Marlow replied. "A deal to save us."

"In return for what?" Pan asked. "What did you give it?"

"Nothing," he said. "It didn't ask for anything, not even my soul. It just . . ." He looked back the way they'd come, gulping like a fish out of water.

"Just what?"

"Nothing," he said again. "I mean . . ."

"Marlow," she said, glaring at him. "What were the exact words you used?"

"I said I wanted to go home, all of us to go home, me, you, and Night."

"Night?" said Herc, looking for her. "She's here?"

Pan shook her head, watched him deflate again.

"And I said that the door should close behind us," Marlow went on. "Not just close, but be destroyed. As soon as we were through, the gateway to hell would be sealed forever. I mean, I thought about it, Pan, I made sure it couldn't follow us."

"What couldn't?" said Herc. "The Devil?"

Marlow nodded

"Behind us," Pan said. "Behind *all of us*?"

"You weren't there," he snapped. "You didn't see what I saw,

Pan. You didn't see what it could do. It . . . It was going to kill you."

"Big deal," she said, jabbing a finger at him. "Death didn't matter down there, I could have handled it."

"I didn't have a chance to think," whined Marlow. "It was too quick."

"You never think," she said. "You never think about anything but yourself."

"Whoa," said Charlie. "Hang on, what are you talking about?"

He was answered not by Marlow but by something else, something that rumbled up from deep beneath them—louder even than the howling storm of the Engine. There was another noise, too, a deep, bone-shaking *uhuhuhuh* that might have been laughter. Pan's blood seemed to boil away, leaving her too light, paper thin.

"Oh no," she said.

"What?" said Herc. "Would somebody tell me what the hell is going on?"

"Behind all of us," Pan said. "You said the gate should shut behind all of us, me, you, and Night."

And she remembered Patrick lifting the girl up, sinking those tombstone teeth into her face. Night was still in hell.

"I got us out," said Marlow. "I got us home."

"Yeah," said Pan. "You got us out of hell, Marlow."

She heard the roar get louder, felt the whole building shake beneath the force of it, and that laughter rising up above everything else.

"You got us out of hell, but you left the goddamn gate wide open."

HEARTBREAKER

"What have you done, Marlow?" said Charlie.

He couldn't answer, he just stood there like a fish out of water, gulping air.

What have I done?

Mucus was building up in his lungs, fast, making up for lost time. He coughed to clear it, breathed in with a wheeze. This couldn't be happening, because he'd been so careful, he'd made sure the gate would close behind them.

Behind *all* of them.

And it made a sudden, awful sense, what the watchmaker had said. By making the deal, Marlow had united the Engines—this Engine, and the one in hell. He'd united them and opened the gates between worlds.

"It's not my fault," he croaked, and was on the verge of pleading his case when the stairwell bucked like a mule, a crack ripping open the wall beside them and unleashing a storm of dust. It lurched again, as if they were riding a train, Charlie almost tumbling down the stairs.

"Okay," said Herc, grabbing the banister with a white-knuckled hand. "We can talk about this later, but we need to get out of here."

That subterranean growl was growing louder and Marlow

couldn't help but picture a shark beneath them, rising through the dark ocean, its jaws open wide.

"I'm with Herc," said Charlie, bounding up the steps. Pan followed, Herc waiting for Marlow to pass before bringing up the rear. Marlow's body felt like an unoiled machine, every joint grinding, his thirst unbearable.

That wasn't the reason he stopped, though.

He clung onto the banister, knowing that there was something he was missing. Everything had happened so quickly, he'd been through so much, that his thoughts were nothing but shrapnel. He couldn't make sense of them.

"Hey," yelled Charlie from the next flight. "You insane? Come on."

He took another step but stopped again, thinking back. The Devil was coming, yes. He'd left the door wide open for him, yes. But there was something else, something the watchmaker had said to him.

"Marlow?" said Pan. "What is it?"

The stairwell shook again, dust raining down from above. It made breathing even harder and Marlow pushed his hand against his chest, clawing in another breath. He could feel the rattle of his lungs through his skin, that and the frantic, erratic beat of his heart.

His heart.

And there it was, detonating inside his skull—the Stranger, a hole in its chest where its heart should be, pipes and tubes and machinery pumping poisonous blood through its rotting body.

Without its heart, it is just a devil. With it, it is a god.

"Holy . . ." He snatched in another breath, yelling to the others. "Wait, hang on."

They were almost too far up the stairwell to hear him, and when Herc stuck his head over the banister he looked like a gargoyle on a cathedral spire.

"Huh?" he yelled down.

"We can't go," Marlow said. "There's something we have to do."

Even as he said it he hated himself. Because he could almost see daylight, he could almost feel the breeze on his skin. All he had to do was keep walking and he'd get to the Red Door.

But the Devil would follow.

"Just leave him," he heard Pan say. "His problem, let him deal with it."

And she was right.

He would deal with it.

He turned, clattering back down the steps. Another tremor shook the vault room as he ran through it, pieces of broken glass and metal dancing over the floor. Marlow had to stop, his heart feeling like a water balloon in a child's fist, ready to pop as he burst into the madness of the Engine.

If anything, it was even louder in here than it had been, although the source of the noise had changed. A deep, thunderous bellow was pouring from the Black Pool, so thick and so loud it was almost like liquid—Marlow could feel it against his skin. Over it all he heard a roar, looked to see Ostheim on the other side of the cavern. His obese body had reared up in triumph as he understood that his job was done, that the gates were open.

Then he was moving this way, *fast*.

Marlow started down the steps only to feel a hand on his shoulder. He flinched, looking to see Charlie there.

"What the hell, dude?" Charlie yelled.

"There's something we need to do," he shouted back. "Something we need to find that will stop him."

Ostheim was on his way across the Engine. For a second Marlow thought they'd been spotted, half expected Ostheim to scuttle up the stairs, for one of his bladed legs to punch into him. But he was running for the pool, plunging two of his tentacles into the boiling water like he was fishing for something.

"What are you talking about?" said Charlie. "What are you looking for?"

"A heart," he said.

"A *what*?"

Marlow stared out into the Engine, into that mass of a billion parts. How was he supposed to find a heart in all of that? It would be easier to find a needle in a million haystacks. He wasn't even sure the heart would be there, because what if Meridiana had taken it with her, hidden it somewhere else. It could be anywhere on the planet, anywhere in time.

Except hadn't Meridiana told him, when he'd been here last, that the heart was right here, in this Engine? She had commanded him to look for it.

"What are you doing?" The hiss behind him was scalpel sharp. Pan was there, Herc looming over her, shrugging for an explanation.

"He's looking for a heart," Charlie went on. "Beats me."

"There's no time to explain," Marlow said, still watching Ostheim, scanning the bus-size mass of bulging flesh. "You just have to trust me."

He heard Pan spit out a laugh.

"Oh, sure, Marlow, I trust you completely."

He ignored her, dread rising in him like a cold tide.

"We'll never find it," he said. "It could be anywhere, it will take—"

"Is that it?" said Pan, pointing at Ostheim.

Marlow squinted, seeing a glimmer of brass clutched in one of Ostheim's eel-like limbs. It was a canister of some kind, the size of a propane tank, maybe, one that emitted a weird not-quite-light. And she was right, wasn't she? It made perfect sense.

Ostheim had been there, back when the watchmaker had taken the heart. He'd have known exactly what it looked like. And he'd have known the Devil would need it as soon as it shed the machinery that was keeping it alive and stepped back into the world.

But surely they wouldn't get so lucky?

"That thing in his weird tentacle-hand-thing," said Charlie. "Doesn't look much like a heart."

Not a heart, maybe, but the residue of the memories the watchmaker had led him through was still smeared on Marlow's brain. He closed his eyes, looked back, saw the watchmaker locking the heart inside a mechanism of copper and steel.

"It has to be," he said, more to himself than anyone else. And there was a brief flood of relief that he didn't have to search the Engine, that he didn't have to find it by himself. It didn't last long, though, because what he had to do now was a hundred times harder.

He had to pry it from Ostheim's greasy, lethal bug fingers.

"I'm so confused," said Charlie.

The howls were growing louder, a tremor shaking the cavern so hard that pieces of stone were raining down from the ceiling. The Devil was on its way, and its heart was right here waiting for it.

Marlow turned to the others. "Look, I can't explain how I know, but if the Devil gets here and sticks that heart back into itself, then we can say goodbye to everything. That heart, it's like the Devil's Engine, the *real* Engine, it's what fuels it. It's gonna be hell on earth."

Charlie and Pan both pulled a face, but Herc—good old dependable Herc—just swallowed, then nodded.

"So we need the heart," he said. "And that fat bastard is in the way. And we've got, what, a couple of minutes maybe?"

161

"If that," said Marlow.

Herc reached down to his holster, patting it like he had just remembered it was empty. He looked left, then right, then behind him, walking to a locker in the corner of the room. He wrestled it open, pulling out two massive flashlights and a bright red pistol.

"Not much," he said, running back to them. "But it might help."

"A flare gun?" said Charlie.

"In case somebody got lost out there when they were mapping," Herc said. "It's a big Engine, in case you hadn't noticed." He popped the chamber, checked to make sure it was loaded, patted the spare flare clipped to the side. "You got two shots, make them count."

He handed the gun to Marlow but Pan snatched it from him.

"He'll just set fire to his pants," she said. "I got this."

They stood there for a moment in silence.

"That it?" said Marlow. "We just rock up and cap Ostheim in the ass, steal the heart? That's the plan? You got nothing else?"

Herc shrugged.

"Run fast," he growled.

Great. Once again Marlow thought about just turning around, making his way up to the Red Door, stepping into the sun. The idea of it was overpowering; he felt like he had to physically wrestle it out of his head.

No, this was his mess. He would deal with it.

Just give me a minute, he said to himself, rocking back and forth in a starter's sprint.

"Dude, what is that?" said Charlie, and Marlow followed his finger down the stairs, across the platform, past the bulk of Ostheim to the bubbling surface of the Black Pool.

To the thing that was pushing out of it, blinking its spider eyes.

"Ah crap," he said, and before he even knew what he was doing he was running, his arms wheeling, the roar of the Devil drowning out the sound of his feet. He missed the bottom two steps, lurching onto the platform, falling, rolling, scrabbling back up. The cavern was close to imploding, a hail of rock pattering down around him as he sprinted. Ostheim was ahead, a behemoth whose body oozed like a slug's. A dozen of those tentacles whipped around him in a frenzy and Marlow had to follow them like a magician's fingers, searching for that glimpse of metal.

There. Clamped to his side.

He cut right, running along Ostheim's flank. The monster was too busy to notice him, plunging more of his limbs into the pool, wrapping them around the shape that floated there. Marlow caught a glimpse of a face made of moving parts. The Devil reached out with a stick-thin limb, wrapping its fingers around Ostheim, hauling itself up like a drowning man. Pieces of machinery were still attached to it, threatening to drag it back down. It opened its mouth and loosed a cry that might have belonged to a million newborns.

Marlow swore, his own fear burning star-bright inside him. He was close enough now that he could see the canister. He could *feel* it, a subsonic pulse that vibrated through his bones, through his soul. All he had to do was reach out and . . .

The Devil turned its eyes to Marlow, and even though they were just pits in its head, holes punched into space and time, he could see the alarm there, the understanding. It opened its mouth and howled out a warning. Suddenly Ostheim was turning, his limbs darting out. Marlow ducked beneath one, his fingers snagging on the canister.

"Eat this, you ugly—" Pan's voice, followed by a hiss, a roar.

A ball of fire thumped into Ostheim's flank. It had to have

been like shooting a bear with a potato gun but it worked, distracting Ostheim long enough for Marlow to grab the mechanism and wrench it free. It was heavier than it looked, slamming to the floor and bringing him with it. He scrabbled back up, dragging the canister across the platform. Where the hell were the—

One of Ostheim's limbs cracked into the canister like a train, launching Marlow into the air. He let go of it, slamming back down onto the stone and rolling into the bottom step. The world was midnight dark, filled with a hurricane of noise, but there were hands on his arm, hauling him up. By the time he was on his feet he could see enough to make out Charlie next to him, Herc there too, hugging the mechanism against his chest.

"Move!" the old guy roared.

Ostheim was a blur of panic and fury, most of his limbs trying to pull the Devil out of the water. Pan was still there, the flare gun reloaded and pointing at his back. It wouldn't do much good—the first flare had burned itself out—and she must have known it because she angled it up, aiming it at the fractured ceiling.

She pulled the trigger, the flare arcing up and thumping into the disintegrating rock. It wasn't exactly a grenade launcher, but it was powerful enough, a chunk of ceiling breaking free and hurtling earthward. It thumped into the Black Pool like a fist, and Marlow wasn't sure if it was Ostheim or the Devil that howled in outrage.

He shrugged Charlie away, limping onto the stairs. The cavern was disintegrating, another stalactite slicing down and shearing away the banister, almost taking out Herc as it toppled past them. Pan was racing up, barging past Marlow and Charlie, yelling, "Ladies first!"

Don't look back, Marlow ordered himself, but he couldn't stop, craning over his shoulder with every other step, seeing

Ostheim haul the Devil out of the water, seeing him turn his bulk their way, seeing those limbs fire out like harpoons.

"Shi—"

Marlow tripped on the last step, the top of the door exploding into dust overhead. He rolled, screaming, Charlie falling on top of him. Something big dislodged itself, collapsing over the door, crushing the limb that had followed them in. Even then it squirmed, a brutal obsidian blade slicing through the air, feeling for them.

Marlow pushed past Herc, clattering up the steps until his calves burned so fiercely he thought he was about to spontaneously combust. Collapsing, he inhaled a wheezing breath, and when he exhaled he was surprised to find that it was a wild, spluttering laugh. And they kept coming, pouring from him so hard that he couldn't get a breath. He had to wipe the tears away so that he could see, and the first thing that greeted him was Pan's face, twisted into a look of annoyance. Before he could stop himself he was laughing even harder.

"You are such an idiot," she said, passing him. Charlie took her place, offering a hand.

"You really are," he said. "What are you laughing at?"

Marlow couldn't explain, it had to be the relief, the insanity, the terror, the joy of being back on Earth. The emotions were so powerful that they'd reduced him to this.

The stairwell rocked as something exploded beneath them, and Marlow forced himself back onto his feet. He'd made it to the next curve before he heard Herc yelling at them from below. Staring over the banister, he saw the old guy struggling with the weight of the canister, hauling it up step by step. He glowered up, furious.

"Any of you lazy bastards want to help?" he roared.

And Marlow was laughing again as he ran back down the stairs.

BACK THROUGH
THE RED DOOR

They stood there, the four of them. They stood there and stared like they were expecting it to open by itself.

And the Red Door just stared right back.

"You gonna do it?" said Charlie.

Pan wiped a hand over her face and it came away smeared with blood. Herc's nose was bleeding too, something to do with the canister he cradled in his arms. It was pumping out a vibe of pure evil, a pulse that ripped through every fiber in Pan's body.

"Pan?"

She wasn't sure why she couldn't seem to move. She wanted to open the door more than she'd wanted anything in her life. But what would happen if she twisted that handle and the door didn't open? She'd be sealed in here forever—or at least until Ostheim and the Devil hauled their way up from the cavern. She could still hear them down there, their rage threatening to shake the Nest to dust.

"Pan," said Herc, struggling with the weight of the canister, his arms knotted with veins. "Just crack the damned thing before I give myself a hernia."

She swallowed painfully, walking the last stretch of corridor, reaching for the handle, pausing again. The Red Door linked to a dozen other places—maybe more—and they had no idea which of those it would open onto now. For all they knew, it might take them back into Meridiana's lair, where Ostheim's demonic offspring would chew them to pieces. Or maybe back into the graves beneath Paris where they would slowly rot in the Liminal.

For all they knew, it might open up to a brick wall.

Pan turned the handle and the door clicked, but when she pulled nothing happened.

"Dammit!" she yelled, kicking it, shouldering it, hanging off it. The door didn't so much as tremble. "Locked."

"No," said Marlow. He limped to the door, Pan stepping out of his way.

"Yeah, right," she said. "Like you'll be able to—"

He grabbed the handle, twisted it hard, then pulled. The Red Door made a sound like a gunshot, which echoed down the corridor. Pan's ears popped, and she felt her stomach cramp as she rode out the wave of horror that always followed. Marlow pulled and the door opened smoothly, without the slightest creak.

Pan swallowed, leaned out, feeling the awful sensation of crossing the Liminal. She saw a barren stretch of stone, empty of life.

Beyond it, clustered on the horizon, distant buildings that might have been ruined skyscrapers.

And ash, so much ash, a world drowning in the stuff of the dead.

"No," she said, her body carved from ice. "No, no, please God no."

The door had opened up into hell.

They were *still there*.

"Please," she said again, less than a whisper. She looked at Marlow, his face gaunt, everything good sucked right out of him.

Pan heard the drumming of feet, pictured a demon running

for them, ready to burst into the corridor and pull them to pieces.

"Close it," she yelled. "Close the door!"

And Marlow was doing just that when a woman in yellow gym gear and pink sneakers jogged past, a huge pair of headphones resting on her head.

What?

"Did you just see that?" Marlow asked.

"The demon in Lycra?" Pan said, nodding.

They craned out of the door together, watching the jogger run along an overgrown path then turn out of sight. Pan saw that the door was in a huge brick wall covered in graffiti tags. Ahead of her was a wasteland, crisscrossed by rusted railway tracks, but she could see a shopping cart, and past that a burned-out car, and past that a shingle drive thick with weeds.

Something honked from close by and she suddenly heard traffic, the growl of engines, somebody yelling. And it was those muffled words—*"Go screw yourself, pal!"*—those beautiful, incredible words, that finally stripped the strength from Pan's legs, sent her crashing to the floor. She felt like crying, but the truth was she was too exhausted, she couldn't even remember how to do it. She just knelt there, sucking in air, listening to the sound of home.

"Oh my god," said Marlow, taking a step outside. He ran his bare foot along the ground, leaving trails in the ash there. Only, it wasn't ash, Pan realized. It was *sand*. She could smell the river, that gut-wrenching stench that had made her want to chuck her guts every summer but which was now as welcome as fresh bread. Marlow looked back at her, his shy smile like a bird, ready to take flight at any second. "We're here."

"Here?" said Herc, pushing gently past Marlow. He looked around, studying the distant skyscrapers—not abandoned, not ruined, just shrouded in mist. "This is New Jersey."

"I thought you said hell was *behind* us," said Charlie, joining all of them in the doorway.

"We're in Greenville," Herc said. "Near the railroad yard in Jersey City. This building, I know it. I *bought* it."

"Huh?" said Pan.

"Well, technically the Fist bought it," he said, spitting. "Ostheim. It was supposed to be another safe house, we bought dozens of them in New York and Jersey; Philly, too."

"Like the walk-up in Hoboken?" said Pan, thinking back to the place they'd camped out before their battle with Patrick—before *one* of the battles. Herc nodded, studying the Red Door, swinging it back and forth.

"I didn't know he'd put one of these in," he said. "I didn't even know you *could*. How'd we get here anyway?"

"I asked it to take us home," said Marlow. "Must have been the closest exit."

"Doesn't seem real," said Pan, finally taking a step away from the door. She felt like an astronaut pushing away from the safety of the airlock. The buildings on the horizon were Manhattan, she saw, and the sight of them sent a spear of longing through her ribs, enough to snatch her breath away.

"*Smells* real," said Charlie, holding his nose.

Pan looked back along the corridor. It was still shaking in there, dust raining down. She could hear that low rumble, more like a dog growling.

"Close the door," she said. "Make it real."

"Wait," said Marlow, holding out his hand. "Night."

She looked through the door again, imagined Night running from the stairwell, heard her calling—and knew it could never happen.

"Make it real," she said, nodding to Charlie.

"Done," said Charlie. He grabbed the handle and, without hesitation, slammed the door shut. The growl was cut off, the tremor beneath Pan's feet thrumming into nothing. And there was just New Jersey, grinding and honking and swearing.

It was *real*.

Charlie was turning the handle again, bumping the door with his shoulder.

"No going back now," he said. "It's locked."

Nobody challenged him. Nobody wanted to go back. Not ever.

Please let it be over, Pan said. It felt like a nightmare already, like she'd just woken from a yearlong sleep. The horror was draining from her head, too awful to be contained in the real world. If it wasn't for the layers of metal in her skin she might have convinced herself that none of it had happened at all.

Please let it be done.

She knew it was an empty wish because Ostheim was down there. And Marlow had finished the job for him, he'd opened the gates and unleashed something terrible.

But it was all a little easier to handle now that the Red Door was locked and sealed behind them.

"First things first," started Herc, resting the canister on the ground, leaning on it. Up close Pan could see that it was a monstrosity, it was something from a museum of freaks and curiosities. It was a cylinder, the top and bottom of which were made of an impossibly complex tapestry of copper parts. The middle was made of glass, streaked with dirt and gore. It seemed too dark in there, but in the inky black water she thought she could see something move, something *beating,* emitting that weird, bowel-loosening pulse.

Gross.

Herc was still speaking but she interrupted him with a hand, trying to swallow down a throat that was lined with carpet.

"First things first. We get water," she said. "And food."

"But—"

"Herc, if you get between me and a meal then I'm gonna end up eating yo—"

And then she remembered seeing Patrick feasting on his sister, ripping chunks off her. Her words died in her throat, and Herc must have sensed the pain there because he nodded.

"Sure, Pan," he said softly. "Food first."

He hefted the canister up and lurched off one way, doubling back, finding his bearings. The track meandered around countless boxcars, then half a dozen warehouses, some shuttered, their windows smashed, before joining a busy street. Workshops and garages spilled noise, the air thick with exhaust fumes and cigarette smoke. There were people everywhere, real people, and Pan watched them warily, half expecting to see their jaws distend, their skin tear, black limbs slicing out. When it didn't happen, she wanted to throw herself onto each and every one of them, just hug them.

It wasn't going to happen. Those few who noticed them walking up the street took one look at their clothes, their bare feet, or just breathed in their stench, and backed out of the way.

Herc cut left, through a wooded patch beside the road—the trees swaying overhead, caught in the same breeze that caressed Pan's skin—and onto another street, this one packed with apartment buildings.

"Uh . . . there, bingo," the old guy said, pointing across the road. There was a coffee shop or something that looked like it belonged in a storybook. It had flowers painted all over it, and the name on the window was *Petals's Cake's*.

"Really?" said Charlie. "I dunno, Herc. That place looks like it has serious code violations, all involving apostrophes."

"Who cares?" said Pan, practically running across the street. She barged through the door hard enough to smack it against the wall, the half dozen customers inside all flinching. "Sorry,"

171

she said, bolting for a soda dispenser and putting her mouth beneath the nozzle while pressing the Dr Pepper button.

"Hey!" said the old lady behind the counter, presumably Petal.

Pan ignored her—she'd have ignored her if she'd been standing there holding a bazooka. The taste of the soda was incredible, she could feel it travel every inch of her body, then a soft, cool detonation in her stomach.

Two people were already walking out the door, the rest of them definitely considering it. Petal had a phone in her hand, holding it as a warning.

"Hold up," said Herc, the canister thumping to the floor with a sound like a cathedral bell. "No rush. She . . . she just got stung. By a bee. In the mouth." He tried to smile at her, his horror-show face making her twice as nervous. "No need to panic, we're . . ." Herc looked at Marlow, dressed in nothing but shorts, his torso covered in dirt and scars, at Pan in her just-hanging-on ensemble, and at the metal that glinted in their faces. All of them were filthy, and there was more than one bloodstain among them. Not to mention the canister that hummed like a generator. "We're doing a play, over in the high school." He waved his arm in a full circle. "Uh . . ."

"*Of Mice and Men,*" said Charlie. "I'm . . . the man."

He looked at Marlow for help and Marlow shrugged.

"I'm the mouse," he said. He lowered his head beneath the soda machine, drinking deeply. Pan grabbed a bottle of water from the fridge and gulped it down, finishing the entire bottle. It seemed to go up rather than down, settling in her skull.

"Brain freeze," she said.

The woman was actually dialing now and Herc walked to the counter, dwarfing her. He reached into his pocket and she flinched, but it was a wallet he pulled out. He shook the dust from it, opened it up, and pulled out a wedge of cash. He placed it on the counter, trying to smudge a bloodstain from the top bill.

"This should be enough to cover everything they need, and everyone else's meals," he said. "It should be enough for exclusive use of your café, if you get what I mean."

She put the phone down, her jaw dropping.

"Uh, shop's closed," she said. There was a trickle of blood winding its way down from her ear and she smudged it away without noticing. "Sorry, folks."

There was a round of groans, but nobody seemed too sorry to leave—especially as their bills had been settled, and especially as half of them were starting to bleed. Petal scooped up the cash, and fled after her customers.

Pan walked through the door behind the counter, finding a small kitchen. She wasn't sure what to take so she grabbed everything she could—taking a bite out of a block of cheese, stuffing an entire bun into her mouth, almost choking herself with it. She saw Marlow ripping open a bag of chips, devouring them like a demon.

"It's like feeding time at the zoo," said Herc, watching them.

"You go four days without eating," Pan tried to say, but there was too much in her mouth and all that came out was food.

She ate until she could eat no more, until she actually had a stitch—like her sides were physically splitting. Then she limped back to the table where Herc and Charlie and Marlow were waiting. Herc had a mug of coffee in his hand and the smell of it was so good it nearly knocked her out. She breathed it in and it seemed to calm the monster inside her. The sun was burning through the morning mist outside and she basked in it, closing her eyes, sleep there almost instantly. She welcomed it, happy to let it come. All she wanted to do was forget.

"So," said Herc, drumming his fingers on the table, snapping her out of the doze. "Tell me everything."

EVERYTHING

She did. She took a breath and told Herc everything.

Not before she had a wash, though. There was no shower here, but there was a sink in the kitchen and she stripped, using dishwashing soap and a sponge to scrub away the blood, the filth. There was so much of it that she didn't think it would ever come off completely. She wondered if she'd have to simply scour away her skin until there was no trace of hell left. But even then there were those pieces of shrapnel woven through her. They would never let her forget.

At least her wounds had healed. The big one in her side had clotted with something so dark and so hard it might have been plastic, the scrapes and grazes just poor memories of themselves, as if reality had rejected everything that had happened outside its boundaries. She wondered if it would last, or if the injuries would catch up with her eventually.

She rooted through the cupboards until she found a box of black polo shirts, *Petals's* stitched on the breast in pink cotton. She found her size and threw it on. There were no trousers, sadly, so she used a pair of scissors to cut off the filthy bottoms of her sweatpants, turning them into shorts. Putting them back on was like crossing the threshold again. She could feel the blood, feel the fluid of the Black Pool. But what choice did she have? She couldn't exactly stroll through Jersey in her birth-day suit.

There was nothing in the lost property box that was any use, but she spotted an inhaler there. It was nearly empty, the noz-zle chewed out of shape, and she handed it to Marlow as he met her at the door.

"Oh, cool, thanks," he said, taking it, then firing off a shot into his mouth.

Pan left him to it, walking to the others. Herc and Charlie had hefted the canister onto the table and they were trying to pry it open with a spoon.

"Stuck fast," Herc said, the spoon pinging across the café.

The door opened and Marlow strolled out with another of the polo shirts, brushing crumbs from it.

"Anything else you need to do?" Herc asked them both when Marlow had taken a seat. "I think there's a barbershop across the street. And I spotted a nail salon down the way."

Pan flashed him the nails of her middle fingers, just to show him how clean they were.

Then they began.

Pan didn't want to speak, didn't want to relive any of it. She was happy to let Marlow do the talking. But he was making such a meal of it—going over every little detail, missing half the stuff that Herc needed to know, that she kept interrupting him. After the third time she just told him to shut up and took charge, telling Herc and Charlie about the mountains that grew from dead people and black blood, the demons and the ghosts and the war that was waging between them down in hell, the fact that it looked like an old city, ruined by time. She told them about the fact you couldn't die there, that you were murdered and reborn in endless violence, about the fact that Patrick and Brianna had been there, driven insane by time and terror. She told them about meeting Night, how she'd saved them. She was still down there, Pan said. She'd have regenerated, and opened her eyes to see that she was alone again—and at this point Pan put her head to the table and wept.

"We can do this later," said Herc, but she waved him away, speaking into the tablecloth, telling him about the sun that didn't do what suns were supposed to do, the ash that covered everything, and which might have been all that remained of the living. She told them everything, because it was like she was purging herself, like she was extracting some kind of poison from her system. She just talked and talked and talked until an hour had passed and the last few drops of truth had spilled from her lips.

For a while, there was only silence. Herc and Charlie had both turned gray. Herc stroked his stubble, shaking his head.

"If I'd known . . ." he started. "I mean, I had no idea, Pan. I knew it would be bad, but I always thought . . ." He put a hand to his mouth. "All those people. I sent them there. God forgive me."

She took his hand, squeezed it.

"None of us knew, Herc," she said. "Nobody but Ostheim."

He nodded, smudging a tear away. Then he looked at Marlow.

"So there's just the bit with the Devil," he said. "Cough it up, Marlow."

Marlow spluttered, lifting his hands as if to say *where do I start?*

"It . . . it wasn't one thing, it was two," he said after a moment. "The Devil, and something else. Some*one* else. Trapped together."

"Whoa," said Charlie. "Slow down. Who?"

"A man. His children died—five kids, including Ostheim, and Mammon, and Meridiana. A long time ago, like centuries. They were killed in a fire, and then he tried to rescue them, but the Devil was there, it set the whole thing up, I think, it made a deal with him. Only, it wasn't really a devil. I don't know what it was, something powerful, and really, really old. Anyway, this thing had been making deals with people since forever, letting them drink its blood, and giving them powers. It made a deal with the man, to bring his children back."

"In return for . . ." prodded Herc.

"The man had to build it an engine," said Marlow. "*The* Engine. It took him ages, trapped in time just like Meridiana. But he did it, he built it."

"But what was it for?" asked Pan.

"To keep it alive," Marlow said. "It was so old, and it needed a way to stay alive. Its heart—that thing." Marlow tapped the canister and the reverberations from inside seemed to double in volume for a moment before settling again. "It's what powers it, it's like, I don't know, Iron Man's Arc Reactor or something, like its energy source. Only really, really evil. The Devil's body was giving out, so it gave this man a blueprint for a life-support machine, helped him build it in return for bringing the man's kids back. Only they weren't really his kids, they were . . . I don't even know. They were something bad."

Pan thought of the way Ostheim had become a monster, the way that she'd barely been able to look at Mammon, the way Meridiana kept murdering her clones. Yeah, they were bad all right.

"They had the Devil's blood in them, they were *his* children, really, not the guy's. Anyway, he knew he'd been tricked. So he changed the design of the Engine. He took the Devil's heart and he hid it, he turned the Engine into a prison. I think."

"His heart," said Herc. The mechanism sat there, pulsing away. Every now and again the lump of meat and gristle inside seemed to squelch from one side to the other, like it was trying to study them. "This?"

"I guess," said Marlow.

"But what does it do?" Charlie asked.

"Makes him whole," said Marlow. "The man—he was a watchmaker—said that without the heart, the Devil is just a devil, but with it, it becomes a god. So maybe if we destroy it, then the Devil dies, too." He shrugged. "Maybe."

Herc shook his head. "You mean all this time we're sitting here with this thing and we're supposed to be destroying it? Marlow, pull it together."

The old guy bent down, fiddling with the brass ends of the canister, grunting with frustration. Then he stood, lifting the heart over his head and slamming it down on the floor. It landed with a thump that seemed too loud for its size, leaving a crater in the tiles. Herc stamped on the glass but it didn't crack. He sat down, wiping his brow.

"We'll find something," he said. "Just give me a sec."

"So yeah," said Marlow, continuing. "The watchmaker turned the Engine into a prison. The Devil was in hell, the heart was here, and so long as they were separated it was powerless."

"Whoever holds the Devil, hold him well," muttered Herc.

"Huh?" said Pan.

"Nothing," he said. "It's just a quote. So this man hid the heart, trapped the Devil, but where?"

Marlow chewed his knuckle for a moment, lost in thought, then said, "I think he might have trapped him in the future, I think that's how he did it."

"The future?" said Pan. He nodded.

"Yeah, you know how the Engine does that, can mess with time. I think the man, this watchmaker, changed something so that the Engine ended up thousands of years from now."

"What good would that do?" asked Charlie.

"Well, no good, if you live in the future," said Marlow. "But if you lived back then, in the past, then it would have saved you.

The Devil can't hurt you if he's moved to another millennium, can he?"

"That would explain the city," said Pan. "The *world*."

"Yeah, that's what I was thinking," said Marlow. "All those dead. Millions, billions of them. He killed them all."

"Hold on," said Herc. "This doesn't make sense. Because if he used the Engine as a prison, holding the Devil until the future, then why does the Engine grant wishes?"

"Because it's powered by the Devil's blood," said Pan.

"Yeah," said Marlow. "Its blood runs through it, and it's powerful, it can give you, I don't know, superpowers and stuff. It's black, it's got these weird sparkly things in it."

"Like the Black Pool," said Charlie.

"Yeah, like the pool. I'm not sure, but I think that's where the power comes from. The blood flows through the Engine, through every part of it, then it ends up in the Black Pool. The Engine, it kind of filters it, customizes it to what you've asked for. What was it Seth always said? It cracks the code of this little pocket of reality. Then, when you go into the pool, I guess the blood gets inside you, you drink it, and you change, too."

Pan took a sip of Herc's coffee and felt it churn in her stomach. The food, which had tasted so good, was sitting there like a lead brick.

"This is all good, but what was that thing? I mean, was it actually the Devil?"

Marlow shook his head, drawing a pattern in a pile of salt on the table.

"I'm not sure. The man said it wasn't the Devil. I think it was something worse. He called it a Stranger."

Pan didn't know how, but she knew he'd given it a capital S.

"Stranger," said Herc, chewing on the word. "What did it look like?"

"You've seen it," he said. "You all have. It's that thing in the pool."

Herc was scratching his head, his frown lines like surgical scars.

"Okay," he said. "So there's the Devil, Stranger, who is evil. Then a man who made a deal with the Devil, who managed to keep it prisoner. And he's good. And the five kids?"

"He loved them," said Marlow. "The Devil made them look like real children but they weren't, they were monsters. But . . . I think the watchmaker's love kind of changed them back." He looked at Pan. "Love can do that, right?"

She blushed, but she nodded. Yeah, love could do that.

"But the Devil turned one of them against him, one called Mephistopheles."

"Who's that?" said Charlie. "I know that name."

"Think about it," said Marlow. Pan did, working the word around her head, seeing something there and then losing it. Herc slammed a fist on the table, making her jump.

"Mephistopheles," he growled. "Sheppel Ostheim. It's an anagram. I'm so goddamned *stupid*!"

"Nobody saw it, Herc," said Marlow. "Nobody."

For a moment there was quiet, just the bustle of the city outside their window, oblivious, the sound of traffic and a distant siren—the lullaby of home. Pan waved her hand through a shaft of sunlight, scattering dust.

"And the demons?" asked Herc. "Why do they come for you? How do they know when your contract has ended?"

Marlow popped his lips. "He sends them, I think, the Stranger. The deal is with him, ultimately, through the Engine, so he knows when your time is up. He controls the demons, he makes them, right? We saw people, they were drinking his blood, turning into demons. They can breach the divide, but because the Engines aren't united only their energy makes it through."

"Sure," said Herc. "It's why they possess walls and stuff."

"Yeah, so he sends them, and they take your . . . your soul, I guess. The bit of you that's *you*."

"But why?" said Herc. "I've been doing this most of my miserable life and I understand less now than ever. Why would this thing want to possess your soul?"

Pan looked at Marlow, and he looked back, and when their eyes met she suddenly knew.

"That's it, isn't it?" she asked him. "You said it yourself, Marlow, that we were there because we had something to give him."

He didn't answer, just turned his attention back to that mess of salt.

"This," she said, gesturing at the heart that pumped inside its cage. "We could give him this. We could make a deal to open up the gates and bring him back, reunite him with his heart."

"But somebody would have done it already," Marlow said. "Right? I can't have been the first person to have reached the Devil. It was nothing to do with me."

Pan slapped her forehead. "I'd almost forgotten. He was living in your *house*, Marlow."

"*What?*" barked Herc.

"Yeah, his house. You wanna explain that one?"

"I don't know," Marlow said, and when she started to push it he swiped a hand over the table, scattering salt and condiments. "Yeah, it was my house. The Devil was in my kitchen. The watchmaker told me only I had the power to change everything. What does that mean, Herc?"

Nothing, just silence, punctuated by the same siren. Marlow grated his chair back, walking to the wall and resting his head there. Herc cleared his throat, studying his fingernails like there might be answers written in the dirt. That siren was definitely louder, and Pan could hear the gunning of an engine. She squinted through the dirty window, seeing the street outside, a couple of customers, and Petal, too, phone in her hand, looking impatient.

"I think she screwed us," she said.

Herc looked at her, then out the window, then he pushed up so hard his chair flew backward.

"Goddammit, Petal!" he roared, pointing at her through the glass. "That was eight hundred bucks! Come on."

But even as they were getting to their feet the squad car screeched to a halt, bumping up onto the curb. Charlie swore, leaping the counter and disappearing through the staff door. He emerged a second later, shaking his head. Herc sighed, his fist flexing.

"Just let me do the talking, yeah?"

He lifted the canister with the heart and they filed from the shop one by one. By the time they were out the cops were scrambling from the car. One of them had his hand on his sidearm, the other actually pulling her gun from its holster when she saw Marlow and Pan.

"Take it easy," said Herc, thumping the canister onto the sidewalk. "There's nothing to see here."

"Yeah," said the second cop, looking at Pan's blood-marbled shorts, at Marlow's face, at the canister, which kind of looked a little like a nuclear weapon. The woman pressed the fingers of her free hand to her forehead as she sensed that awful pulse. "Sure."

"They said they were in a play," said Petal. "But I don't—"

"Shut it, Petal," growled Herc, and the other cop slid his gun free, too.

"I'm going to need you to get on the ground," he said to Herc. "Hands where I can see them. That a problem?"

"With these knees," Herc said. "Yeah."

The cops glanced at each other, the guy stepping wide, pistol clamped in both hands. He was twitching his head like he was trying to shake water from his ear.

"Look, everything's fine," said Pan. "It's not what it looks like."

"Wanna tell me what it looks like?" said the woman.

"No," she said, but at the same time Marlow started blurting.

"We were in hell, me and her. That's why our clothes look weird. That's where the blood came from. We just got out, these guys are our friends, Herc here is mission commander. We're like a Special Forces outfit, but for supernatural stuff. Because there's an Engine, which can kind of give you powers, only we found out it wasn't the Engine, it was this thing, like the Devil only not the Devil, something else, and its blood is what gives you powers, and I might have accidentally left the door open after we got out of hell and it might be, you know, coming. Like, now. For this. That's its heart, in there, it's sorta still beating and if he gets it back everything will be over. So yeah, that's what happened. And there are no shoes in hell, just so you know. We couldn't see any shoes."

Herc slapped a hand to his forehead and Charlie actually burst out laughing for a second or two until the cop glared at him.

"You think this is funny?" she said. She pressed her collar radio, never taking the gun off Herc. "Yeah, Dispatch, we got a 10–33 at 162 Industrial, four suspects being detained so we need a bus, over."

Her radio fizzed, then made a sound like a screeching cat. She flinched, trying again.

"Ten-33 at 162 Industrial, send a bus, over."

The radio screeched again, and this time something fizzed

out of it—a spark that lashed up and struck a streetlight. The bulb exploded, raining glass, and the cop panicked, pulling the trigger. Her gun barked, the bullet skimming Herc's head and punching a hole through the café window.

"Hey!" yelled Herc and Petal together.

The woman's radio was still sparking and she ripped it away, tossing it to the street. The other cop was shouting something into his own radio—"Shots fired! Shots fired!"—but the only answer was that cat screech again. It wasn't just coming from them, Pan realized, it was being blasted from the car radio, too, from every car radio, the sound of it filling the street.

"Stay where you are!" the woman yelled, her gun hand shaking. "Do not move."

The air hummed, every light on the street, every headlight, suddenly blazing even though the day burned brightly. Something was raging inside Pan's head, too—panic, pure and terrible.

"No," she said.

Farther down, the way they'd walked up from the Red Door, the street bucked like a rodeo bull, the force of it bumping cars into the air, shattering the windows in the apartment buildings. That generator hum grew in volume until, as one, the lights on the street exploded. Pan ducked, breathing in a stench that made her want to vomit. There was no denying what it was, that rotten egg smell she knew so well.

Sulfur.

"What—" the cop started, and the ground thumped up again, pieces of asphalt popping like corn. She toppled back into the squad car, spinning to the ground. Her gun clattered halfway across the street. The other cop had no idea what to do, swinging his weapon wildly left and right. Everyone else was fleeing the scene.

"Hey," said Herc, both hands raised as he addressed the man. "Listen to me. Something bad is coming. Something *really* bad. If I was you, I'd get in that car, go find your family, and get the hell out of Dodge. You hear me?"

The ground lurched up again and Pan could almost see it, a shape of darkness bouldering against the Red Door, demanding to be released.

"What is it?" the cop asked, his weapon finally dropping to his side.

"Hell," said Pan. "Hell is coming."

And he must have seen something in her worth believing because he holstered his weapon and dived into the squad car, screeching away. The other officer was scampering into the road, an SUV skidding past her, horn honking.

"You, too," said Herc. "Nothing you can do here."

He turned to Pan, to Marlow.

"So, this is it. The thing we've been working to prevent since all of this began. We've somehow made it happen."

"It wasn't my fault," said Marlow, when Herc threw him a look.

"Doesn't matter," he said. "We've been outplayed." He looked down to where the canister sat like a vat of toxic waste. "I'm guessing the Devil is going to be gunning for that, so we'd better—"

Another explosion beneath them, a sonic boom that almost reduced Pan's brain to mush. She could hear another sound, woven around the first, an echoing thunder of laughter. The cop obviously heard it too, because she turned and ran, her weapon abandoned.

"Dibs," said Charlie, waiting for a semi to hiss past before running out and claiming it.

It wouldn't do him any good, Pan thought. There was no

weapon here capable of defending against the thing that pounded at the door. This was a world made of straw, not bricks, and the Devil would blow it over with a single breath.

Unless they destroyed the heart before he could find it.

Herc had obviously thought the same thing because he'd taken the gun from Charlie. He aimed it at the canister, flicked off the safety, fired off a shot. Pan flinched, her ears ringing. She heard Herc fire three more times, then swear. When she looked back the canister was unchanged, the glass not even scuffed. The heart beat inside, the sound of it almost mocking them.

And the Devil answered its call, roaring.

"What do we do?" she asked Herc.

He stood there, muttering something so quietly that she couldn't hear it over the growing storm. She moved closer, trying to make sense of his words, finally catching them.

"Whoever holds the Devil, hold him well," he said, turning to her. He was trying to look strong, but Pan saw the way his lip trembled, saw the watery fear in his eyes. "Because he will not be caught a second time."

And even as he said it, all hell broke loose.

HELL ON EARTH

It started with a scream.

Marlow coughed the gunk from his lungs, turned to look past Pan, past Herc, past Charlie, past the cop car, past the traffic—which was like a demolition derby now, as the chaos set in.

Somebody was on fire down the street, their entire body engulfed in flame. They made it three or four feet, loosing another shriek into the day, then they exploded.

Literally exploded.

The flames were doused by the force of it, the figure blooming into a flower of dark ash, which drifted outward. A second woman ran through it, oblivious, then she, too, became a screaming immolation, flailing, collapsing, detonating into silence.

"Move," said Herc, grabbing the canister, struggling up the street with it.

Marlow couldn't seem to remember how, his body made of stone. The air was poisonous, that reek of sulfur clawing into his lungs, dissolving them. In the distance, two more people erupted, the fire burning through them like they were paper soaked in kerosene. They both exploded together, the sound of it arriving at Marlow a second or two after the visual. He still couldn't move, watching the ash—ash that had just been skin and bone, smiles and laughter—catch hold of the wind, riding it up the street.

"Yo!" Charlie shouted. "Marlow, come on!"

He concentrated, found first gear and floored it—turning and running after the others. The awful trinity of sounds chased him, shrieks, and whumps of ignition, then the gunshot pop that ended it all. Traffic streamed past, the cars in the other lane crunching into one another as they tried to turn. Marlow heard a metallic prang, looked over his shoulder to see a dry cleaning van mount the curb behind him, closing fast. The windshield was blackened, an inferno raging inside.

He dived to the side, colliding with a bike messenger who was tearing up behind him. They both hit the ground, the van crumpling the bike and slamming into the side of a building. The door blew off, a cloud of ash billowing out, choking Marlow. He spat, the taste of it impossibly familiar. He'd been breathing it in for the last three days.

It was the taste of hell, pure and simple.

He got to his feet, sucking in air, feeling his windpipe shrink as the asthma caught up with him. He fumbled for the inhaler as he broke into a run.

Behind him, the street was a war zone. There had to be ten cars piled up and burning, punching a fist of smoke into the sky. The windows of the apartments were exploding like firecrackers as the people inside—watching the carnage, no doubt—caught fire then burst. Others were sprinting toward him, twenty, thirty yards away, the farthest of them twisting into shapes of flame, vanishing a second later. They were pumping out so much heat that the trees had caught fire, swaying like the arms of burning men.

And the ground under them—it was growing soft, the asphalt melting, the rock beneath starting to glow. Their shoes were sticking to it, rooting them in place.

It wasn't this that drove Marlow on, though; it was the thunder in the air. It rose up over the screams, over the shriek of rending metal, over the sound of his own painful wheezing. It was like a radio being tuned, impossible to make sense of—until he'd covered another few yards and suddenly it fizzed into clarity, bursting into his thoughts as sharp as a scalpel.

A voice—a voice that spoke a language the world had not heard for centuries, but which Marlow understood like his own.

I AM FREE.

It was like a concussive wave of dark sound, one that ripped up the street and knocked him flat on his face. He lifted his head, a string of drool hanging from his lips, his forehead smarting where he'd scraped the sidewalk. Groaning, he turned onto his side, trying to remember what to do with his feet.

I AM FREE.

It came again, as powerful as the shock wave from a nuke— the force of it extinguishing the burning trees, scattering cars, rolling Marlow along the asphalt.

It was too much, he could make no sense of the vortex of his thoughts. He just looked through that sea of burning people, through the dancing clouds of ash. He looked, and he saw.

He saw the Devil step out of the dark.

It rose like an inverse sun, blistering a path up from the horizon. It dragged the darkness with it, like it was wearing the night as a cloak—only it wasn't really night, Marlow saw, it was something so much worse. It was as if reality were a photograph and this thing was burning a hole in it, scorching it from existence. He wrenched his head away, blinking. It had left an imprint on his vision, a shape inside that darkness—a too-tall figure who walked unsteadily on sapling legs, whose arms were curled up to its empty chest, who dragged a yoke of machinery behind it, and whose face arranged itself from shape to shape, which turned to him and spoke.

GIVE IT TO ME.

Marlow pushed himself onto his knees, then onto his feet, so night-blinded that he didn't even know which way he was supposed to be running. He turned back again, by mistake this time, almost falling into that ink-spill dark. The Devil was walking, anyone close to him bursting into flames, exploding with such force that they left craters in the sidewalk.

He staggered, feeling like his mind had been overridden, the controls taken over by somebody else. The world was a tornado of sound and fury, battering him. All he could see was the dead and the dying, all he could hear was their screams. He could smell them, he could taste them, he could feel them settling in his nose, in his ears. He had the sudden image of their spirits clambering onto him, into him, whispering, *It's your fault, Marlow. This is all because of you.*

And they were right, this *was* his fault.

"Hey," said a voice, quiet and yet the loudest sound on the street. Marlow looked to see Pan there. Her fingers rested lightly on his elbow. "We need to go. Whatever you're thinking, we need to go."

She steered him like he was a horse, leading him away. But they'd only taken a couple of steps when they saw Herc barreling back toward them, canister held to his chest, his cheeks puffing with the effort.

"That way!" he roared, skirting around them, heading straight for the Devil.

"What?" shouted Pan. "Are you—"

The apartment building to their left flew apart in a tsunami of bricks and steel. There was something inside it, a mass of twisted muscle, easily as big as a house, tendrils of darkness whipping around it. Even though it didn't really have a face it looked *pissed*.

"*Ostheim*," Marlow said.

The monster fell clumsily from the building, flopping and rolling onto the road. One of its tentacles punched into the street, skewering a truck and shattering asphalt, and it somehow managed to push its bulk up. A split opened up in its ass-ugly face and it vomited out a wet howl, dragging itself down the street.

Marlow didn't hesitate this time, turning and bolting after Pan. The ground was shaking as Ostheim followed, another immense howl right on their heels. The Devil was closer than ever, striding across its stage of dancing dead.

IT IS MINE.

The hole in its chest seemed to stream with darkness, those pieces of machinery hanging there, but if it was weaker without its heart it showed no sign of it. The heat was unbearable, Marlow's feet stinging from the steaming sidewalk.

Herc was ahead, running faster than Marlow thought possible. Running right for the Devil. He reached the van, the one that had almost hit Marlow, and ripped open the passenger door. He was inside in a flash, Charlie jumping up after him. By the time Pan and Marlow reached it Herc was hunched over the wheel, trying to turn the key. The whole of the cab was a sludge of melted plastic, the seat covers gone, the windshield burned and cracked.

"Seriously?" said Pan.

"Shut it, Pan," he said. "Get in."

The key was fused in the ignition, but Herc wrenched it hard and the van sputtered. Marlow looked over his shoulder, the skyline dominated by the tumorous mass of evil that was rolling toward them.

"Herc," he said, backing against the van. "You'd better hurry."

Somebody else ran past, devoured by fire. Marlow watched him go, watched as he ran straight into the path of Ostheim. The monster flicked him aside with a tentacle and he soared out over the street, exploding like a firework and releasing a dark starburst of ash. Then Ostheim was coming even faster, galloping, the whole world seeming to tremble.

"Herc," Marlow said again.

The van roared to life. Herc stuck it in reverse and slammed his foot on the pedal. The engine rattled, screamed, but the fender had welded itself to the wall.

"Get in," Herc yelled again, and Marlow did as he was told, Pan throwing herself onto his lap. Herc tried the gas again, the van shaking like a washing machine. Then, with a mighty clank, it ripped free from the wall, leaving its bumper behind as it lurched backward.

A blade of darkness sliced through the space they'd just vacated, hammering into the side of the building and reducing it to dust. Another followed, but Herc was reversing fast, the van sliding from side to side as he fought with the wheel. Pan swiveled around on Marlow's lap, kicked at the broken windshield with her bare feet until it popped free from the frame. Then Herc was spinning them in a circle, Ostheim filling the empty windshield.

All four of them swore together as Ostheim's mouth split into a cavern big enough to swallow the van in one go. Herc punched it into drive, the van's gearbox stuttering. Then he spun them to the right, the van bruising off a parked car. Another vehicle slammed into them from behind, shunting them toward Ostheim. He threw another of those giant tentacles at them but Herc flicked the wheel and the weapon grated down the side, powerful enough to knock the van onto two wheels.

"Christ on a bike," Herc yelled, wrestling with the wheel like it was a bear. They landed, rocked hard, Ostheim looming up in front of them. The beast roared, spraying black spit, Marlow's mouth full of it. For some reason Herc had flicked on the wipers and they flopped back and forth over the glassless windshield. "Hang on!"

He spun the wheel the other way and they one-eighty'd. Ostheim vanished, replaced with the carnage farther along the street. The Devil was there in its pocket of burnt earth, closer than ever, that subsonic boom still radiating from it.

YOU CANNOT KEEP IT FROM ME.

Herc turned the van around again, steering past a car that was tearing the other way, engulfed in flame. Another one cut in from the side, like they were riding bumper cars, this one crunching into them hard enough to ring Marlow's head off the sidewall.

He shook the flurries from his head. Herc was driving up the middle of the street, weaving between the stationary cars. Through the windshield was nothing but traffic, the Devil behind them and Ostheim nowhere to be seen.

"Where—"

Pan's question turned to a scream as a woman ran in front of them, blinded by terror.

Herc swerved as she exploded, the force of it bursting a front tire, the van skidding around again. Ostheim was closing in fast, one of his limbs cleaving a path along the metal flesh of the van, exploding Marlow's window. It curled up into the air in front of them, angling down like a striking cobra.

"Mother of—" Herc spun the wheel to the left but Ostheim was too quick, that razored limb spearing through the hood. The van stopped like it had hit an invisible wall, Marlow slamming into Pan, Pan slamming into the dash. The back of the van lifted up and spun around its new axle, then they were airborne, Ostheim jacking the entire vehicle up off the ground like a landed fish.

Marlow rolled over the back of the seat, falling, thumping

into the rear doors hard enough to smash them open. He flailed, fingernails scraping the metal, sliding over it, catching on the handle. Beneath him the world shrank, thirty, forty feet below, Ostheim's immense bulk holding them up like a trophy. Bags of dry cleaning dropped earthward, landing on the burning cars, on the exploding people. Marlow clung on with everything he had, the pain of it like he had plunged his hands in boiling water.

"Marlow? *Marlow?*"

He couldn't tell if it was Charlie or Pan calling his name, he couldn't make out either of them in the darkness of the van. There was only the drop, and Ostheim, and past his freakish mass the Devil carving a path their way. The air pressure was changing, Marlow's ears protesting. It was like the tide receding before a tsunami, because that awful call came again, shaking the street.

IT IS MINE.

The words hit them like a strong wind, the van swinging wildly. Marlow's left hand slipped free and for a second he thought he was going, then he recovered, crying out as his back cramped from the effort. Ostheim seemed to recoil from the Devil's call as well, as if even he was afraid of what stalked the shadows behind him. He moved fast, his bulk flattening cars, pushing through the trees. Marlow saw another road ahead, and past that the silver scar of the Hudson.

"Marlow, what the hell is he doing?" Herc called.

He had no idea, and even if he knew he wouldn't have been able to say it. His jaw was clenched with the effort of holding on, his teeth on the verge of shattering. Ostheim's mouth sagged like an open wound, spraying a guttural noise that might have been words. He raised his snaking limbs, the world shrinking even further as the van rose and rose.

Then suddenly the ground was rushing up to meet Marlow—a heartbeat of stomach-churning acceleration. Marlow screamed, letting go. He landed awkwardly, the van crumpling next to him.

"Pan!" he tried to shout, but his lungs were empty.

Ostheim lifted the van again, shaking it. There was a thump, a rattle, and this time the canister tumbled from it. It hit the ground hard, not even bouncing, sending a ripple across the earth. If anything, the pulse from inside was beating harder, calling to its master.

Ostheim was too busy to notice it. He was still shaking the van, his tendrils rummaging inside like he was trying to find the last Skittle in a bag of candy. Marlow could hear Pan shouting, Herc, too. Then Ostheim was off again, sliding into the river.

"No!" Marlow yelled, but it was too late. With a roar, Ostheim plunged the van beneath the water.

Marlow started toward them, then stopped, looking back. The canister with the heart was lying there, and behind it the world grew dark. How long before the Devil found them? How long before it pushed that rotten organ back into its chest? How long before it became a god?

The van was sinking. They were going to drown, all of them. But what were three deaths next to a million? A billion?

But it's Pan, it's Charlie, he thought, knowing even as he said it that if the Stranger was made whole again then they would die anyway.

"I'm sorry," he said to them, watching for a moment more, until he could find the strength to tear himself away. He doubled back, heading for the heart.

DROWNING

The van hit the water like a sledgehammer.

Everything went dark, freezing water boiling up through the open doors, covering Pan's head, forcing itself inside her ears, her nose. She reached out, grabbing Herc or Charlie, feeling them grab her, too.

Something sliced through the wall of the van, as easily as a knife through butter. Another of Ostheim's limbs cut in from the other side, this one gripping the metal and pulling it. The van crumpled like a soda can, halving in size. Pan screamed into the water as the ceiling crushed down, pinning her against the seat. Ostheim squeezed again and the van shrank even more. A body pressed against her, hands groping at her face, her hair.

She tried to push up, to get to the windshield. Another limb wrapped itself around the front of the van and tightened, catching Pan in a metal straitjacket. They were sinking fast, into the cold, into the dark, and she was trapped, pinned tight. The van was her coffin, she would die here, at the bottom of the river.

There was an explosion of something right in the center of her, something bright, something golden. Because death didn't seem so bad now. Death was a good thing, compared with the horror of eternal life in hell. There would be no waking up on a mountain of bone, no new scars, no more pain, no more suffering.

Just oblivion.

It lasted a second, then she tried to breathe in and her lungs roared. Suddenly she was in the pit again, back in hell, trapped in the suffocating dark beneath a hundred frenzied, dead Engineers. The adrenaline hit was like a slap and she knew she didn't want to die, not here, not like this. What had Night said? Hell destroyed all hope. If she died here then hell would have beaten her. It would have won.

Never.

She planted a hand on the crumpled roof and pushed, wriggling, the warped metal gouging into her kidneys. Her lungs were in spasm, her whole body screaming for air. The seat finally let her go and she wormed backward. There was no room to turn around, the dark like a cloth held over her face.

And where were the others?

She smacked the front of the van with her feet, trying to find a hole, but Ostheim had crushed it completely. White streaks cut through the dark, her brain running out of oxygen, preparing to shut down.

No.

There was a dull thump as the van hit the bottom of the river, groaning as it toppled onto its side. Pan kicked away, clawing over the tops of the seats, fumbling through the dark. Where were the doors? Where were the goddamned—

There, and they were open. She swam into the dark, floundering up, her lungs on fire.

Comeoncomeoncomeon.

A smudge of silver, growing. Pan had nothing left to give but she forced herself to keep going, even as a deeper, more awful darkness started to creep into the edge of her skull. She kicked, she pulled, then she burst into the light, into the air, sucking down a breath before she was all the way clear and swallowing water. She coughed, tried again, the oxygen entering her bloodstream like a drug.

Something exploded from the water beside her and she flinched, expecting to see Ostheim. It was Herc, screaming in a breath, clawing at his throat. He disappeared, then bobbed back up, treading water, blasting out hoarse swearwords as he fought to stay afloat. Pan called his name and he turned his head, his eyes big and red and full of panic.

"Where . . ." he spluttered, but she could guess the rest. There was no sign of Marlow or Charlie but Ostheim was rolling into the water, his tentacles churning it into a foam as he ripped the van to pieces, probably looking for the heart. Behind him the world was slipping into an unholy twilight as the Devil closed in.

"Come on," Pan said, swimming to the side, trying to flank Ostheim before he spotted them. The river took pity on her, carrying her in its flow. It took her four attempts before she found the strength to pull herself onto shore. She flopped down onto a concrete walkway, shivering so hard she could barely breathe. Herc grunted as he rolled next to her, landing in a wet pile.

"That guy . . ." he said, forcing himself up and offering her a hand, "is a major asshole."

Ostheim had finished dismantling the van but hadn't found what he was looking for. He roared, his tentacles cutting through the flow like lamprey eels.

"Pan!"

It took her a moment to find Marlow, another moment to make sure she wasn't imagining it. He was on the other side of the green, overshadowed by a slice of night that emerged from the trees behind him.

And he was trying to wrestle the canister toward her.

She struggled onto her feet, Ostheim howling again behind her. The ground lurched as he started to chase and she knew he would be too quick, she knew he'd be on them in seconds. They were trapped between him and the Devil, and this time there was nowhere left to run.

Then the Devil spoke.

His word was a ten-megaton blast, a shock wave filling Pan's head with darkness. It rolled over the Hudson, roiling the water into a churning frenzy.

CHILD.

Pan slammed her hands to her ears, a gout of blood squirting between her fingers. Behind her, Ostheim froze, those grotesque limbs retracting like a snail's antennae. Pan could see Herc farther down, helping Charlie out of the water, the boy coughing out half the river.

The Devil was standing on the bank in a bubble of blistering shadow, and even though it hurt to look at it Pan forced herself to, trying to make sense of what she was seeing.

It almost looked like the Devil was about to keel over, its jointed legs buckling. It was still trailing pieces of Engine behind it but they were failing, the mechanisms collapsing, shedding, a trail of them left in its wake. It called out again, a word so loud, that carried so much force, it was just a concussive boom that shook the ground on which she stood.

"Is it . . ." started Charlie as he hobbled to her side. "I mean, what's it doing?"

"No idea," growled Herc, walking in the direction of the mainland. "But this ain't the time to play tourist."

"Wait," said Pan, her jaw dropping as the Devil actually collapsed onto one knee beside the river, its arms unfurling to stop itself from landing on its face. Watching it was like a blade in her eyes but she couldn't turn away. Chunks of black light were dropping from it, fizzing into the ground. She was too far away to see its face but it looked like it was rippling, the mechanisms of it going into overdrive. It curled one hand to its chest, those too-long fingers probing. Pan squinted, trying to work out what she was seeing there—a gaping absence in that body of writhing shadow, where its heart should be. "What is it doing?"

Marlow had almost reached them, dragging the canister behind him.

"Dying," he said, snatching in a breath. "Please, just die."

It called out again, the booming low of a cow being led to slaughter. Ostheim had nearly reached it, his limbs curling protectively around it. His moan was the sound of a child mourning a sick parent.

"Please," said Marlow. "Please, please, please."

The Devil's body was spasming as Ostheim lifted it up. It looked like it was melting, dissolving, great gobs of inverse light fizzing as they hit the ground. Ostheim pulled it close, smothering it in his limbs. Flames were erupting from the earth, from the river, weaving a curtain of smoke and steam. Pan felt a shift in the wind, in the air pressure, buffeting her against the railing.

"Come on," said Herc. "This ain't gonna end well."

But she had to see. Because what if it *was* dying? What had Marlow said, that it was old? It had been suspended in hell for all this time, cocooned in that freak show. But this was the real world, the rules here were different. What if it just crumbled, like a museum artifact taken from its hermetic box and exposed to the environment?

Please, she found herself chanting along with Marlow. *Please, please . . .*

Ostheim screamed, a feral, industrial sound. His body reared, splashing down in the boiling water, two dozen limbs flailing. Only when he stumbled back, collapsing into the river, did Pan see why.

The Devil was burrowing into the mess of Ostheim's face, a blazing core of darkness that seared its way inside. She had to turn away from the sheer force of it, but nothing could stop her looking again, seeing Ostheim thrash and howl, seeing that insect shape pull itself inside him like it was disappearing under a comforter. Black blood sprayed upward, casting colorless rainbows in the sun. The Devil was drinking it, gorging itself on it, feeding from its own child.

"Pan," said Herc, right beside her. He had taken the canister and was backing away. "I'm serious."

She staggered after him, still watching. Ostheim's movements were growing weaker, his body deflating like a blimp. His obscene mouth hung open at the waterline, the skin bubbling in the heat of the river. And still the Devil dug deeper. The sound of it feeding mixed with Ostheim's cries, his mewls, then the wet struggle of his breaths.

"What's it doing?" she asked again, but the truth was right there in front of her. Without its heart, and without the Engine that had been keeping it alive, the Devil was dying. And the only thing left to feed on was its own sick progeny.

It was almost enough to make her feel sorry for Ostheim.

Almost.

"Come on," said Herc, hefting up the canister, slapping a hand against it to try to silence the organ inside. "We've got to work out a way of destroying this, and something tells me we don't have long."

He was right, they didn't have long. Minutes, maybe, before the Devil reclaimed its heart.

Before it became a god, Pan thought, and ate the world whole.

BE WHO YOU ARE

Marlow struggled away from the river, following Herc until the old man's arms gave up on him and the canister fell.

Herc dropped on top of it, growling. Marlow slumped down next to him, taking a shot of his inhaler. The carnage behind them was screened off by the burning trees but he could still hear the Devil feasting on Ostheim.

It was a good sound.

"Hey," said Herc, clicking his fingers. "Focus. All of you. I need your full attention. We've got one shot. One shot to make this right. Maybe not even that. And if we don't take it . . ."

He let the world answer for him, the air shuddering with the force of Ostheim's screams. Herc wiped his face with a shaking hand.

"I've worked my whole life to stop this from happening," he said. "But I don't think it was ever really up to me. I don't think there was ever anything I could do. I think it was always supposed to be like this."

He was right. Ostheim had used them all; he'd been able to look ten moves ahead and he'd played them like pawns, like fools. And behind it all had been *it*, a creature of dark intelligence that had been planning this for a hundred thousand years. How could anyone, any mortal, ever stand a chance against that? How were they supposed to know whether the next move they made was their own thinking or part of that same infernal plan?

"I don't understand any of it," Herc said. "But I won't let it end like this. I won't let him win, not while I've still got breath in my lungs. And I know you've been through too much to give up now. I know you've *seen* too much to let him win."

The ground shook, the Devil almost done.

"Nobody else is coming to help," Herc said. "It's us, that's all. The four of us against all of hell."

"But what do we do?" Marlow said. "How do we stop it?"

"Open it," Herc said, nodding at the canister. "Open it and then destroy that bastard thing inside."

"What if we can't?" said Marlow.

"Not an option," Herc said. "You do it."

"What if it doesn't work?" he said, and Herc's face fell for an instant before he caught it.

"Not an option," he said again. "You *do* it."

"Me," Marlow said. "So where are you going?"

Herc looked back, his teeth grinding, his eyes bulging.

"I'm going to show that creep what happens when you mess with the U.S. of A."

"I'm with you," said Pan.

Herc shook his head. "I'm not sure if there's any coming back from this one, kiddo."

"I'm with you, Herc," she said again. "We'll buy you some time, Marlow. Find a way."

"No," Marlow said, shaking his head. "We can't split up, we . . . We have to stick together."

"Eggs and baskets," said Charlie. "Marlow, I'll come with you. You guys see if you can slow it down a little, we'll get it open."

"No," said Marlow again. He looked at Pan, felt himself reaching for her. She shrugged, smiled sadly.

"You play the game, you take the pain," she said. "Always knew it would end like this."

"With the Devil chasing us through Jersey, looking for its heart after betraying Ostheim after Ostheim betrayed us?" said Marlow, and she almost managed a smile.

"Well, *almost* like this," she said.

"Please," he said. And what he wanted to say to her was *we can go, we can all just get in a car and drive the other way, we can survive.* But it was a lie, because however far they went, it would catch up with them eventually. The Devil wouldn't stop here. Sooner or later, the whole world would be reduced to silence and ash.

And it was a lie because he knew that however scared they were, however much they wanted to run, none of them would abandon their post. His brother, Danny, had been the hero, but somewhere down the line Marlow had become a soldier, too.

You play the game, you take the pain.

He wondered if, deep down, he too had always known it would end like this.

Farther down the river a fleshy shape bounded from the trees, a fury of bunched muscles already slick with blood. A demon. It looked the other way, loosing a cry from the ragged hole in its head, then set off toward the sound of traffic. More were coming, though, announcing themselves with their hyena calls. The gate was still open, the nightmares flowing through.

"We're still alive," said Herc, watching a helicopter wobble into the air from nearby, somebody lucky enough to be able to escape. "We're still fighting. Just remember that. However much we've played into the Devil's hands, however much it's used us, it hasn't managed to kill you yet."

Because it needed us, thought Marlow. *Because it was trying to keep us alive so that we could open the gates.*

"And we saw it fall," Herc went on. "I don't know what it is.

I don't know where it came from. But we all saw it fall, right here. We saw it struggle. It calls itself a devil but it's not one, it's not a god. It's a piece of crap, nothing more. You remember that, okay? You remember it."

"What are you gonna do?" Charlie asked. Herc smiled.

"I got something in mind," he said. "Now say your goodbyes, 'cause we gotta move."

Marlow stared at the floor. He couldn't bring himself to look up.

"Marlow," Pan said. Still he didn't look, he just studied her bruised and bloodied feet as she walked in front of him. "You can do this."

"What if I can't?" he said. The exhaustion pressed down on his head, his shoulders, so heavy he thought he might snap. "What if I can't?"

"Then you can't," she said. "Then it all ends."

"No pressure," muttered Charlie.

"You're only human," she said. "All of us, we're only human."

He felt her hand on his chin, pulling gently. He resisted for a moment, then he raised his head and met her eyes. They glinted like copper pennies, those little pieces of hell that they had brought back with them. They were so alien, but they were so real. They were her eyes, the same ones that had glared at him back in the parking garage, a million years ago, when he'd first seen her die. The same ones that had watched him as he stepped into the Black Pool, as he emerged a superman. The same ones that had melted as she'd moved in for the kiss. He and Pan had died together, they'd gone to hell together. Somewhere in the last few days he'd resigned himself to the idea that they would lose themselves to eternity together, living forever in that nightmare underworld. However bad it would get, he'd always have her by his side. He'd never have to let her go.

Yet here he was, saying goodbye.

"I'm sorry I rode you so hard," she said, swallowing something big. "You were a good soldier."

"Pan," he said.

"We wouldn't have got this far without you," she said, shrugging. "Even though it was kind of all your fault."

"Pan."

"Don't spoil it," she said. "Don't be your usual douchey self and ruin the moment. Yeah?"

He opened his mouth, then closed it, nodding. He wanted to hug her, wanted to kiss her, but in the end, for a reason he couldn't quite understand, he just stuck out his hand. She looked at it, then back at him, then she grabbed it and shook it like they'd just finished a business meeting.

"You really are a dick, Marlow," she said, but she didn't let go, and after a moment she threw herself onto him, wrapping her arms around his shoulders, squeezing him like he was the only thing stopping her from drowning—so hard he could barely breathe. He hugged her waist, held her, felt the sobs there rather than heard them, felt her tears against the skin of his neck, so warm.

Then, just as suddenly, she pulled away, scrubbing at her face. Marlow wiped away his own tears but they kept rolling out of him, impossible to stop. He felt as if there was a piece of him connected to her, an invisible line that would pull him in her wake.

"Go on," she said. "Let's give the Devil something to cry about."

Marlow sighed, nodded. He looked down at the beating heart, locked away in its metal-and-glass cage. The thought of having to open it, of having to destroy it, was like a neutron star tied around his neck, heavy enough to pull him into the ground, to make a grave of the earth. Charlie was already wrestling with it, his skinny arms trying to pick it up. Marlow grabbed the other end and together they managed to get it off the ground. If anything, it seemed heavier now than ever.

"As soon as it's done with Ostheim, it's coming after you," said Herc. "And I'm guessing it's gonna be juiced. Find a way. I would say stay safe, but it's a little late for that. Just do what you do. Be who you are."

Marlow nodded. Charlie was walking away and he had to follow, but he kept his eyes on Pan and Herc.

"What are we, Herc?" Marlow called out. The old guy looked back, smiled.

"You're Hellraisers," he shouted. "Go raise some hell."

PAYBACK

Pan watched as Marlow and Charlie struggled back toward the street, the canister slung between them. It seemed to dwarf them, even though she knew it was just an optical illusion caused by the pulse of black light it threw out, one that rippled through reality, that called to its master.

What were the chances of them being able to open it when even a bullet couldn't shatter the glass? And more to the point, what was the chance of them opening it before the Devil finished its meal?

"You've really got a plan?" said Pan when the boys were finally out of sight. "Or shall we get on a boat and leave them to it?"

She was exhausted: four days in hell with no food and barely any sleep would do that to anyone. But she'd lasted longer than this without rest. However bad hell had been, the few sleepless days she'd had after caving Christoph's head in with a lamp, when she'd hidden out in the sidings near the Harold, sobbing and screaming and knowing she could never go back, had been worse.

Herc started to run, old but fit, jogging like a drill sergeant. He looked back, and there was a smile on his face. She ran after him.

"I hear the Keys are nice this time of year," he said. "Grab a couple of cocktails, moor the boat offshore, front-row view of the end of the world."

She laughed as best she could, picturing Marlow's face if he could hear them. But the vision of him there was a weight tied to her soul, like she was pulling the world behind her. She had to stop, sucking in air until everything stopped spinning.

Herc realized that she'd halted, turned back to her.

"They'll be okay," he said. "Marlow's the luckiest son of a bitch I know."

The words hadn't even left his mouth before the Devil howled, a noise that churned the river into a frenzy, that snapped trees in half. Pan ducked instinctively, Herc dropping with her, both of them watching as a tornado of shadow twisted up over the land. It began to move, carving out a path of darkness. She had to turn away after a few seconds, but there was no denying which way it was heading.

It was going after Marlow.

Pan swore, was halfway to telling Herc to hurry up when she heard it—a noise coming from the space the Devil had just vacated. It took her a moment to recognize the voice, and it was the sudden twisting jolt of realization that made her double back, that made her step between the corpses of the trees, into the spiraling clouds of ash.

Ostheim was there, or a mess of parts that had once been him.

And somehow, he was still alive.

He was trying to claw his way out of the river. He had one half of his enormous mass on the bank, but he was bottom heavy, beached. He was an empty bag, most of his limbs lying flat and still. Only those at the front seemed to work, churning grooves in the mud as he tried and failed to escape.

"What do we do with him?" asked Herc, catching up with her, but Pan was already on the move, driven by fury. She broke into a run, tripping along the walkway that tracked the river. The air here was dense with smoke, fire devouring trees and buildings.

"Pan!" yelled Herc. "Wait!"

But she couldn't. Her rage was too much, it was overpowering. All she could think about was Ostheim, his voice on the phone telling her that she was doing the right thing, that she was saving the world; the joy she'd felt when he had sent her down to the Engine, on a new mission. She had done something terrible, she had killed Christoph, and it was Ostheim who had offered her a way back to something good, a way back to *herself*.

And it had all been a lie.

She'd killed for him, she'd sent people to hell, for *him*. He'd played her like a puppet, and he'd brought about the end of the world.

Whatever happened now, he was going to pay for that.

The closer she got, the more immense he became. His deflated bulk had to have been fifty yards long, trailing into the unsettled water like a fishing net. The top half was a chaos of movement, his skin made up of what looked like leeches, millions of them squirming and coiling. There were glimpses of machinery there, too, flashes of bronze cogs, obsidian bones. Pan skirted around him, scanning the riverfront for anything she could use as a weapon, finding nothing. She splashed through puddles of black blood until she stood before what could only be his face.

He looked just like he had when he'd slaughtered Mammon, an engine of moving parts, as far from human as it was possible to be. And yet there was something there in that kaleidoscope of motion, a glimpse of humanity in the alien chaos. Half of his face had been eaten away, a gaping, car-size hole where the Devil had made a meal of it.

"Ostheim," she said, surprised at the strength in her voice.

"Careful, Pan," said Herc, standing by her side, the cop's gun clenched in his hand.

The sound of the Devil was growing weaker as it chased its heart, but it was still like standing in a storm, the wind tugging at her clothes, her hair. The beast before her groaned, the movements becoming more frenzied. The leechlike components of it twisted around each other and a circle of flesh peeled open to reveal a single piggy eye. There was a mouth, too, but when it opened the only thing that fell out was a spew of liquid filth, one that reeked of forgotten food, of rot, of death. One of its working limbs spasmed into the air but fell flat again almost immediately. Pan stood her ground, wondering if the look in her eyes was enough to finish Ostheim off.

"You bastard," she said. "You bastard. You did this."

She stepped forward, slammed the heel of her bare foot into Ostheim's flesh. It cracked like an old egg, more of that rancid gunk flowing out, steaming over her bare skin. She scraped her foot on the ground, using every ounce of restraint she had not to throw herself on him, finish off what the Devil had started.

"Not so cocky now though, huh?" she said. "You happy? All this time, everything you did, and this is your reward, bleeding out in the mud."

Ostheim groaned, the noise of a thousand men dying in sync.

"You didn't see this coming, did you?" She noticed one of his tentacles, flopping limply. There was a blade on the end of it, as dark and as sharp as flint. She stamped on it, crushing the jelly out of it until it was almost completely severed.

"Thank you," she spat, grabbing it. It was surprisingly heavy, like an oversized baseball bat, great drops of blood falling from it, thumping when they hit the ground. But that blade was lethal. She'd seen dozens just like it slide into Mammon, reducing him to so much mince. Ostheim's face had been sucked back in again, like he was hiding in there. The stump of his arm twitched, brushed over her face, leaving a trail of slime.

She hawked up a ball of spit, launched it at him.

"You'd better look at me. I'm going to kill you, so you'd better look at me."

He loosed another demonic growl, one that formed guttural, bestial words. They fell from him in clumps of meat and blood, more liquid than sound.

"Hell is loose . . . and everything will die . . . It's over."

"For you," said Pan. "Your master saw to that."

"No," he groaned, his body shuddering, slipping farther into the river. His last remaining limb poked at the ground, trying to find purchase. "I was made from him . . . It was always his blood. I will . . . live on . . . in him."

"You tell yourself that," said Herc, joining her. "Then watch as we crush its ass."

Ostheim laughed, a sound that quickly became a cough. Pieces of him were literally dropping away, hitting the ground like rotten carcasses. He was decomposing as they watched. Pan put a hand to her mouth against the smell of it.

"There is no . . . way to . . . fight it," he vomited. "It has already . . . begun . . . and it has already ended. Once he has his heart, there is nothing . . . nothing left to do but fall . . . to your knees . . . embrace him."

"It won't get the heart," said Herc. "Marlow will destroy it."

Ostheim just laughed.

"It cannot be destroyed," he said. "Even if the body dies . . . the heart lives on. It will find . . . a new home, new flesh. Marlow . . . Marlow is the biggest fool . . . of all . . . blind to it . . . How can he not see . . . the truth? How can he not see . . . ?"

"*What?*" asked Pan.

"It does . . . not matter," Ostheim said. "Something as holy as this . . . can never die."

"You sure about that?" Pan said. "Mammon sure died. Meridiana died. How are you any different from them?"

Ostheim's face fell, his mouth grinding on some unthinkable truth. His body was collapsing into itself like a bounce house after a party, corrupting instantly, blossoming into mold. He looked at her through the rotten hole of his eye, his face growing slack.

"I will never die . . . hell is coming . . . and I will be—"

Pan rammed the blade into Ostheim's head, her body acting without her permission, without her even knowing it was happening. She felt the thick bone of his scalp give, and when she tried to tug the weapon loose it was stuck fast. A spasm passed along Ostheim's entire body, shaking him down the bank and farther still into the river.

"You could have waited, Pan," said Herc. "He could have told us how to destroy the heart."

She didn't care. She kept her eyes on Ostheim as his face dissolved into a nest of vipers, squirming into nothing. Then gravity took hold, dragging his bulk beneath the waters.

She should have felt some sense of victory, she should have been laughing. Ostheim was dead, they'd never have to hear his lies again, never have to follow his orders. But she felt hollow inside, a doll. Ostheim was dead, yes, but his job was done, he'd birthed something so much worse.

A demon screamed from nearby, but the sound of it didn't even shake her. She'd just killed Ostheim, after all, and this was just a demon—mindless, stupid.

"So," she said, wiping the blood from her hands. "The plan."

"Remind me never to piss you off," said Herc. "Come on, we need to find something—"

He cocked his head, listening.

"Chopper."

She could hear it, too, above the grind and roar of the Devil, over the screams, over the sirens. She couldn't pinpoint where it was coming from, but Herc obviously had better ears than she did because he was running along the river, heading for a pontoon that jutted out into the water. There was a warehouse there, and once they'd cleared it Pan saw a helicopter rocking on its landing pad, a handful of suited men climbing inside.

"Move!" roared Herc, shoving through the crowd. They protested and he bunched his fist, smashing a big guy in the nose and dropping him like a sack of bricks. The pilot was panicking, the chopper's runners thumping out a rhythm on the pad as it struggled to rise. Herc lifted the cop's gun, pointing it inside.

"What's happening over there is bad," he said. "But I'm worse."

He gave them one of his specials, a glower that had scared Pan half to death more than once. It did the trick, the chopper emptying. Herc aimed the gun at the pilot.

"You, too."

Herc took his place, squeezing into the pilot's seat. Pan jumped in next to him.

"You know how to fly this?" she asked.

He smiled. "How hard can it be?"

Suddenly the chopper was lifting, wobbling like a spinning top at the end of its spin.

"Where are we going?" she asked.

They were high enough now to be able to look down on Jersey. The land was filled with smoke but she could still make out a trail of devastation that led away from the river. There was a pulse of black light there, a hole in the world. The sight of it made Pan giddy, made her dig her fingers into her seat until the tips of them burned. She wondered if it already had Marlow, if it had turned him to fire and ash like everyone else.

"To get a little surprise," said Herc.

"A nuke?" she said, and she saw his face fall.

"It was supposed to be a surprise," he said, pouting.

"Bloody hell, Herc, how many of those things do you have?"

"More than you'd think," he said, spinning the helicopter around. "I just hope there's time."

JERSEY DEVILS

There was no time.

They weren't moving fast enough. They *couldn't* move fast enough, the canister was just too heavy. It was getting heavier, too, Marlow was sure of it, like the heart inside was a black hole, anchoring itself with its own gravity. It knew its master was close and it wanted out of its cage.

Marlow risked a look back, through the trees, past the grid-locked cars, to see that evil cloud of shrieking death rising behind them, swallowing the sky whole. Inside it he could just about make out that flickering mass of antimatter, the holes in its head staring right back at him.

IT IS MINE.

He almost threw the canister to the ground, almost screamed "Take it!" Instead he gripped it even harder, lumbering across the road. Behind them came a scream, then that awful *pop* as someone exploded. Marlow felt the shock wave billow against his back and he picked up speed, running into the street just as an SUV barreled past.

"Hey!" Charlie yelled at the driver. "Stop!"

Marlow swore, staring back into the chaos, almost blinded by it. The Devil was closer now, gaining fast. He shook the shadows from his head, stumbling down the street. It was choked with trucks, one semi straddling the road where the driver had left it. Cars had been abandoned, too, the drivers fleeing on foot rather than risking the gridlocked roads.

"There," he said, steering Charlie to the nearest car.

"A Honda?" Charlie said. "Do you want to die? Try that one."

He set off so fast that Marlow lost his grip on the canister. He scooped it up again, his fingers cramping with the effort, following Charlie to an eighteen-wheeler, driver's door open, the engine still running.

"A truck?" Marlow yelled. Together, they hefted the heart inside, Marlow climbing the steps into the passenger seat. Charlie clambered in next to him, staring at the giant wheel, at the complicated gearshift. "Please tell me you can drive this?"

Charlie stomped the clutch and grated the transmission into gear, the truck groaning, protesting like a stubborn mule.

"Charlie," said Marlow, staring out the windshield at the storm that swept toward them. The Devil was a pocket of absolute darkness in the day, radiating inverse light. It had shed almost all of the machinery that had accompanied it out of hell, powered by the blood that it had stolen from its child. It was still struggling, but it was a different kind of struggle—like it was learning to use its body again.

"Are you nuts!" he screamed at Charlie. "Go!"

"I'm trying!"

Charlie wrestled with the wheel, the truck lurching forward, turning as slowly as a tanker. The Devil closed in, its voice shaking the street, shaking the sky. But the truck was picking up speed, the darkness swimming from the windshield and replaced with what was left of the day. The road was a fortress of metal, dense with cars, but Charlie floored it, the truck thumping its way down the center lane. Marlow checked the rearview mirror to see the Devil giving chase, scattering cars with its too-long arms, turning everyone it passed into creatures of fire and ash.

"Faster!" Marlow yelled.

"It's on the floor!" Charlie replied, the semi growling, shuddering as they plowed past a smaller truck. "Just try to get that thing open, yeah?"

Marlow wrestled the canister upright between his legs. Inside, the heart beat faster than ever, squelching grotesquely against the sides of the jar. The top of the canister was like something that had been pulled from the Engine, a mess of clockwork parts. He pulled at them, poked at them, but nothing seemed like it was designed to move. The glass was one solid tube, smeared with gore. There wasn't even a mark where Herc had shot it.

Charlie steered right, hard, accelerating through a chorus of horns. The truck hit a railroad crossing and almost took off, tilting wildly as they accelerated around a bend.

"Damn thing's indestructible," Marlow said. "We need a bomb to get it open."

"Can't help," said Charlie.

IT IS MINE.

Marlow looked back again, even though he knew it was a bad idea. It was like a tornado there, a churning vortex of darkness that picked up cars and hurled them against the buildings.

"Go!" yelled Marlow. Charlie kept his foot on the floor, the semi cleaving past cars as they smashed through the sign for the 440 and wobbled onto the highway. Marlow grabbed his seat with both hands, screaming "Go! Go! Go!" He looked in the mirror again as they built up speed, hoping to see the storm recede, but if anything the sky back there was darker, that hideous shard of negative light reaching out for them.

IT IS MINE.

Marlow grabbed the canister, held it to his chest. What the hell were they supposed to do with it? At this rate the only option open to them was finding a place to steer the truck off the road and into the harbor. With any luck they might be able to sink without a trace, at least long enough for Herc and Pan to come up with something to fight the Devil.

IT IS MINE.

The voice was a hurricane and this time Marlow felt the words hit the back of the truck. Charlie swore, struggling with the wheel. By the time he'd gotten control again it was too late, the truck demolishing the barricade and slamming into a parking lot. Charlie kept his foot on the pedal, knocking cars aside like they were toys. But there was nowhere left to go, a Walmart looming up in front of them.

"Hang on!" Charlie screamed. Marlow waited for the brakes to kick in but if anything the truck seemed to be going faster.

"Wait!" Marlow tried to say, but before the word was even out of his mouth they hit. The semi plowed through the wall, Marlow's head ringing off the canister. Bricks and dust rained down on the windshield, the truck demolishing aisle after aisle until it hissed to a halt.

For a second he didn't dare move, then the pain started to creep in. His face felt like it had been held to a blowtorch and he grabbed his nose, feeling the broken cartilage.

"Ow," he said, his thoughts settling like falling snow. He turned to Charlie, the boy wrapped around the steering wheel. He wasn't moving.

"Hey," Marlow said, grabbing his friend's arm. "Charlie?"

"I," he replied, lifting his head. His face was a mask of blood, but his eyes were clear and somehow he managed a smile. "I've always wanted to do that."

Marlow smiled back—or at least he tried to, the pain straitjacketing his face. He reached for the canister, disappointed to see that the crash hadn't so much as dented it. He wedged his feet against the door and kicked it open. The canister fell to the floor and he followed, the whole world spinning. Only part of that was concussion—the store was shaking like there was a tornado overhead, people streaming toward the main door.

It wouldn't do them much good. The darkness that greeted them there was worse than any storm. The Devil was outside in the parking lot, turning flesh to ash with just a thought.

"Where do we go?" said Charlie, jumping down from the cab.

Marlow had no idea. They couldn't run, the Devil was too fast. He wasn't even sure they could hide, because the heart was pounding against the walls of the canister, hammering out a pulse that seemed louder than sound, that seemed like it triggered some *different* sense. He got the feeling the Devil could track that noise from the other side of the world.

It was his heart, after all.

They could always wait until the Devil just died, until its blood ran dry like last time. There was nothing left for it to feed on. But how long would that take? Minutes? Hours? Centuries?

The desperation hollowed him out, made him feel like every limb was a paper shell. He didn't think he'd even be able to pick the canister up again. It was too much. He looked around him, the aisle full of kids' toys, nothing they could use as a weapon. There would be chain saws here, he knew, maybe even guns, but they'd need an atomic bomb like the one they'd had in Paris if they wanted to win this war, and he was pretty sure not even Walmart carried them.

Marlow dug deep, both of them dragging the canister down the aisle. He could hear that awful *pop pop pop* as the Devil closed in on the hole they'd made in the front of the building, the ash riding on the current of its subsonic voice.

IT IS MINE.

It was too much. Marlow dropped the canister. It landed

with a clang, rolling back like it was going to find the Devil by itself. Charlie collapsed, looked as if he was about to faint.

"What do we do?" Charlie said. "How do we break it?"

Marlow didn't know. And what if they *did* break it? All they'd be doing was handing the heart back to its master.

"You should go," he said to Charlie. "This is my mess, let me handle it."

Charlie smudged the blood from his face, his teeth the brightest thing in the room as he flashed a smile.

"No way," he said. "Did you learn nothing last time? You ain't leaving me, Marlow. I'm part of this as much as you." He looked toward the front of the store, the aisle gradually darkening as that evil cloud of death drew closer. "Whatever happens next, it happens to both of us."

He grabbed Marlow's shoulder, squeezing, and Marlow had almost managed to smile when the Devil stepped into Walmart.

ENOUGH.

It's over, he thought. *We've lost.*

A different sound, a thunderous roar, and the front of the building exploded. A hammer of noise and heat slammed into Marlow, shunting him back across the floor on a wave of glass and shrapnel.

He tried to sit up, found that he couldn't. He looked for Charlie, looked for the Devil, but there was only smoke, seen through a red haze. If his face had been bad before it was a mess now, blood flowing freely from his scalp, his shirt sodden with it.

He swore, rolling onto his side. The canister was there, almost close enough to touch, and he squirmed toward it. He couldn't see the Devil through the carnage, but it was still there—waves of dark energy pulsing from it, churning the smoke and fire into a frenzy. Something had slowed it down, though.

Not that it mattered.

It was over, he knew. In seconds the Devil would simply do its thing and turn him into a sculpture of fire, then he'd explode into ash and everything he ever was or could be would drift into the day, up into the warmth. There was something almost peaceful about the thought.

No.

He managed to get a fingertip to the glass, leaving a smudge of blood there.

No.

He wouldn't lie down and die. It wouldn't end like this. He'd faced up to the Devil once, he'd do it again—even though it would be the last thing he ever did.

"Come on," he groaned, finally managing to sit up. He rolled the canister toward him, his bloodied fingers grabbing the gears and cogs, pulling it to his side. All the while that bodiless heart beat and beat and beat, growing ever faster. "Come on, you mother—"

The canister clicked, a pop like the universe was snapping its fingers. Its mechanisms were moving, those clockwork pieces grinding in unison. They were slick with blood, he realized, *his* blood. He looked at his hand, a ragged gash across his palm.

Marlow pushed his hand against the mechanism again, felt those pieces rotate against him. Then there was something wet, like a tongue, and he pulled his hand back only to find that he couldn't. Something had hold of him. He grunted, kicking, his hand finally coming free as the canister rolled back along the floor.

Empty.

He looked down, saw something embedded in the wound in his palm—something that wriggled like a leech. He followed it down, saw a grotesque lump of meat and gristle, of obsidian and bronze, of dark light and blinding shadow, hanging from the other end of it. It pulsed madly, its infernal mechanisms gyrating as more of those veinlike threads fired out and plunged into his hand. He could see them there, writhing beneath the skin of his wrist, and the scream was in his throat, burning its way out of him, when the world went black.

TRUTH KILLS

If the view from the ground had been bad, the view from up here was worse.

Pan stared through her gaunt reflection at the burning world beneath her. The destruction was limited but it was spreading fast. The Devil was a pocket of seemingly infinite absence, one that carved a path away from the harbor and through the vast warehouses that sat next to it. A churning cloud of smoke and debris revolved around it, so Herc was keeping them to the side at a steady two hundred feet, low enough to make out the people on the street below.

Low enough to see Marlow and Charlie trying to get themselves killed.

"What the hell are they doing?" she said, speaking into the mic of her headphone set. They were running with the canister, almost getting hit by a silver car. Marlow dropped his end, scrabbling for it. They looked like two of the Three Stooges trying to carry a ladder, and at this rate they were both going to be dead in about four seconds.

Herc had obviously seen it too, because he spun the chopper in a wide, lazy circle.

"If you're going to get this weapon of yours, you'd better do it fast," she said. His growled reply was fed into her headphones.

"Huh?"

"I said there's no time. Goddammit, the nearest weapons cache we have is in Queens. By the time we get halfway there Marlow's gonna be toast."

She ran a hand through the knotted mess of her hair.

"There must be something else," she said. "Come on, Herc. No pressure or anything but the whole world is counting on there being something else."

He angled around again and it took Pan a second to find them.

"Can Charlie drive a truck?" she asked, but the boy answered her, the semi swinging around in a wide arc and dragging its trailer behind it. It had to be the slowest mode of transport they could find—*stupid stupid stupid*—then the semi started thumping through the motionless traffic and she took the words back. The roads were pretty clogged, and the Devil was fast, but at least in a truck they might be able to shake him off.

They'd stand more of a chance if Herc could think of a plan.

"Anything?" she said.

"Something," he replied.

He wasn't sharing, though. Instead he pushed the stick and followed the Devil, staying low. She looked out over the buildings of Jersey, New York glittering on the other side of the bay. How long before everything fell, before the whole country turned to ash?

And suddenly she was thinking of her old house, over the East River. She wondered if her foster mom was still there, if she still thought about her missing child. Christoph's apartment was out there too. It was like a punch to the gut, the knowledge that all of this had started there, with her hand wrapped around the cold, metal base of a table lamp.

Thunk. Thud.

"Hey, Pan," said Herc. "You still with me?"

She realized he was waiting for an answer to a question she hadn't heard, stared at him until he repeated it.

"They still alive?"

"Yeah," she said, watching the eighteen-wheeler smash its way through traffic. The roads were opening up as they tore south into Bayonne, whoever was driving pulling them onto what looked like the 440.

Her stomach lurched as Herc accelerated after them. She could feel him looking at her, and when she turned to him again he was wearing an expression that was one part misery to two parts guilt.

"You were somewhere else, there," he said. "Wanna tell me where?"

"Home," she said, shrugging. "Just thinking back. Never actually thought that it would lead me here."

"Christoph?" he said, and when she nodded something shifted in his expression. He took a deep breath, like he was about to dive out the door. "Look," he said, not meeting her eye. "I never planned to tell you this, but . . . But it's changed, hasn't it? Everything has changed."

"What are you talking about, Herc?" she said.

"Maybe there's something you need to know," he replied, clearing his throat. "Maybe there's something you need to know, and I don't know if I'll get another chance to tell you."

"Herc," she said, trying to laugh. "I know you love me, but it's your face, I could never love somebody with a face like . . ."

"It's about Christoph," he said.

And she clamped her mouth shut. Christoph was dead, Christoph was long buried, Christoph was nothing but a memory.

Herc finally turned to face her. He looked old, like one-foot-in-the-grave old.

"You have to understand, we needed Engineers. We were

losing the war, we were losing too many people." He stalled, his red eyes blinking like he was trying to send her a message in Morse code. "I didn't think you'd say yes unless . . ."

"Unless what, Herc?" she said. Her palms were stinging and she realized her fists were bunched, nails digging into the flesh.

"Unless you thought you didn't have a choice."

Choices: it's what Herc had offered her when he'd walked into her cell that day. She'd been thirteen, she'd killed a man. It had been self-defense, but the cops hadn't exactly gone easy on her. What had the detective told her? Juvie, prison, and a life flushed down the can.

Then Herc's face, smiling at her as he offered her a way out. *Pick door number one.*

"What are you saying?" she said. But she knew, she knew exactly what he was saying. She just had to hear him actually say it.

"You didn't kill him."

He spat the words out like they were rotten fruit, running a hand through his thinning hair.

"You didn't kill him, Pan. You knocked him halfway to Sunday, caved in his head so much he had to have a metal plate fitted. Hasn't ever been right, he's been under medical supervision for four years now. But he didn't die."

The chopper might as well have crashed, because Pan's world was suddenly burning phosphorus-bright; she was blinded by it. She pushed her head between her knees, a low, awful groan spilling out of her.

He wasn't dead.

She hadn't killed him.

And the numbness was suddenly something else, something that rose up inside her, erupting from her mouth. She screamed, pounding at Herc—his chest, his face—scratching at him. The chopper rocked wildly but he didn't fight back, he just sat there and let her hit him until the rage drained out of her, the shock, the fear, the relief—until there was nothing left inside her but that sound—*thunkthud*—the one she'd carried inside her for so long. She fell still, unable to move because Herc had cut the strings that had held her up for so long, that had kept her going.

He wasn't dead.

"I'm sorry, Pan," Herc said. "I had to. You never would have come. You never would have come."

She tried to speak but she couldn't summon the words. Something inside her had fundamentally shifted. Christoph's death had defined her, it had made her a killer, and everything that followed had been drawn from that. It felt as if the child she had been, the one who had picked up that lamp and swung it at Christoph's head, had somehow been erased—and everything she had been since then was disappearing too, eradicated from history. She felt like if she sat here she would gradually fade away, never have been.

"I'm sorry," Herc said again. "I'm sorry. But you were the best we had, Pan. I didn't know it at the time, but I know it now. You were the best we had, and if I had to do it again, if I had to look you in the eye and tell you you were a murderer, I would. You saved the world; everything you did, you held off the darkness."

Until now.

She looked down to see the Devil as it burned after Marlow, whipcracks of dark lightning carving through the skies above it.

"It would have happened a lot sooner without you," he said, reading her mind.

Where would she be if Herc had never shown his ugly face? The cops might have let her go and she'd be sitting in her room right now, maybe, or in a class at school, or just walking down the street, oblivious to everything. There would have been no Engine, no Ostheim, no Marlow, no hell.

There would have been the Devil, though. She'd have looked up from her desk, from her phone, from her ordinary life, and she'd have seen the darkness overhead, the impossible storm that gathered. She'd have been just like the others, running and screaming and lost.

At least here, now, she knew what it was. At least she could fight it.

Herc had given her that.

She sat up in her seat, so woozy that she might have been drunk. Herc flinched as if she might start hitting him again. He had a smudge of blood beneath his nose, and when she looked at her knuckles she saw more of it there.

"I'm sorry," he said again. "I never should have—"

"Priorities," she said, her voice robotic. "We survive this, we can talk about it then."

He nodded sadly, offering her a hand. She stared at it for a moment, thinking back to her cell. He'd offered her the same hand then, so much bigger in her memory, so much stronger.

Choices.

Pick door number one and you join us, you help save the world.

What he'd done to her was wrong, was unforgivable. But it was done. She had to live with it. Christoph might still be alive, but it was his death—his *not*-death—that had driven her into the arms of Ostheim, and how many more had she killed in his name? How many more had she sent to hell?

So nothing had really changed. She was still a killer.

"Let's do it," she said, taking his hand. "What are we waiting for?"

Herc nodded, banked the chopper, and the end of the world rose into view.

The Devil was a spiraling vortex with a core of absolute darkness. Pan couldn't look directly at it but she kept seeing staccato bursts of light at street level, there for a second and then gone. They were almost like gunshots, only Pan knew what they were—men, women, children, exploding into fire and then dust. It trailed a wake of nothing, the land scorched to dust all the way back to Greenville.

The chopper shook, caught in an updraft from the destruction below. An alarm sounded and Herc mashed the heel of his hand against the control panel until it stopped.

"Damn thing," he growled.

A pulse of black light rippled up through a building beneath her, blasting out the windows like demolition charges. Herc yanked the stick, Pan's stomach trying to clamber to safety out of her mouth. The chopper shook, hard, the windshield full of the inferno that churned into the clouds.

The building slumped—not collapsing, just leaning to the side like it was exhausted. Glass and metal rained to the earth in what looked like slow motion, reflecting the sun. Most of its skin had been ripped away, girders sticking out like bare bones.

Pan looked at it, at its skeletal form, at the clouds of ash that danced around its burning base. She looked, and she suddenly understood what she was seeing.

"Hell," she said. "This is where it begins."

The toppled buildings, the wasteland, the mountains of the dead.

None of it made sense, it made her head hurt just trying to think about it. But wasn't that what the watchmaker, or whatever Marlow had called him, wasn't that what he had said—he'd kept the Devil prisoner until the future.

Until *this* future.

And the fear that washed through her was like acid, burning every cell. Because if they didn't do something now—right now—then there would be nothing left here but corpses and cursed souls. It would be hell on Earth, pure and simple.

"Time's up," Pan said, staring through the dust, looking for Marlow. It wasn't hard to find him again, the Devil chasing them like a shadow, all of them heading for what looked like a shopping mall. Even as she watched she saw a pulse of black light burst from the Devil, a shock wave that shunted the semi off the road and into a parking lot. They didn't slow, just churned their way through cars heading right for a store.

"Goddammit," said Herc, craning up in his seat to watch them. "They wouldn't . . ."

They did, the truck slamming into the front of the building, vanishing in a cloak of smoke. The Devil was halfway across the parking lot, and even up here, even over the roar of the rotors, she could hear it speak. Herc pushed the stick and the chopper angled earthward.

"Drop me down there," she said. "I'll . . . I'll think of something."

"Pan," said Herc, swinging the chopper around. "I can tell you absolutely and positively that isn't going to happen."

"Where are you going?" she said, watching as the Devil closed in on the building—she thought it might be a Walmart. "Herc, if Marlow's in there we have to do everything we can to stop it getting to him. Because if there's a chance, even the slightest chance, that we can stop this from happening, then—"

"I know that, Pan," said Herc. "You know, you really do have a habit of stating the bloody obvious."

"Then what?" she asked, the chopper aiming for a low building across the street. "How are we . . ."

The chopper juddered as Herc lowered them, Pan gritting her teeth until they were hovering over the roof. She looked down, and suddenly she knew what he was planning to do.

"Don't you dare," she said. "Don't you even think about it."

"Hey," he said, shrugging. "I'm getting too old for this, kiddo. And I've done too many bad things."

"Herc," she said, taking hold of his hand. "I mean it. There's another way. You don't even know if this will work."

"We don't know it won't," he said. "You're clear."

She glanced out the window to see the roof ten feet below, the chopper weaving dangerously from side to side. She ignored it, turning back to Herc, holding his big bear's paw as tight as she could.

"I won't let you," she said. "We can think of something else."

"Listen to me," he said, squeezing her hands in his. He fixed those watery eyes on her, and he smiled—all scars and broken teeth. "Listen to me, Pan. We've been through a lot together, you and I. Christ, we've been through a lot. But everything we've done has been to stop that thing over there. That's all this is, a job."

"But—"

"It's been an honor working with you, soldier," he said, his jaw trembling. He wiped his eyes. "I'm sorry I did what I did. I'm sorry for it all. But I did it for the right reasons."

"Don't be sorry," she said, brushing away a tear of her own on her shoulder. "It doesn't matter. I wouldn't have done it any differently either. I would still have picked door number one. I'd pick it every single time."

He smiled again. His face was a mess but that smile was the brightest thing in the world. It had welcomed her home from a hundred missions, the first thing she'd seen each time she'd escaped hell. The thought that she might not see it again was like a piece of her own being had been torn away. She gripped his hand, hard enough to hurt her fingers.

"This is my penance, Pan. It's my way of making it all right."

"You've got nothing to make right," she said. "Nothing."

He nodded, the tears rolling freely now.

"I can't land this damned thing anyway," he said. "Doing it this way just saves me the embarrassment."

The laugh escaped her before she could stop it and she lunged at him, wrapping her arms around his shoulders. He yelped, fought to control the chopper, hugging her back with his free hand. She pushed her face into his chest, breathing in that Old Spice smell of him one last time. Then she let go, a sob forcing its way up from somewhere deep inside her.

"I love you, Pan," he said. "Whatever happens next, if this thing survives, kick its goddamned ass back to hell."

"I will," she said. "I promise."

"Go on," he said, turning to the windshield, hunched over the stick like a big kid on a toy. "Go on now."

She popped the door, suddenly gripped by noise, by the howling wind. She shuffled out onto the runners—looking back once, barely able to see him through the tears.

"You're a good man, Herman Cole," she said.

Then she dropped.

The fall was longer than she'd anticipated and she struck hard, a spasm riding its way up her spine as she toppled backward. By the time she'd recovered, the chopper had banked back the way they'd come, the thrum of the blades fading as it disappeared beneath the roof. Pan tore off her headphones and ran after it, through the heat, skidding to the edge and almost losing herself to gravity. She called Herc's name but her voice was a ghost's, lost in the storm.

The helicopter rose, circled clumsily, then dropped fast, its angle too steep, heading right for the cloud of darkness that stepped up to the shopping mall. She held out a hand to Herc, wanting him to pull up, to race back to her, to grin that toothless grin out the chopper window and say "I've got another plan." She just wanted the Devil to curl up and die, to falter and fall like it had done last time.

But it wasn't going to happen.

The helicopter thumped into the Devil, seemed to pause for a second, then erupted into fire. The air around Pan shook, as if the entire world had taken a breath in shock, and she took a breath in shock too because she couldn't believe it. She couldn't believe what she was seeing. A peal of thunder broke out, rolling toward her like a physical thing. It knocked her to her knees, to her elbows, and she did the only thing she could think to do. She put her head on the rooftop, whispered Herc's name, and started to cry.

ONE LAST DEAL

The darkness sluiced into Marlow's head, deeper than the night, worse even than the Black Pool. It filled his skull, his heart, his lungs, it occupied every cell, drowning him from the inside out. But it wasn't a close darkness, it wasn't suffocating. There was something different about this because he knew, somehow, that this was all there was—an endless void of nothing. The thought of it, of that gaping absence, made him open his mouth and loose a silent, deafening howl.

He could feel the poisonous arteries of the Devil's heart burrowing into him, working their way up his arms, searching. But he couldn't fight them, he couldn't move. They wriggled beneath his skin, beneath his muscles, coiling around his bones, as cold as ice and as hot as molten lead. He screamed as the first of them brushed against his spine.

A voice that wasn't really a voice filled his head—a language without words bursting inside him like a lightless firework. There was somebody there, some*thing*, a shadow against the night. Marlow understood that this thing was as old as time, older, even—a creature that had burned its way through reality before there was even a reality to explore, a creature that had *created* reality as it went.

The wordless voice showed him things he couldn't even comprehend—explosions that birthed universes, played out in the blink of an eye he couldn't actually blink, stars forming from the chaos, and planets forming around those stars. And even amid all this light, there was darkness, *its* darkness, that pulsing core of inverse matter that stalked the unthinkable distances between the galaxies.

And it was not alone, this thing. It was not safe—Marlow could sense an emotion that was unlike anything he had ever felt, so powerful he might melt beneath the sheer force of it. It was terror, the terror of a creature who knows that soon it will die.

More churning motion, and Marlow watched as this shape of infinite darkness split itself—not through space but *beyond* it, separating into seven shards of impossible light that scattered through the universes. It was the only way, the voice showed him, the only way to stay safe, and to stay hidden. Seven pieces of the same being, hiding in seven alternate realities.

Seven Strangers, that unvoice said. Because in dividing they lost one another, they lost themselves.

The scene shifted again, bringing Marlow home—to a place he knew so well now, a burning watchmaker weeping for his lost children, and one of the seven Strangers coiling out of the smoke. It had been hiding there for so long, waiting for the right time, for the right person. It had watched, it had learned, it had a language now and Marlow heard that voice again.

IT IS DONE.

And he saw the creature's blood—blood that had boiled in its veins since the very start of everything—bubble and blister its way into the watchmaker. The man's scream was so loud it shattered the vision to pieces but Marlow could still hear his voice, his desperate pleas.

Give them back to me. Bring my children home.

THE LOVE FOR A CHILD IS THE MOST POWERFUL THING IN THE UNIVERSE.

Marlow wasn't sure if the voice came from the memory or from somewhere else. It was a whisper rather than a shout, sliding into his ear like a needle. He tried to turn his head but he had no control, and there was nothing to see, just that infinite void.

Until something began to swim out of it, a scene like a movie in fast-forward. He saw Ostheim, the boy who wasn't really a boy, the boy who was born from the Stranger. Marlow saw him live in the Engine with his true father, with this serpent of smoke and shadow. He saw him feed on blood, saw him grow into something monstrous, something that wore its human face like a mask. And that face changed, losing its hair, its vitality, its youth—but never losing the darkness that swam just beneath the skin.

"I don't understand," Marlow said in a voice made of silence. "I don't know why you're showing me this."

YOU WILL, said the voice.

Time and matter imploded again, Marlow's stomach flipping like he'd been launched from a catapult. He fell into more light, so bright it was like a blowtorch held to his retinas. For a moment he didn't understand where he was, then he saw the stones, arranged in perfect lines, one for each dead body resting beneath the earth, and he understood.

Arlington.

He heard her before he saw her, sobs that echoed off the stones, which rose into the sky like doves. And when he turned his head there was his mom—so much younger, so much healthier. Only her face was the same, warped with an expression of grief that she'd tried to hide in the years since Danny's death, but which she'd never managed to remove. She was holding on to somebody Marlow didn't recognize, somebody in full ceremonial uniform. There were dozens of people there, all clustered around a small, dark hole in the ground. Marlow knew who was inside the coffin that lay there.

His brother.

Danny, he said, reaching out for him with a hand he didn't possess. He scanned the crowds, looking for himself. He didn't remember the funeral, he'd been too young, surely. Or maybe it was because he hadn't been there, because he couldn't see himself. His mom wouldn't have let him go, he realized. It would have been too traumatic. He reached back into the fog of his memory but he couldn't recall her even talking about it. There was nothing there at all.

The scene scrubbed forward, his mom alone now, inside their house—the walls freshly painted, the carpets clean, photographs hanging on every wall. He tried to make out who was in them, seeing his mom, seeing Danny.

But no photographs of Marlow.

He squirmed against the memory, wanting to go to his mom as she opened up a grocery bag, as she pulled out a bottle of Bacardi, sobbing uncontrollably as she unscrewed the cap. And in the moments that followed—a hundred days bunched into one awful, endless swallow—he saw her age, saw her deflate into herself, saw her home crumble into ruin.

And there was still no sign of him.

It didn't make any sense.

The memory shuddered back into real time with the sound of a knock on the door. And even here, bodiless and alone, Marlow felt that pinch of terror at the base of his spine. He wanted to tell her not to open it, just to sit in the dark and wait for the caller to leave. But his mom wobbled to her feet and called out a word that broke Marlow's heart.

"Danny?"

She rushed from the room, down the hall, bouncing off the wall. A silhouette filled the glass panel, something that looked too big to be a man, shadows squirming there like they were trying to find a way in. But they didn't need to, because his mom wrenched open the door, letting them flood forward, drowning the house in darkness.

A man stood there.

A man with an impossible face.

A man who pushed lank strands of hair back over his balding head and flashed his mom a vicious smile.

Sheppel Ostheim.

No, said Marlow, trying to pull the memory inside himself, trying to rip it away from the man at the door. But he was powerless here, and all he could do was watch as Ostheim strode into his mom's house, walking into the living room like he owned the place. And his mom just followed him. She didn't call the cops, she didn't ask him to leave, she just trod in his shadow like a beaten dog, collapsing onto her knees before him.

Leave her alone! Marlow screamed, watching Ostheim run a hand down her face, cup her chin. His fear was like an ocean in a storm, enough to pull him to pieces. But he couldn't fight the paralysis, couldn't help his mom, couldn't even turn away. He could only watch as Ostheim leaned in, brushed his mom's greasy hair from her ear, and whispered.

"I can give you back a son."

No, Marlow said.

"I can make you a mother again."

No.

"It won't be the one you lost, of course, but he will be just as good, and just as kind."

No, please.

"And you will love him as if he were real."

Please, God, no.

"All you have to do is say yes."

Please, Mom, don't.

"All you have to do is say yes, and your house will no longer be empty, it will no longer be sad."

239

Mom!

"All you have to do is say yes."

Say no! Marlow screamed, but it was pointless because all of this had already happened. It was pointless because he already knew what his mom had said. Hadn't he always known it, somewhere in the very deepest part of him? Because there had never been any memories, there had never been any childhood. There had only been that one, awful word.

"Yes."

Ostheim lifted his head and howled his laughter out into the memory, shattering it. When it reformed Marlow saw a bedroom—*his* bedroom—the floorboards bare, wallpaper hanging like peeling skin. One corner was shrouded in darkness, sinkhole-deep, but something was walking out of it—a boy, maybe five or six, his eyes two black marbles. They were doll's eyes, looking like they might just roll out of their sockets.

His mom ran into the room, her sobs the loudest sound in the world. She dropped to her knees before the child and swallowed him up in a hug. The boy didn't react, he just rolled those dead eyes to where Marlow floated and smiled.

Nonononononono, Marlow screamed, fighting the memory, watching *him* as he watched back and feeling the fury like a cold, dense explosion inside him.

THE LOVE FOR A CHILD IS THE MOST POWERFUL THING IN THE UNIVERSE, said the voice, that scalpel-sharp whisper.

There was no escaping the truth, it sat in Marlow's head like a beacon. But the Stranger spoke it anyway.

YOU ARE MY CHILD.

The boy was *him*.

YOU ARE MINE.

And the creature that had begun its life before the universe had been formed, before the stars, before worlds, before time.

The creature whose blood had corrupted countless souls,

whose touch had reduced men to monsters, and children to something even worse.

The creature who was tearing its way through the world, who wanted to turn the living to dust, who wanted to make this place into hell.

It was his father.

PART III

THE DEVIL'S
IN THE HOUSE

LIKE FATHER, LIKE SON

His rage was powerful enough to blow away the last scraps of the memory. It picked him up in a fist of sound and fury and dragged him back to the world.

It was like waking from a nightmare, and he opened his mouth and screamed—a noise that roared from him like fire, which ripped through the shelves of the aisle, which tore loose the steel beams from the ceiling. He was on his knees and he clenched his fists, pounding at the ground, filling the air with dust. There was no pain, there was just anger, cold and infinitely deep.

He was born from a deal with the Devil.

No!

He had been forged with the blood of the Stranger.

No!

He was not real.

No!

He was not real.

He screamed again, searching for anything in his head that might undermine the truth. But there was nothing there, nothing to remember. Because everything he was, everything he had ever been, had begun when he was five years old and he had stepped from that web of shadow.

"Marlow?"

He looked up, the world swimming in shades of black and silver, like he was watching an old-fashioned movie. Somebody was standing in front of him, a rabbit caught in the dark light of his rage. It took him a moment to remember a name—*Charlie*—but he didn't speak it. There was no point. How could he have had friends, real friends, when he was not real?

"Marlow!" Charlie yelled, holding out his hand. "Just hang on, I can help . . ."

But his words were insect-small and Marlow waved them away, seeing the Devil's heart still hanging from his fist. It threw out sickening waves of dark light like a lighthouse, thrumming so loudly that the vibration traveled through every one of his bones. A dozen thick, ropy veins had penetrated his skin and more were shivering up his wrist, stretching like plant fronds. He saw that they were inside his shoulder, they'd bridged the gap to his chest, his neck. He could feel them inside him, probing, reaching, the disgust dwarfed by that same violent tide that roiled inside his skull.

I am not real.

He growled like an injured dog, but there was nothing weak about him now. The Devil's heart was pumping, the arteries bulging with the force of some new circulation. His own veins had turned black, straining against his skin, that poisoned blood hurtling through his system like a drug. He arched his back and screamed again, a wordless cry that flew from him like a weapon.

Charlie dived away, head in his hands. Marlow stood, took a step. The heart swung from his wrist but the stringy tendons that connected it to him were retracting. It was reeling itself closer, resting wetly against his skin, pumping, pumping, pumping.

Somewhere, in some distant part of his mind, he knew he

should tear it loose, knew he should grab a knife and saw at those veins until this rancid piece of the Devil fell to the ground, knew he should stamp on it until it was jelly.

But he didn't.

He felt stronger than he had in years, stronger than ever— stronger even than when he'd burst free from the Engine after his first deal, with the strength of ten men. He felt like he had the strength of a hundred men now, a thousand. He had the strength of the entire human species. And he knew why.

Because I am not real.

Another sound forced its way from him, a guttural, choking laugh.

I am not real.

It should have terrified him, but there was still only anger, his skull full of the dark horror of it—only anger, and a flicker of something else, something he hadn't felt since the last time he made a deal.

Excitement.

The Devil was on the threshold of Walmart, but something had happened to it, pieces of machinery scattered across the blackened ground. The world was burning there, the creature squirming inside the flames. It was hurting. It needed its heart more than ever now. The corrupted organ beat against Marlow's skin and he put a black-veined hand to it. Somewhere he could hear Charlie screaming at him.

"Destroy it! What are you doing?"

Marlow's rage burned too fiercely, too brightly. He couldn't see anything past it.

Except one thing.

He ran through the ruin of the store, punching out of the side wall like it was made of paper. The Devil's heart clung to him, beating out a frantic rhythm, filling him with cold fury. It must have known that its master was close because it was twitching, the veins in his arm tugging at him like a horse's reins.

No, he said again, but his own voice seemed farther away than ever—like he was drowning inside himself, sinking into an ocean of blood. He bunched his fist and struck himself on the head, screaming *get out get out get out*. But the call of it was too loud, too powerful.

I am not real, I am not real. He chanted it, because surely it was easier if he just accepted it, if he accepted that he had never been born, that his mom had never loved him, that he was just the terrible union of loss, grief, and a deal with the Devil.

I am not real.

The heart was pounding so fast its beats were just a blur, Marlow's vision pulsing red and black. He was growling, a noise that sounded as far from human as anything he had ever heard. It was the sound made by a monster.

Because he *was* a monster.

He thought of his mom, the way she'd never looked at him like she'd looked at those photographs of Danny, the way she'd always compared him with Danny, the way she'd said she could never love him like she loved Danny.

His mom had made him a monster.

He loosed another animal howl that rocketed over the city. The darkness behind him was growing deeper, the Devil recovering.

But it wasn't the Devil he wanted answers from.

Snorting like a bull, he turned south. He sniffed the air— smoke and blood and burning flesh—then started running again, away from the darkness. He galloped on all fours, his fists gouging holes in the asphalt as he bounded through the parking lot. He vaulted onto a burning car, leaping onto the roof of a van, leapfrogging his way through the carnage. The world tore past him in a blur, like it, too, was no longer real.

Ahead was a bridge, clogged with traffic, and he carved a path through it. People swarmed like ants, their mouths open as if they were screaming, but all he could hear was the roar of the Devil's blood in his skull, and the endless howl of his own rage.

He ran, and he ran, and he ran, until, at last, he began to slow. Each ragged breath was like a grenade going off, sending plumes of dust out across the street. The houses to either side of him were shut tight but he could sense the people inside, watching him.

He didn't care. It meant nothing to him. He was only interested in one house and he had reached it now. It sat there, slumped and miserable, its blue paint peeling. The curtains were closed the way they had been since Danny's wake.

Since the moment that Marlow had crawled from the shadows.

He stood in front of it, trying once again to remember anything, trying to remember one scrap of truth that would make the Devil's story a lie, finding nothing.

I am not real.

He opened his mouth, fired out a single word that shook the street, that exploded the windows of his house and ripped open the door.

"Mom!"

CHASING DEVILS

Pan burst out of the stairwell into the lobby, stopping for a moment to catch her breath. She was in a home improvement store, people either streaming out the doors or hiding in the aisles. The air was drenched with smoke and screams.

What did you do, Herc?

Thinking about him was too painful—she almost hadn't been able to stop crying, almost hadn't been able to get back up. But she had to see if it had been worth it, if his sacrifice had blown the Devil to pieces.

She burst into the parking lot, half of it erased by the Devil, half by Herc. The fire was moving quickly, devouring the Walmart where Marlow had hidden. There was a mass of shadow in front of it, a pocket of darkness that seemed to fight with the flames. She squinted, seeing a broken figure there, patching itself together again. Then she had to turn away, momentarily blinded.

A scream, nothing human about it. She peered through her fingers, seeing somebody explode from the side of the same building. It moved like a demon, too fast, but when she managed to focus on it she understood it wasn't a demon at all.

It was *Marlow.*

He opened his mouth and screamed again, a shock wave of sound ripping across the street. There was something wrong with his skin but she couldn't work out what. Then he was moving again, dropping onto all fours and galloping down the street. He was moving so fast that by the time she'd called out his name he was gone.

She saw it, though. She saw the thing that had burrowed into the flesh of his arm.

The *heart*.

Behind Marlow, the Devil was pulling itself free of the wreckage, of the flames. It loosed a roar that threatened to shake the city to dust, a column of darkness rising into the sky, flickering tendrils of inverse light winding through it.

The bastard was still alive.

"You *idiot*, Herc," she said, fighting her way through the panicked crowds. Somebody grabbed at her, clutching a handful of her shirt—a man, his eyes on the verge of madness.

"Please, please, what's wrong?" he said, and then he took her in, the copper filaments of her eyes. "What's wrong with *you*?"

She had her mouth open to answer but she never got the chance. A mass of rippling pink muscle thumped past her and slammed into the man, ripping him away in a shower of blood. The demon pinned him to the ground and tore him in half with a single snap of its jaws. It didn't even stop to eat, just looked back at Pan.

"Come on, then," she said.

It charged for her and she threw herself behind a parked car, the vehicle shunting into her as the demon shouldered past it. There were too many people here, all of them screaming, and it rampaged among them. She knew what it felt like, to be torn in two, and the thought of those claws inside her neck, the teeth crunching her skull like it was an ice cube, drove her back onto her feet.

She punched her way through the maelstrom, leaving the shadow of the buildings, the highway coming into view again.

From the look of it Marlow was still heading south, the Devil on his tail. Pan put her hands to her head, another cold, dark vortex spinning inside her. She was powerless here, no weapons, no contract, no backup. Herc was dead, Night was in hell, Truck was a thousand miles away. For all she knew, Charlie had been torn to pieces as well. And Marlow, Marlow was something else, something *bad*.

She had never felt more alone.

More demons were appearing; she could hear the ugly *uhuhuh* of their laughter as they went to work. There was nowhere left to run, and even if she did make it out of the city, what then? She'd have to keep moving as those waves of darkness chased her. The East Coast would fall in hours; how long would it take for the Devil to devour the world?

She swore, looking at the storm again as it moved south. Where the hell were they going?

Think, Pan.

But it was impossible, because even now somebody behind her was pinned beneath two demons. Another appeared, running past her like she didn't exist. More were stampeding that way, as if they'd spotted something over there, spotted prey.

Or as if they'd been called.

Think.

The Devil was moving south. The demons were flocking the same way.

Think!

"Pan!"

The sound of her name was so alien she wasn't sure it was real. She turned, looking through the crowds into the mess of Walmart. Was that *Charlie* there? He was so covered in blood and dirt that he didn't even look human. He clung to the wall, limping, and she saw the tear in his pants, the bone poking out of his leg. Checking the coast was clear, she bolted to him.

"What happened?" she asked.

"The heart," he said, grimacing against the agony. "He got it free."

"Where's he going?"

Charlie shrugged, staring at the shrinking cloud of darkness.

Pan's mind was a mess of noise, of blood, of smoke. It was like she was back in hell, back in that hurricane of confusion. She watched the buildings burn, she breathed in that choking cloud of ash. She might as well still be there, sitting on that damned pyramid as the Devil or the Stranger or whatever the hell it was strode from the ruin of Marlow's house.

A thought flickered right at the back of her head, blown out as another demon bounded past, its muzzle spraying. She tried to ignite it again, her mind soaked through with blood and sweat.

Hell. The Devil's lair. The impossible building that had sat right in the middle of it all.

She looked up, everything still swarming, that cyclone of darkness almost on her. She stared at Charlie and he'd obviously had the exact same thought, because they said it together.

"Staten Island."

Marlow was heading home.

"Come on," she said, but Charlie didn't move.

"Not this time," he said, looking at his mangled leg. "Go get him, Pan. Be careful, yeah?"

Pan took a breath, pushed herself forward. The crowd was moving in every direction now, and she put her head down, charging through them, wishing she still had her electromagnetic charge so she could scatter them like pigeons.

She scanned the lot, searching the cars. Somehow or other, she'd get to Staten Island, she'd get to Marlow.

There was only one thing she was sure of.

She was going to be there when it ended.

CONFESSION

"Mom!"

Marlow howled her name again, and this time his voice was strong enough to rip down the porch, scattering wood. The whole house seemed to shudder in fear, the front door flapping on its hinges like a mouth.

Goawaygoawaygoaway, it seemed to say.

The heart pulsed against his skin, its echo inside every cell as it called to its master. Somewhere behind him, the Devil was coming, driven by the last of Ostheim's blood. But there was time. Marlow wasn't going anywhere until he heard the truth,

Barking, from inside. A shape appeared in the doorway. It was Donovan, the dog worked up into such a frenzy that he was spitting foam. He threw himself from wall to wall, his hackles raised, his eyes boring into Marlow. The sight of him was almost enough to break through the fury, a beam of sunlight in the storm.

Then *she* appeared, staggering up behind the dog, and a supernova of emotion boiled his heart to dust.

His mom stood there, a shadow of herself. Even from here, in the middle of the street, he could see her trembling. Donovan ran from the house, standing at the top of the steps, barking at Marlow like he'd seen the Devil himself. And the dog was right, wasn't he? Marlow might have had him fooled for all these years, but the truth was he was the spawn of something infinitely evil. Who else could stand here with the Devil's heart fused to his body, with the Devil's blood pounding through his arteries?

"Mom!" he yelled again, his voice a weapon that blasted shingles from the roof, that sent Donovan skittering back. The dog barked again, then launched himself down the stairs, teeth sharper than they had ever looked. Marlow held out a hand, those black veins pulsing. "No!" he said, and the force of the word hit Donovan like an invisible boot, kicking him down the street.

The gears of his rage seemed to stick, his head roaring as they ground, strained, then burned into motion again. He ignored the whining dog, started up the stairs. His mom was backing away, screaming at him, but there was nowhere for her to go. She couldn't escape it. She had to have known this day would come sooner or later. You couldn't make a deal with the Devil and not expect to pay the price.

He had to duck to get through the door, his body growing, swelling with the volume of infernal blood that pumped through him. His mom backed into the living room, bouncing off the wall. She couldn't take her eyes off him. She was muttering prayers beneath her breath but it wouldn't do her any good. The only god here now was him.

He followed her through, punching the wall and showering her with bricks and dust. She was too scared to scream this time, tripping on an empty bottle and falling onto the couch. Her mouth opened and closed like a landed fish, like she was trying to call his name. He walked toward her, his head hitting the light and filling the room with sweeping shadows.

It was here that it had happened, he realized, *right* here. Ostheim had sat on this very couch, his mom had fallen prostrate before him, and together they had conjured him into being. His anger, his hate for them both, didn't even need a voice anymore. It radiated from him, shaking the walls so much that plaster dust rained down from the ceiling, gathering in his mouth like ash. The heart thumped its demented rhythm, the loudest sound in the world.

"Why?" he said, his voice filling the room like a thunderclap. His mom clamped her hands to her ears, still mumbling those prayers. Marlow leaned over her, resisting every urge to just pick her up and throw her into the wall.

Wait, part of him said, but it was a part buried so deep that it was nothing more than a whisper, quickly forgotten.

"Why?"

She sobbed, holding a cushion to her face like she meant to suffocate. He bent down and pulled it away, the fabric tearing, spitting feathers. His mom moaned, scrubbing at her eyes with her fists. She said something but it was lost behind the jet engine roar of Marlow's emotions.

"Why?"

"Danny!" she screamed at him, and the last trace of doubt burst from his head. Here was the truth, right here, written in her tears, in the lines that etched her face, in the defiance as she stared up at him. "Danny, I need you. Please! Please!"

Marlow shook his head, grabbing his face like he could just tear it off to reveal something else behind it. An inferno was raging inside him, the pressure of it too much. It was going to detonate, and he felt like he might take the entire world with him. And what did it matter if he did?

I am not real.

Because he'd never truly been a part of it anyway.

"I loved him so much," said his mom, curling her legs up beneath her, her eyes big and wet and frightened—a child's eyes. "I don't understand . . ." She groaned again, as if the truth were being physically ripped out of her. "I don't understand what you are. It was never supposed to be this way, It would never have been this way if Danny had still been alive. Please, Ma—"

She stopped, like she couldn't speak his name. She had to be lying—or maybe she didn't remember. Maybe the years of drink had just washed the shame and the horror away. But there was no denying it, was there? His mom might not have forged a contract with the Engine, but she'd traded with the Devil, it had used its tainted blood to build Marlow from darkness.

"I thought I could love you," said his mom. "I thought it would make it better, I thought I could love you like you were . . . you were my son. And I did love you." Again, his name got caught in her throat like a chunk of rancid meat. "I did love you. I did love you."

She glanced up at him and her face seemed to slide off the bone.

"But I couldn't love you as much as I loved him. I couldn't forget where you'd come from, and what . . ."

She burrowed her head into her legs, sobbing, but he could still make out her muffled words.

"Or what you would become."

The pressure inside his head was so great that it was whistling, a shrill sound that might have been his skull about to shatter. The scream rose like vomit and he turned, opening his mouth and loosing it toward the window. It ripped out of him, a fist of sound that tore away the entire front wall, blasting wreckage into a street that had turned twilight dark. The house moaned, the ceiling cracking above his head. He didn't care. Let it bury him, let it be done with them both.

"I always knew it," she said. "I always knew I'd lose you, too, but not like this, not like this. I loved you, I loved you almost as much, I swear it. But I knew . . ."

"What?" he asked.

"I always knew you'd raise hell."

Marlow reeled, reaching for the wall to steady himself. His hand punched into the bricks and he squeezed them into shrapnel, ripping them away and blasting them out into the street like bullets. It couldn't be real. Ostheim had known everything, he'd planned everything—everything Marlow ever was had been orchestrated for one simple purpose.

To open the gates of hell.

To let the Devil step out into the world.

He saw the way he'd been kicked out of school, the way that Pan and Herc just happened to be battling demons across the neighborhood. What were the chances of that? Ostheim had sent them there for one reason, to draw him in. He remembered the way he'd stumbled into that parking lot, gun in hand. Why would anyone sane, anyone real, step out of the daylight and walk toward chaos? It had been inside him all this time, the part of him that somehow knew he'd be raising hell. And everything that had happened since—telling Charlie he couldn't join them, setting him up to meet Mammon and infiltrate the Engine. Then working out where Mammon was and leading Ostheim right to him, paving the way for him to unite the Engines and open the gates. Finding Meridiana, sentencing her to death, and getting a contract that would expire in minutes. Hell, too. He'd always been destined to go there, to meet his maker first-hand, to broker one final deal that would open the gates and allow the Devil to come home.

Every single thing he'd done had been programmed into him.

He was a puppet, a shadow thing, soulless and corrupt.

The Devil's heart thumped, still swelling, as big as a football now. The veins that stretched from it, that had burrowed into his skin, were as thick as fingers and as hard as steel, still pumping him full of blood.

And there was a good reason for its excitement.

Outside, the world was gripped by night, as if the sun had been shot from the sky. The room was juddering, and across the street the houses were caught up in a frenzy of dark light, tearing themselves to pieces. The air pulsed with a voice, with *its* voice. Marlow stumbled toward the ruined wall, out into the fury of sound and violence.

The Devil was walking up the street.

It was almost impossible to look at it: the world seemed to blister as it approached, pockets of reality burning away. But its blood still blazed through Marlow, through every cell, and he peered inside that bubble of black light with his new eyes. That too-tall figure was there, its face opening and closing like origami, its eyes like black holes, pulling Marlow in. It unfurled those insect arms as if it meant to embrace him, and as it did so he understood the final piece of the puzzle, he understood the last thing that the Devil needed him to do.

THE LOVE FOR A CHILD IS THE MOST POWERFUL THING IN THE UNIVERSE.

The Devil's voice wrapped itself around Marlow. It threatened to shake his bones to dust, but there was no pain—the heart saw to that. Marlow smiled as the Devil stepped closer. The world hadn't made him. The world had never wanted him. But this thing, this *god*, had given him life, and given him meaning. And all it asked for in return was his love.

YOU ARE MY CHILD.

"I am your child," he said, the shock wave from their voices cracking together, opening up a crater in the earth, splitting the clouds. The sheer power of it made Marlow's smile stretch even farther. He thought of his mom, of his principal, of Patrick and Ostheim and everyone else in his life who had told him he was weak, told him he was not worthy of love.

But wait till they saw him now. He would be a king here.

YOU WILL BE A GOD.

The Devil floated forward, cradled inside its storm. The closer it got, the more Marlow could see of it—those mechanisms still turning inside its skin, the empty space in its chest that screamed for a heart. It looked different from the last time he had seen it, its skin ragged, oozing dark blood, its movements hesitant. Despite its fury it was weak, and Marlow knew that without him it would die. *Then let it die*, he screamed from inside the well of himself. But even as he spoke the words he was walking, then stumble-running into the hurricane.

ALL YOU HAVE TO DO IS SAY YES, the Stranger said.

All it wanted was his love, and that was all he had to give.

Smiling at the thought, Marlow reached out, opened his arms.

And said yes.

THE END OF EVERYTHING

The Devil's arms uncurled, the cracking of its joints even louder than the howl of the storm. It held them out, threatening to swallow Marlow whole. There was a moment when he almost heard his own voice, his *old* voice, as weak and pathetic as a kitten's mewl—*nonono what are you doing?*—then it was gone again, drowned out by the thunder of the Devil's heart, by the roar of its blood.

He took a step toward it, close enough to touch. Its whole body was made up of parts, a mix of organic and inorganic that moved as one. It was an engine of flesh and machine, one that stank of blood and oil and something ancient, something awful. He watched as pieces of it peeled loose, more of those black veins sliding from its greasy torso, angling at Marlow, feeling for him. The heart that beat against his flesh reached out tendrils of its own, black threads that mingled with those from the Devil.

GIVE IT TO ME.

Again, a splinter of doubt. He looked at his house, trying to find his mom, and the thought of her rocked him back, rekindling the anger. It was her fault he was here. She was the reason he was what he was.

Right?

THE HEART BELONGS TO ME.

Marlow turned back, the Devil towering over him, growing taller. Its arteries fused with those in the heart, blood pumped from the Devil straight into Marlow. Time and space seemed to shudder into fragments, the very stuff of the world—cells, molecules, and the quantum universes inside each individual atom—coming apart, unwinding.

THIS STORY WAS WRITTEN SO LONG AGO, the Devil said, its voice not outside but inside Marlow's head, a flashbang going off in his skull. BEFORE THE VERY FIRST FLICKER OF MATTER, THE FIRST GRINDING INSTANCE OF TIME, IT WAS WRITTEN, JUST AS ALL THINGS ARE WRITTEN.

It reeled Marlow in like it meant to absorb him, pulling him against the shifting mirage of its body. A thousand tongues of skin fluttered out, taking hold of him. Its touch was like cement, as if he were being buried alive. More of them fed into the heart and he felt the gentlest of tugs as the Devil tried to pull it loose. Marlow didn't fight it because this was who he was. This was *why* he was.

I am not real.

YOU ARE REAL TO ME, it said. YOU ONLY HAVE TO GIVE ME THE HEART, AND LOOK AT WHAT WE CAN DO.

Something slid up the base of his neck, inside the column of his spine, and the street blasted away into dust. He saw New York, a dead city, its people corrupted into ash, the buildings gutted. The rot and ruin spread outward, crossing the country in a wave of carnage. Demons teemed like ants, painting the streets with rent flesh. And through it all walked the Stranger— the Stranger *and* Marlow, held together by an unthinkable bond, a terrifying union of blood and old magic.

I DO NOT BELONG HERE, the Stranger told him, embracing him, pulling him closer. He felt his skin start to bubble and blister. I WAS TRAPPED HERE. BUT THIS UNIVERSE CANNOT HOLD ME FOREVER.

The vision showed a world crumbling into dust, the trees erupting, the crops withering, the people screaming even as their bodies disintegrated. Marlow watched animals throw themselves into the inferno just to avoid the creature who walked among them, and the final few people, the last of his species—*no, not my species, never my species, I am not one of them*—fight tooth and nail, and then fade, blown into spirals of ash that settled into calm. He watched, and he couldn't help but smile, because the stillness that fell over the world was beautiful.

IT IS WHY I MADE YOU, it said. A UNION OF HOLY AND UNHOLY. THE WATCHMAKER WAS CLEVER, BUT EVERY DEAL CAN BE UNWOUND, EVERY CAGE CAN BE UNLOCKED. THIS WOULD NOT WORK IF YOU WERE HUMAN, IT WOULD NOT WORK IF YOU WERE A DEVIL. YOU HAD TO HAVE COME FROM ME, AND BECOME LIKE THEM. YOU ARE THE LINK BETWEEN OUR WORLDS, AND THE END OF YOUR WORLD IS THE BEGINNING OF MINE.

But how? Marlow asked, the words plucked from his head. *Why?*

WHEN MY KIND SPLIT, WHEN WE BECAME STRANGERS, WE LOST OUR STRENGTH, WE LOST ONE ANOTHER. WE LOST OUR ABILITY TO TRAVEL THROUGH THE UNIVERSES. THE WATCHMAKER WAS SUPPOSED TO HELP ME, BUT HE DECEIVED ME. THE ENGINE THAT HE BUILT TO KEEP ME ALIVE, TO MAKE ME STRONG AGAIN, BECAME A PRISON—NOT JUST FOR ME, BUT FOR ALL OF US.

Marlow saw it like he had seen it before, that entity which had roamed the universe even as it was forming, which split itself into seven shards of darkness to keep itself safe. The Engine hadn't just contained this Stranger, he realized, it had threaded a linchpin through all of them.

WE YEARN FOR ONE ANOTHER. WE NEED ONE ANOTHER. WE WILL CARVE A HOLE IN EVERY UNIVERSE UNTIL WE FIND OURSELVES AGAIN.

The Stranger showed him: the world burned but it was just

the beginning—the more the Stranger destroyed, the stronger it became. It would swallow planets, he saw. It would devour stars. It would become something infinitely more powerful than a black hole—a creature inside a storm that would rip a wound in the very fabric of time and space.

And eventually, when it had carved a hole deep enough, those universes would have nothing left to hold them. They would collapse down on one another like a house of cards.

AND WE WILL BE ONE. JUST LET GO OF THE HEART, CHILD, RELINQUISH IT TO ME.

It was almost too much to take in, almost enough to drive Marlow to madness, but again the Devil's blood kept him sane, kept him safe. He was not mortal, he was not one of the insects that crawled around him. He was part of something immense, something that had played out long before the first star had sparked itself into being, something that would continue even after the last of them had sputtered into darkness.

He held out his hand to the Devil, offering it the heart. As he did so he laughed, and something echoed it, a noise that might have come from the Devil but that was too familiar, too much a part of his old world. Marlow ignored it, until it came again, as small as a needle but one that pierced through the thumping haze of the Devil's blood. He peeled his face away from the mechanisms of the creature's chest, saw the street, saw the houses, saw the raging skies.

And there was Donovan, the dog back on his feet, one front leg hanging like a broken branch. He was the only living thing in sight, standing fierce against the storm. He barked, but the aggression had gone. His eyes were big and round and wet and they fixed on Marlow with a look of such pain, such longing, that for a moment the darkness boiled away, the unbearable song of the Devil fading almost into silence.

It was as if the skies had parted, something golden beaming

right into the center of Marlow's mind. Before he could under-stand it, though, the Devil had pulled him close again, tugging at the heart, ripping it from his skin. The blood roared back into him, so loud.

It was just more proof. The dog hated him because he knew Marlow wasn't human, because he knew Marlow was some-thing rotten, something dragged from the foulest part of hell. Pan had said the same thing, that animals could sense evil. It was only telling him what he already knew, that he wasn't real.

But it wasn't always like that.

And there it was again, a guttering break of light right on the edge of his thoughts. He saw himself, much younger, roll-ing over the living room floor with the puppy his mom had just given him. It had licked him, bitten him with those dagger-sharp teeth, but only in play. He'd spent every single day with that dog and it had loved him.

He growled into the Devil, wrenched his head free. Some-thing was jamming the mechanisms of his brain, his thoughts screaming as they fought to free themselves. Donovan just stood there, pacing back and forth as best he could with his bad leg, not barking now but whining.

GIVE IT TO ME.

The dog had trusted him.

The dog *still* trusted him.

No, he thought, and he spat the word up, howling it at the devil. "No!"

It carried a force of its own, the tainted blood giving the word power. It tore from his mouth and slammed into the Dev-il's torso, the filaments of its skin rippling with the force of it. The creature pulled back, startled, and Marlow loosed a scream.

"It's a lie!"

The Devil had recovered, was reeling him in, the blood ham-mering through the web of arteries that joined them.

IT IS A SMALL GIFT, BUT ONE YOU MUST GIVE. YOU ARE MY CHILD, YOU HAVE ALWAYS BEEN MINE. LET US END THIS WORLD TOGETHER, LET US PIERCE THE SKIN OF THIS UNIVERSE AND FIND OUR WAY HOME. JUST GIVE IT TO ME.

He could feel the Devil's rancid joy, it overwhelmed him, overpowered him. The world was nothing, he knew, just a rock that harbored a meaningless swarm of accidental life, a speck in the unspeakable vastness of the universes. What lay beyond this place was so much more, it was infinite, and beautiful, and silent. The idea of it vibrated through Marlow's mind, through his soul; he felt as if he would melt beneath its glory.

IT IS OURS.

It would be. Marlow would see the impossible truth, he would be a child of eternity, a deity who roamed the space behind space.

But Donovan was still whining, the sound of it an anchor in rough seas, enough to keep him steady, but at the same time enough to tear his mind apart. He cried out again, the power of his voice cracking the street, crumpling a house into rubble. The Devil was working at the heart, peeling it free.

SEE HOW EASY IT IS.

A handful of veins still joined the heart to Marlow and the blood coursed into him like fuel thrown on a fire. He wondered if his mom were still alive in there, or if she'd been blown to dust as well.

And the awful truth was that he didn't care.

One way or another, she'd die today.

Everyone would die.

No!

He reached inside himself, to the boy he'd once been, and prepared to snuff him out like a candle.

IT IS THE BEGINNING OF SOMETHING WONDERFUL, the Stranger said—*Marlow* said. Their voice was the same now. JUST LET GO.

He turned to the city before him, the one that he had once called home, the one where he had spent his entire life, ready to scream it all away.

But Donovan was still there.

The candle flickered, burned again. That was his dog. That was his Donovan. And whatever Marlow was now, he hadn't always been this way.

It's a lie, he said. *It's a lie.*

AND WHAT DOES IT MATTER IF IT IS?

"It matters," he said, clenching his hand again, feeling the energy inside it, inside *him*. The Devil's heart beat, and beat, and beat, a neutron star of darkness, powerful enough to carve a hole in the universe.

Only it wasn't the Devil's heart anymore.

"It matters," he said.

And once again, he opened his fist.

WAR OF THE WORLDS

It was like he'd been holding a pulled bow, an arrow of black light pulsing from his hand and hitting the Devil. A cave opened up in the myriad parts of its face and it grunted in shock, staggering back. The storm gyred around them, like they were in the eye of a cyclone. The street was disintegrating, pieces of wood, of stone, of asphalt, of people rising into the tar-black sky.

Marlow held out his other hand, his whole arm trembling with the power inside it. The Devil's heart hung there like a tumor, but it was still beating hard, filling him with darkness and with strength.

It doesn't care, Marlow understood. *It doesn't care who uses it.*

It was *Marlow's* heart now.

He opened his fingers and the air fractured, a bolt of inverse lightning slamming into the Devil. The thunder was deafening, kicking up a shock wave of dust, and Marlow pushed through it. His face ached, and it was because he was grinning. The thrill of it was like nothing he had ever experienced. He knew he could jump up right now and burn his way into space. He knew he could punch a hole in the street and crack the world in two.

The heart thumped, and thumped, and thumped, like it was chanting his name. *Mar-low. Mar-low. Mar-low.*

THIS STORY HAS BEEN WRITTEN FOR TOO LONG, the Devil roared, finding its feet again. IT CANNOT BE CHANGED.

Marlow grabbed hold of the web of veins that still joined them, tearing. They came free from the Devil's chest with a series of wet pops and it howled, clutching at its flapping skin.

IT IS MINE, it said, reaching out with those too-long arms. YOU ARE NOTHING WITHOUT IT. NOTHING.

Nothing without it.

But with it he was a god.

This time he didn't open his hand, he clenched it into a fist, striking the Devil in the machinery of its face. It was an unstoppable force hitting an immovable object, the concussive force of it juddering out through the air, scattering pieces of asphalt. A jarring pain rode up Marlow's arm even past the cry of the blood. The Devil moved in, its fingers wrapping themselves around his throat, tightening like a noose. Marlow's stomach lurched as he was plucked from the ground, the Devil staring up at him with the rot holes in its face.

It punched him into the ruined street, *through* it, burying him grave-deep. Then he was in the air, long enough for a single breath before the Devil slammed him down again, and again, each time the darkness settling a little deeper into his thoughts.

YOU ARE NOTHING, the Devil said.

A sudden agony tore through his body, radiating from his arm—a pain the likes of which he didn't think was possible. He stared through the haze, through the mask of black blood, seeing the Devil harvesting the heart from his arm. It came free reluctantly, trailing wormlike veins that twisted and thrashed.

NOTHING.

"No!" Marlow yelled, grabbing hold of it. It rocked between them, pulsing dark light. He was powerful, but the Devil still had Ostheim's blood inside it, it was still too strong. It was pulling the heart toward the cavity in its chest, its flesh peeling open to make room for it.

Marlow lunged forward and the Devil lost its balance, falling. The heart bounced off its chest, and in the confusion Marlow managed to gain purchase. He plunged his other hand into the hole in the Devil's ribs, into the impossible coldness there. There was nothing but darkness to grab on to but he pulled at it, ripping out chunks of oily matter. The Devil arched its back, uttered a noise that might have been a scream, but whose frequency Marlow couldn't detect.

He ripped, and he pulled, and he punched, pounding the Stranger's face over and over until its ancient skull crumbled and the mess of its brains slopped out.

Only then did he rock back and howl into the sky. The heart swung beneath him, still connected. It was already reeling itself back into place, those filaments reattaching themselves to his skin. For a second, he thought about pulling them free, but he knew that if he did that his injuries would be too great. He would die right here, on what was left of his street.

And even after everything he'd been through, everything he'd seen, the idea of slipping into that darkness forever was too much.

The Stranger twitched beneath him, the subtlest of tremors. Its body was flattened like roadkill. It couldn't be moving, it had to be dead. And yet it twitched again, a bolt of dark lightning searing up into the storm, the clap of thunder knocking Marlow away. There was another sound, too, a deep, booming pulse that could only be one thing.

Laughter.

The Stranger's corpse sat up, crushed so thin it was like a drawing etched on paper. Its top half peeled away from the earth, swaying there, the ruin of its face slowly turning to Marlow.

YOU CANNOT KILL ME, it said. WE WERE NOT MADE TO DIE THIS WAY.

It rose like a puppet, more of that lightless lightning crackling up into the sky. Its face folded and refolded, shaping itself. It took a step toward him, unfurling its arm, stretching it until the fossil of its hand sat right before him.

NO MORE GAMES. IT IS TIME.

Marlow shook his head, forcing himself back to his feet. The Devil's heart beat.

YOU CANNOT DENY WHAT YOU ARE.

Marlow knew. He could feel the heart thump against him, and he knew that it was his now.

What did that make him, if not the Devil?

And suddenly, he knew what he had to do.

He lunged forward, sinking his teeth into the shifting skin of the Devil's face. It came away surprisingly easily, tasting like he'd just chowed down on a month-old corpse. He spat, gagging, then he did it again, aiming for its throat.

The Stranger pulled back, blood spraying from its neck. Marlow didn't give it a chance to recover, his head snapping forward like a viper's, his teeth sinking into its throat again. Blood flowed into his mouth and he swallowed, drinking it down, black light pouring from the wounds, fizzing up into the storm.

Marlow drank deep, devouring the Devil like it had devoured Ostheim. The horror of it was so immense that he lost himself to it. There was just his hunger, and the flesh beneath him, and he grunted and growled and snarled his way through it until what lay there was just a garbage bag of spilled flesh, motionless and forgotten.

He stood, and it was as if he pulled the world after him, as if it would change the direction of its orbit if he only willed it.

Nothing was the same. Even though the sky was dark with cloud he could see the stars there, billions of them. He could see the sun, could see past the blinding glare of it into the atomic machinery that kept it burning. He looked down, through the empty mess of the Devil, saw the rock, and the history of that rock, the billions of years that had brought it here. And beneath it the molten flesh of the world, and the iron heart of the planet that whispered a strange, beautiful song.

The world was nothing. Time was nothing. He could wait here for a thousand years and it would be a blink of his eye. Or he could stop it altogether and live a hundred lifetimes in the stillness he left behind. It was all his to love.

It was his to destroy, too, if he wished.

The thought of it released a charge of energy, one that burned its way through a house down the street, shaking it to atoms. Marlow laughed, and even this was a weapon, carving a trench through the exposed foundations, turning the earth into a memory of dust.

Somebody up the street made a break for it, an old woman running from her front door. He didn't do anything, didn't move, he just thought it and she burst into flame. There wasn't even time for her to collapse to the asphalt before she exploded, a concussive thump casting her ash up above the rooftops.

The horror, the joy, pulsed out of him as an animal roar, a sonic explosion that plowed through the street, which tore away asphalt and stone and earth and pipes, turning it into a tsunami. The ground cracked like an earthquake had struck, one side slumping so much that the houses there collapsed into themselves.

And over it all, the heart beat and beat and beat.

It would beat in him forever.

Marlow lifted his arm, brought the heart toward his chest. More of those eel-like veins slid from it, burrowing into his skin, curling themselves around his ribs. He felt them brush against his own, human heart—*no, it was never human, I was never human*—rooting there.

The storm hung over him like a crown, a cloak of dust and wind and ash flowing after him as he began to walk. A distant part of him screamed that this was his street, that somewhere here was his mom, his dog. Then he remembered that they were probably dead, that he had probably killed them both, and suddenly all there was inside him was that age-old call—the heart needed him to punch a hole in this universe so that it could slide into the next, so that it could be reunited with the other impossible shards of itself.

And he would.

He smiled as best as he could remember, felt the fabric of his face start to shift and turn.

Then he began.

THE FURY

Pan wrenched the wheel, the truck thumping up a section of broken asphalt before slamming down again. The suspension groaned, the cab rocking, but it was an old Ford, practically indestructible, and it was holding itself together.

So far.

She didn't know how much longer it would last, because up ahead the world was ending.

Literally.

The sky was black, as if somebody had peeled it away to reveal the ceiling of a cave—as if everything she had ever been told about the universe was a lie. People were fleeing, painted white with ash that had once been their friends, their neighbors, their families. There was so much blood in the air that she had the wipers on, smearing it across the windshield.

She steered to the side to avoid a man, then ripped the wheel the other way as a demon came bounding out of the smoke. It thumped off the fender, too consumed with bloodlust to even notice her. A bus lay on its side across the broken street and she cut right, accelerating up a hill before screeching left, the apocalypse that gripped Staten Island swinging into view again. Up here she had a better idea of where she was going, that impossibly dense cloud of darkness boiling in the sky maybe three blocks away.

Three blocks, not so far, and the thought had only just entered her head when a peal of thunder detonated beneath the storm. The world seemed to lift, tearing toward her like a tsunami. She screamed, twisting the wheel too hard, the truck bouncing, tilting, then collapsing onto its side. Then the maelstrom was on her, a hurricane of noise and debris that shunted the truck back down the street, rolling it onto its roof, then its side, then its wheels, over and over and over. She gripped the seat but it wasn't enough, the truck spinning her like she was inside a washing machine, thumping against her hips, her head, her arm.

Her skull was an inferno of white fire, and for a moment she was lost to it. Then the world began to settle around her, piece by piece. She heard somebody shouting her name, realized that it was her, like she was calling herself back from the brink, screaming for herself to move.

But she was still alive.

She shuffled around, kicked at the passenger side window. It took a few attempts before it shattered and she crawled through, legs first, her bones made of burning coals. It seemed to take a hundred years before she could stand again, and even then she wasn't sure how long she'd be able to stay that way. Everything was catching up with her—the years she'd spent fighting, injury after injury after injury, the broken bones, her shattered heart, not to mention her time in hell. Her body was a clockwork toy, winding down, the key lost.

But she was *still alive.*

She put one foot in front of her, trying to remember if this was how you walked. It seemed to work and she tried the other one, staggering over the rubble. The people who had once lived here, worked here, watched her with glass eyes.

I'm sorry, she tried to tell them. *I'm sorry I couldn't stop it.*

And she wouldn't stop it. She knew that now. Ahead of her, the storm pulsed into the sky like a torch of black light. In the clear patches between the clouds, through the ash, she could see stars there, in the middle of the day, crowding around like spectators. The world was ending. This thing was going to finish it.

But *she was still alive*.

She walked, seeing a demon up ahead. It was injured, sniffing the air through half a face. She almost fell on it as she walked by, a hand on its fleshy ribs to stop herself from toppling. It snapped at her but it was too weak. She wondered if this demon had once been an Engineer like her, trapped in hell for an eternity, forgetting herself a little more every single day as she lapped at the Devil's blood.

I'm sorry, she said, transmitting the thought down through her fingers even as the bellows of its lungs shuddered to a halt. She pushed up, a sob falling from her. Another demon was hurtling this way, distracted by something, vanishing into the smoke with a shriek of glee.

She walked. One block passed, then another, the scene of ruin growing worse with every step she took. It was only when she'd crested the hill, though, that she understood the true extent of the devastation.

The world ahead was a crater, as if a meteor had struck. Buildings were nothing but matchsticks, the people nothing but dust. The slope of the ground led up into that churning madness of smoke and shadow, its movements leaving black scars on her vision.

In the middle of the storm was a man—no, a devil. She could see its nightmare form, its body strung with fat black veins. It seemed different, somehow, infinitely more powerful. And that could mean only one thing: it had its heart back.

No, she realized. It meant two things.

Marlow was dead.

She scanned the wasteland of Staten Island but there was no sign of life, no sign of anything other than the Devil as it strode over its kingdom of rubble and dust. Pan called Marlow's name but only inside her head. She had no words to give, not now, not here, with the world ending before her. Marlow was dead. Herc was dead. Night was dead.

And in minutes, she would be dead too.

But she'd go out swinging. She didn't know how to do it any other way.

She took another step, stumbling in the dust, in the rubble. The Devil was lost in its own art, releasing a rippling vortex of unlight that shook the street, launching a cloud of detritus. Some of it was sucked into the sky, but the rest hailed down around her. She waited for the end, for her head to be staved in by a brick, but she kept walking. Something clanged off the ground a few feet away and she picked it up as she passed—a length of metal pipe, almost too heavy for her to carry. She rested it on her shoulder like it was a bat, focusing on the Devil's head, digging inside the empty husk of her body for the strength to reach it.

The Devil's head. It seemed to shift, just like it had back in hell, but there was something new there, something familiar. It was only when it turned its face toward her, though, that she understood what she was looking at.

And this time, she had the strength to call his name.

"Marlow?"

It couldn't be him, and yet it was. It was his face, one that clicked and spun like a Rubik's Cube, but which always juddered back to its original form. His eyes were black holes, and that infernal heart clung to his chest, its beat audible even over the chaos of the storm, over the patter of falling rocks. Pan was too far away to read his expression but she could see the emotion there, the story of it etched in lines.

"Marlow," she said again, her voice just a whisper against the storm. It hurt to speak, hurt to breathe, and she wondered if she'd broken a rib. He was fifty yards away now, closing fast.

She called his name again, took another step. It was one too many and she dropped to her knees. The pipe clattered away. It was like she had a demon sitting on her neck, her head too heavy for her to lift. But she grunted, stretching up, watching as that impossible figure crossed the distance between them, pulling the storm overhead like it was covering her with a shroud, like it was about to bury her.

Let it, she thought. Herc had been right, this was their penance. They had done bad things, terrible things. And even though she'd always tried to justify it, she'd always told herself she was doing them for the right reasons, she'd always known. Deep down she'd always known.

Take a life and save a billion, Herc had always said.

But she'd taken a billion lives to save her own. This had only ever been about her. Everything she'd done had been to make up for a crime she hadn't even committed. It had all been for nothing.

"Marlow," she said again, but the storm was too loud. It was like looking up as a cold, dark wave surged toward her. She was dwarfed by the fury of it, by the power there. It would roll right over her and she would never even feel it. She'd just be another ghost of ash, dancing into the night.

"Marlow," she said, louder, as loud as her body would let her. Marlow walked on, his face a Halloween mask that looked ready to fall right off. It twisted from joy to grief so fluidly that she couldn't tell the expressions apart. His eyes blazed with nightmare light, and the sight of it, the sight of those Devil's eyes burning in his face, made her sob out his name, a scream that cut through the storm, that finally caught him.

He stopped, twenty yards from her, the winds that circled

him kicking up huge clouds of dust and ash and smoke. He thrummed like a generator, the force of it making her bones tremble. The ground beneath him was flowering into mold, erupting into spores. The mechanisms of his face opened and closed like a puzzle and he cocked his head, studying her with those empty eyes. She understood she'd already lost him. Whatever the Stranger had done to him, he was gone.

"Marlow," she said again, only this time it was a sob.

It didn't matter what happened next. It only mattered that she wasn't alone. She was in too much pain, death already creeping inside her skull, nesting there.

Marlow took a step toward her. The darkness in his eyes was like nothing she had ever seen before. But he was blinking like he was trying to make her out, like he was trying to make sense of what he was seeing.

"Hey," she said, coughing blood but trying to smile. "And I thought *I* was having a crappy day."

The heart thumped against his chest, blood spilling from his sliced skin, from his broken ribs. The veins that connected it to him rocked like water hoses as it filled him with poison. But still Marlow fought against it, his face falling into a frown. His mouth opened and he shaped a word, one that might have been her name. She reached up to him, so close, and he flinched, as if she were the one who burned with darkness. He took another step in her direction and she could feel the kinetic force that radiated from him, like she was about to erupt into flame. He opened his mouth, and when he spoke it was with the Devil's voice.

I AM NOT REAL.

He shaped her name with his mouth, dropping to his knees in front of her. The sound of it, of the storm, of the ending world, the relentless beat of the heart, was enough to pulverize her. But she was still alive, she was still here, and when Marlow stretched his bloated hand toward her she reached out, she grabbed it.

She saw it in an instant, she saw all of it, his memories played out in a single moment of time—his brother's death, his mom's collapse, Ostheim sitting on that sofa offering an unthinkable bargain. And she felt it, too, felt the crushing weight of his misery.

I AM NOT REAL.

The words echoed around her own head like she was standing inside a cathedral bell. But she saw it as he had seen it, a story told by the Devil. And what had she always been told, that the Devil was the master of lies?

I AM NOT REAL.

She saw him step from that web of darkness, a boy shaped in shadow, whose eyes blazed inkwell black.

I AM NOT REAL.

And she saw him grow, day by day. She saw his mom tucking him in at night, reading to him, she saw her brush his teeth, she saw her teaching him how to swim, how to ride his bike, how to bake, how to read and smile and laugh. She saw them together at school, saw her clapping when he stood and sang his first national anthem on stage, saw them sitting at Chuck E. Cheese sharing pizza and fries, saw her wrapping bandages around scrapes and cuts, saw him crying on her shoulder, saw her crying on his, saw her come home one day with a box, one puppy paw sticking out like it was waving, saw her holding him and kissing him and singing to him and loving him, *loving* him.

And she watched the young Marlow change. She watched him grow. She watched the darkness leak out of him day by day by day. And yes, his mom had grown more distant, she had sunk inside the bottle again. But she had done enough. She had made Marlow twice: once with a deal, but again, with love. She had made him real.

"Don't listen to it," she said, more blood than words. "Don't listen to it."

He pulled his hand free like she had scalded him, lifted his head to the roiling sky and screamed.

"It's not real," she shouted, pulling his hand to her, holding it tight even though it buzzed like a live wire. "What it's showing you. It's a lie, Marlow." She didn't know it, of course, it might have been the truth, Marlow might have been forged from smoke and shadow. But it didn't matter. "Love can do that," she said. "Love can make you real."

She thought back, saw him the first day she'd met him— lying on the floor of a parking lot. He'd saved her life then, there was no doubt about it. And how many times had he saved it since? Not just from the demons, from the Devil, from the wormbags and ghosts and Patrick. How many times had he saved her from herself?

"Love can do that."

Marlow howled again, one hand on his head as if he were trying to tear it from his shoulders. The heart swelled, as big as a watermelon, its organic and mechanical parts thrashing. His face moved like there was something beneath the skin, but Pan could only see that goofy grin, the way he'd always smiled at her, the way he'd looked when he was drifting off to sleep, when she'd tried to kiss him.

"It's enough," she said again. "It doesn't matter what you were. Only what you are. Love is enough, Marlow. Love can do anything."

He fell away, tearing at the heart fused to his chest.

"It's enough," she said again, louder now. "Love makes you real. Your mom's love made you real."

Marlow growled, and even this had force—an invisible hand that rolled her back. And he was there again, his fingers wrapped around her throat, lifting her up like he meant to hang her.

But she was still alive.

"Her love made you real, Marlow."

She forced the words out, even though there was no air to shape them with. She looked Marlow in the eye, and despite everything, she smiled.

"*My* love makes you real."

LOVE

In the heart of the tempest, he heard her.

He heard her say his name.

He was almost lost, caged inside a version of himself that might have been a machine, an engine of parts whose blades thrashed and churned in every direction.

Every direction except one.

He stared up and out of himself, through the ocean-dark smoke, through the ruin. And he saw her there, hanging from his own fist. Her face was so familiar, but he couldn't remember her name.

The Devil's blood still flowed. All there was was all there had ever been—an entity that had burned through the universes before they had even been formed, that wanted those universes to collapse back in on themselves so there would be silence once again, and peace. It was everything he was, because he was a child of darkness, spawned from something ancient, something evil. His fingers twitched, the energy there pulling at him like a leashed dog. He could wipe this girl out with just a thought.

She gripped his hand, her touch drawing something out of him—memories, a golden thread of them, things that he hadn't thought about in so long, a life with his mom that he had somehow forgotten. They were so bright that they seared through the murk of his thoughts.

"My love makes you real," she said again.

The heart roared its chthonic pulse; the girl spoke. He was caught between a storm and a forest fire, pummeled by the force of it. But all he could think about was a journey to hell, a girl he loved being held by the throat—not by him, but by another Devil—the idea that they might not spend an eternity together after all. All he could picture was Pan, held up by a demon on the first day he had met her, her eyes shards of flint.

"Do your worst."

All he could see was Pan, her eyes locked on his, her lips moving, shaping those words, speaking to him even as her eyes rolled up in their sockets.

"*My* love makes you real."

And it was enough. Because love *could* do that.

He let go, putting his hands on the heart that bulged from his chest. The disgust was a furnace that burned in his *own* heart. He sank his fingers into the grotesque meat of it, and pulled.

The Devil's heart had rooted itself deep, and it had the strength of the universe inside it, but it had given that power to him, too. He pulled harder, the pain like he was gouging out his own organs. A wave of vertigo made him feel as if he'd been hurled off the edge of the world, and he staggered, recovering, seizing a fistful of those fat black veins. He wrenched at them, feeling them slide from his arm like hypodermics. They whipped through the air, furious, black blood misting from the severed ends. And already they were worming their way back inside him, seeking out his nerves.

He tore at them, and he was faster—even though the blood was draining out of him, even though his skin was torn in a hundred different places. He was faster.

Then Pan was there, too, clawing at the heart, swearing over and over as she tried to rip it free. He tore at the last few veins then he pulled, pulled as hard as he could. His skin was fused there, and even past the thrum of the blood he could feel the agony of it peeling loose. He was losing himself inside a tunnel of darkness, and he suddenly understood that the heart would kill him rather than let him go.

Maybe that would be the end of it? Maybe if he died, then the heart would die too. The world would rid itself of two demonic creations. He grabbed it again, but it wouldn't come loose, it had burrowed too deep.

He collapsed to his knees and Pan dropped down next to him, her hands on his face.

"I'm going to get a knife," she said. "Cut that bastard thing out of you."

It doesn't matter, he thought, and somehow she picked the words out of the air.

"You're real," she said. "I promise you that."

She leaned forward, pushed her lips against his. He kissed her, and the universe ground to a halt—the storm, the shaking earth, the roar of the Devil, it all dissolved into stillness and silence until she pulled away.

"You're the realest thing I know," she said.

Whether she was right or wrong, it was working. The earth-shattering call of the heart was quieter now, he was sure. Maybe because it knew the lie it had told was disintegrating, un-spooling like tissue paper in water. Or maybe Pan was right. Maybe it didn't matter. Human or devil. When it came down to it, what was the difference?

"Come on," said Pan, struggling up and offering him a hand. "Let's end this."

"Yeah," Marlow said, hauling himself to his feet. His voice was his again, but he could still hear the power of it, bubbling just beneath the surface. "Ending it seems like a really good idea."

She let go of him, running across the ruined street and

snatching up something there. It was a metal bar, almost as tall as she was. She hefted it toward him, the look in her eye so crazed that even with the power of the Devil inside him he still took a step back.

"Pan, wait!"

"Too late," she said, swinging the bar at him. Her aim was true, the tip of the bar slamming into the gristled mess that clung to his torso. It was like she'd pummeled every single pain receptor inside him, the agony like a magnesium flare. By the time it had burned away he was lying on his back, and Pan was standing over him, bar raised for another strike.

She hit hard, and this time the world went dark. Marlow roared, sinking inside himself, sinking into that comforting beat of the heart. He slammed a fist onto the ground, his vision full once again of ruin, of death, of ruptured universes.

"Whoa! Marlow!"

Her hands were on his face and it was like she was reaching for him through black water. He sat up, groaning, fighting to find himself in the fury, in the hate. He grabbed Pan's face, feeling her to make sure she was real. She had abandoned the bar and she pulled him close, muttering, "Sorry, sorry, sorry."

"It's no good. It's inside me. It won't let me go."

"There must be a way," she said. "A knife, a chain saw, we—"

"We can't destroy it," he said. The blood pounded in his ears, in his skull, drumming the sense from him. The heart was patient, because it knew that sooner or later he would succumb. "I can't fight it. It's going to use me to end everything."

He touched it, this piece of filth that had crawled through space and time, that had crossed star systems, that had created hell once already—at this entity that had somehow ended up right here, on the streets of Mariners Harbor. It moved beneath his touch, feeding him, nurturing him, whispering promises of eternity.

"Then what?" asked Pan.

It would overpower him, he knew, it would use him. So long as it was free, it would burn a hole in reality.

So long as it was free.

"I know what we have to do," he said, and Pan almost had a smile on her face before he finished. "We have to go back. We have to go back to hell."

JUST DON'T LOOK BACK

The biggest surprise of all was that Marlow's words didn't surprise her one bit.

Pan looked at him, at this thing that stood before her. The blood-slicked skin of his face rippled like it was trying to pull itself from the bone beneath, his eyes spitting out a light that was so dense she could feel it. He looked somehow less solid, the edges of him bleeding into the world around him as if his presence here was shredding the muslin-thin veil of reality. How long before he broke through completely, before he punched a hole in the universe and drained everything into oblivion?

The Devil's heart still clung to his chest, arteries as thick as fingers puncturing his skin, feeding him with poison. His flesh had been torn in a dozen places where the organ had fastened itself, and where he'd tried to gouge it free. Only the heart, and the blood that flowed from it, was keeping him alive. He needed it now, as much as it needed him. It would cling to him forever, and sooner or later they would be one.

The Devil is dead, she thought. *Long live the Devil.*

"We have to go back," she echoed, her words lost in the maelstrom that churned overhead. The ground was also moving, shifting, like an ocean. Marlow didn't even have to do anything and the world would disintegrate around him.

Because he's not real, she thought, remembering her vision then shaking it from her head. Whatever she'd seen in the madness of Marlow's thoughts, whatever the Devil had told him, it didn't matter now.

"We have to go back," she said again, nodding. Marlow shook his head, one hand grabbing the heart, pulling at it. In response it slid its roots even deeper, she could see them coiling around his ribs. He growled, almost lost himself again, and she cupped his face, whispering his name, bringing him back.

"Just . . . me," he said in a voice that was barely his, a voice that sounded like a hundred voices. The terror roiled inside her and she was so close to losing herself to it, but she clung on, teetering.

"Yeah, sure," she said. "As much as I would love to leave you here, I trust you with this about as much as I trust Truck with my breakfast."

She let go of his face, took his hand. She could feel the power there, it was like holding on to an electric charge or a live grenade. But she didn't let go, she just led him across the ruined earth. There were no landmarks anymore, too much smoke to see more than a hundred yards or so. How were they supposed to find their way off the island?

Something moved in the corner of her vision and she braced herself, waiting for a demon, or something worse. But when she turned she caught a glimpse of fur, shaggy and blood-spotted. There was a dog there, doing its best to walk with an injured leg. It was looking at her as if she could save it, and she shooed it away. Hanging around here, with her, would only get the dog killed.

Then Marlow spoke, his voice cracked with emotion. "Donovan?"

The dog whined, taking a step toward him, its head bowed, its eyes turned longingly upward. Marlow dropped to his knees, calling the dog's name again, and this time it bounded unsteadily toward him, its tail wagging so hard she thought it might take off. It ran into his legs, collapsing against him. Marlow stroked its head, its neck, its belly, and great oil-black tears squeezed from his eyes.

Right now, he looked as far from a devil as it was possible to be.

Then he groaned, the heart contracting, squeezing his chest in warning. The veins jerked as the blood flowed through them, trying to scrub away everything Marlow was, everything he ever had been. The blood would kill him first, and then it would kill them all.

But maybe it was the one thing that could save them.

"Go," Marlow said, growling at the dog. He looked at Pan. The not-light from his eyes made her feel like she had a hand inside her skull, cupping the flesh of her brain, but she gritted her teeth against it, calling to him.

"You can take us there," she said.

He shook his head, growled her words away.

"Seriously, y—"

Something shrieked, close enough that she flinched. To her side, a demon scrabbled over a mound of rubble. It shook its head, spraying a fan of blood. A long pink tongue slid out, licking its lipless mouth. It sniffed the air, angling its head toward her.

"Seriously, Marlow," she said. "The blood, it's *his* blood. It's the same stuff that was in the Black Pool, it's the same stuff that we used to make every single contract."

Another demon bounded up, stopping next to the first, snapping at it. A third announced itself with a scream, closing in from another direction. It cocked its head and she understood it was listening for something—it was listening for the *heart*. Its beat was a bell that pealed impossibly loud, a clarion call that drew the forces of hell toward it.

It knew, she realized. It knew that Marlow was fighting it, it knew she was a threat, and it had called for help. Even with no eyes, even though it was just a football-size parasite of meat and machine, she could feel it watching her, she could feel the icy depths of its hatred.

"Marlow," she said softly, her hands on his face again. The demons were running now, their clawed feet kicking up dust and ash—five of them, seven, then too many to count as they stampeded, as they screamed. "Marlow, please. Get us out of here."

He tilted his head, the tendons in his neck bulging like steel cables. He grabbed the heart with both hands, trying again to pull it free. The demons were almost on them and Pan let go of him, scanning the ground for the metal bar, knowing it wouldn't do her any good. She bunched her fists instead, turned to the nearest one.

"Come on then, you—"

The monster detonated like it had been packed with explosives, blasting out a shock wave of rendered flesh. The second ruptured with such force that its top half was catapulted over Pan's head, its legs spasming in the dirt.

Then she felt arms around her, Marlow's arms, and suddenly the world burned away in a flurry of embers. Pan's stomach lurched so hard she thought she'd been disemboweled, the air punched from her lungs. There was an instant of nothing, of utter emptiness, then there was a gunshot pop and she was back.

The ground, though, had gone. She was airborne and falling, falling into the threadbare carpet of clouds, the world laid out beneath her like a map. Her stomach flipped again and she tumbled through the freezing air, the wind roaring, faster, faster. She turned, saw Marlow next to her, just as shocked as she was. She reached for him, saw him reach for her, too.

Their fingertips touched and Pan felt the thump as she was

kicked out of herself again, reality reclaiming her with a sickening strength, as if it were furious that she had managed to escape. She fell onto solid ground, her head spinning. She pushed her hands into the dirt, into the sand, and only when she felt like she had rooted her fingers deep enough did she dare look up.

Marlow was there, surrounded by a halo of burning ash. He was standing, but only just.

"Little warning," she muttered, somehow making it back to her feet. She looked at the river, at the warehouses, then at the Red Door, which stood open on its hinges. "You ported."

He nodded, then moved his hands to his stomach. If he'd looked sick before he looked half dead now.

"Never again," he said.

He wouldn't need to do it again. Pan sucked in a breath, noticed how quiet it was. The heart was still hammering its demonic tune against Marlow's ribs but they'd left the storm behind. It was catching up with them already, the ground beginning to shake, a ring of debris and sand and water rising up, spinning lazily.

"You sure?" she asked.

"About hell?" Marlow winced, then nodded. "Bastard's in every thought, it's pummeling the crap out of me. Don't know how much longer I can hold it."

He screwed his eyes shut, staggering, and she grabbed his hand, leading him to the door. The Devil had obviously exited at some speed, and with force—the corridor beyond was cracked, the walls fractured, the ground cratered—but the Red Door was undamaged, not even a scratch. Some things were more powerful than all of hell. It just stared back like it was defying her to cross the threshold.

She paused. Whatever happened next, this was a one-way

ticket. Once she crossed over into hell there would be no way home, not this time. Behind her was the world, was freedom, was the joy of knowing that she could leave this all to Marlow. She could push him through the Red Door, close it, and pray that he made it to the Black Pool before the heart took full control.

Yeah, right.

"Just don't look back," she whispered to herself as they walked through together, ignoring the acid-bath sensation that always came with crossing the Liminal. "Don't look back. Don't look back."

She didn't, she just reached behind her, grabbed the Red Door, and slammed it shut.

The sound of it echoed down the corridor like an explosion, Marlow clamping his hands to his ears, then to the heart as it squirmed against him. It almost looked like it was starting to panic, like it knew where they were going. More of those finger-fat arteries were sliding from it, pushing their way into Marlow's skin. Black blood streamed to the ground from the wounds. He took hold of a vein with shaking hands, tried to pull it free. Pan snatched at it as well, the tube too slick for her to get a grip.

"Come on," she said, taking his arm instead, pulling him after her.

Marlow growled, lashing out and hitting her. She flew back like she'd been struck by a moving car, bouncing off the wall and rolling across the broken ground. Marlow was turning, stumbling to the Red Door.

"Hey!" Pan yelled, somehow pushing herself to her feet. "Marlow Green, don't you dare."

He was fighting it, one fist punching through the concrete wall. He screamed and more of the ceiling fell away. Pan limped through the dust, grabbing him, inching him down the corridor.

The heart boomed, but it was just a heart, just an ancient, crumbling ruin.

"You can beat it," she said. "You're stronger than it is, than it ever was."

The door to the stairwell was open but it would take too long. She guided Marlow to the elevator, the cabin missing, the shaft yawning up at them like a demon's muzzle.

"Pan, what are you—"

She pushed them into it, grabbing hold of him as best she could as the ground fell out from under them. She screamed, Marlow grunting as he hit the side, breaking into a spin. Then he had her and she felt the air balloon around them, felt them start to slow.

They still hit hard, the force of it blasting out the doors at the bottom of the shaft, filling the vault room with dust. Pan felt something wet against her face, something probing, and she peeled away from Marlow's chest to see some of those twisted heart veins pushing against her, the tips of them flexing like mouths. She pushed away from him, hauling herself up into the room.

"Little . . . warning . . ." said Marlow from the darkness. She offered him a hand and he struggled up after her. He looked pale, he looked drained, and when he opened his eyes some of that awful darkness had faded from them. The heart was still there but it was doing something new, its arteries flailing through the air like spider legs, spraying a mist of black blood over his face, over his neck.

"You've got a bit of . . . something on you," she said, smudging it away.

"Thanks," he said, just a whisper.

He struggled onward, crossing the room. She held his arm, pushing through the door by his side. The Engine sat there, dead. The Black Pool lay quiet, too, but she was fairly sure the gateway was still open. It had to be, because this was their only hope.

"There's no other way," she said, and she couldn't be sure whether it was a question or not.

"No," said Marlow, waiting until they were at the bottom of the steps before saying, "Not for me, Pan. I have to do this. You don't."

"Marlow—"

"You got me here," he said, clutching the heart again. More of it had come loose and she could see the gleam of ribs there, the wet contraction of his lungs. The blood was trying its best to patch him up but there was only so much it could do. Marlow was right, if they cut the heart from him then surely he would die.

"Better this way," he said. "Better to be sure. And . . ." Another vein popped free and the heart bulged outward. Marlow collapsed onto the rim of the pool, blood trickling from his lips. "I belong there. I belong on the other side. It can't kill me there. I'll just . . . I'll keep coming back. I can hold it."

"You're nothing like it," Pan said, kneeling in front of him. "You're not a devil, Marlow. Come on, if you were a devil would you be covered in dog hair right now? If you were a devil do you think I would have . . ."

He smiled.

"You kissed me," he said, as if he'd only just realized. "Again."

"Yeah, but only because you were freaking out," she said, and even though there wasn't much blood left in her it still managed to rush to her cheeks. "Again."

The heart juddered, fought.

"You need to go," he said, not trying to free it now, but trying to hold it to him.

"And leave you to sort this out by yourself? *Nuh-uh*, Marlow, you'll just screw it up."

"That's exactly why," he said. "Everything else I've done, it's all been for the Devil. It felt . . . it felt so real, my life. But it was all for the Devil."

"No," Pan said. "It wasn't. What did it tell you, that you were *made*? That *it* made you? That's bull, Marlow. Everything you've done, it's only ever been because you're real. Think about it, just think about it. Your decisions were human, they were stupid and idiotic and wrong, half the time, but they were *human*."

The cavern creaked like a boat in a storm, the light fixtures swinging. Pan gripped Marlow even harder, looked him in the eye.

"Come on, Marlow," she said. "Do you honestly think that if the Devil was trying to make the perfect soldier, the perfect machine, it would have turned out like *you*?"

Something burst from the Black Pool, a twisted muzzle that snarled in panic. The demon was trying to swim to the edge, its bulk almost dragging it under. Marlow winced as he held out a hand and unleashed a stream of invisible energy. The creature had time for a squeal of pain before it was ripped into ribbons, the force of the explosion sending a plume of dark water up into the air. It rained down on them, the drops squirming like they had a life of their own.

"This is where we say goodbye," said Marlow.

Pan shook her head, holding him even tighter, hearing his skin tear as the heart fought to free itself.

"It's been a hell of a ride, Marlow Green," she said, ready to push him into the pool, ready to throw herself in as well. "Let's at least end it together."

Marlow nodded, then his face creased and he doubled over, screaming into his knees. Pan heard something crack inside his chest, a rib. She grabbed him, calling his name as he rolled onto his back. Then she let go, scrabbling away, refusing to believe what she was seeing.

The heart was pulling itself from Marlow's chest.

It looked like a giant insect, the veins hardening into limbs as it wrenched itself free. Something opened up in the knotted mass of tissue, a gaping hole that might have been a mouth. It was growing, swelling, as it peeled out the last of its arteries and flopped onto the stone floor.

Marlow screamed again, more blood than noise. He curled onto his side, cradling the mess of his chest. The heart-beast was trying to push itself up on those legs, more of them bristling from its greasy flanks. It was the size of a small dog now, its mouth working at the air like it was trying to speak. Its clockwork pieces caught the light, glinting like the metal parts of her own skin.

Pan waited for the creature to turn and bolt, to make a break for freedom. Only, it didn't. It grew like a wormbag, bladelike limbs bursting free of its rancid shell, muscles twisting beneath its skin. Rot holes burst open and she could see eyeballs bulging there, dozens of them.

She had time to swear, and then it was coming right for her.

LAST STAND

Marlow was in pieces. He didn't even have to look to know how bad it was. He had his hands to his chest and he could feel the holes there, like he'd been riddled with bullets. Blood was pouring from the wounds, cold and hot at the same time, and when he pushed his fingers to himself he could feel bone, and something deeper, something that was never supposed to see the light.

He didn't care, though, because however bad his injuries were, the fact that he could feel them at all meant the heart had gone.

The pain was a blowtorch held against his eyes but he could feel the corrupted blood inside him, pumped by his own battered heart. It was powerful, and already he could feel it knitting him back together, repairing the wounds. There were too many holes in him for it to save his life, he was pretty sure about that. But there was enough to see this through.

Behind the supernova of his agony he heard a scream. Somehow, he managed to roll onto his side, peeling open his eyes to see Pan. She was retreating across the platform, and there had to have been something wrong with Marlow's vision, because it looked like there was a shadow chasing after her, a creature so dark its shape had to have been cut from his retinas.

Only when it reared up—taller than a man, as fat as a pregnant sow, its jointed legs cleaving through the air—did he understand what it was. It was still pulsing, its flanks bulging and splitting with each beat, more limbs slopping out of its belly like newly birthed snakes. Pan had tripped onto her ass, looking like she was about to drop dead on the spot. She never took her eyes off it, she just bunched her fists and gave it a look that would have been enough to blow a lesser evil into pieces.

It slammed its front legs down and Marlow moved without thinking, stretching out an arm. The heart wasn't part of him anymore, but the Devil's blood still ran in his veins and when he opened his fingers a weak surge of energy slipped loose. It scudded along the ground, thumping into the ass end of the heart. It was barely enough to nudge it, but the creature swung around anyway, its cluster of rotting eyes rolling wildly.

"Yeah," Marlow grunted. "Still got it, asswipe."

Pan had made it back onto her feet and she had a chunk of rock in her hand, pulled from the fractured platform. She brought it down on the top of the creature's head and it squealed, backing away. She lifted the weapon and threw herself at it, but this time it saw her coming, snapping out a leg and swiping her feet from under her.

She spun, landing on her back, uttering a long, low groan. Marlow dug deep, flicking his hand and seeing another channel of inverse light cut through the air. The heart scuttled to the side, then it was charging at him, its bladed feet carving trenches in the stone.

He cradled his chest, sitting up, everything going dark.

Don't pass out.

Fluid leaked through his fingers but a thick, oil-black scab had grown over the worst of the injuries, the blood patching him up. He risked a look, still seeing a glimpse of rib.

Do not pass out.

There was enough of him left, though. He lifted both hands, the heart looming over him, its limbs raised like scorpion tails. The blood could give him any power, all he had to do was think of one. He cast the charge out like he was throwing a baseball—not a pulse of darkness this time but a ball of burning plasma. It hit the heart in its open mouth, spreading like napalm. The creature was squealing again, batting pathetically at its own skin.

Marlow tried to get to his feet, failed. He willed another attack but his batteries were running low, the blood deserting him like rats from a sinking ship. He managed to conjure a forked blast of blue flame but it went wide, arcing into the ceiling.

A scream, not from the heart this time but from Pan. She had thrown herself on it, something glinting in her palm. Whatever it was, it was powerful, chunks of flesh and blood erupting from the heart like she'd blasted it with a shotgun. She stabbed it again and this time the blade spun from her hands, scraping across the ground.

A crossbow bolt, Marlow saw, carved from the Engine. Pan had brought it here a lifetime ago, he remembered, to fight Mammon.

Pan ducked beneath the creature's limbs, running for the bolt. She didn't make it, an obsidian blade suddenly erupting from her stomach. Her mouth turned into a perfect O, then she collapsed into herself, the heart tossing her away like she was garbage. She landed, rolled, close enough to Marlow for him to be able to grab her and pull her to him.

The heart was recovering, the wound in its side bubbling closed. It hauled its ugly bulk toward them, more of those daggered limbs poised to strike.

Marlow could hear splashing from the Black Pool, knew there were more demons on the way. And just like that he understood it was over. They had lost.

The anger was powerful, but it was brief. He just didn't have enough left of himself to give to it. Pan groaned and he pulled her close, her head resting on his stomach. Blood flowed from her torso, so red, the brightest thing in sight.

"Sorry," he said, to her, to everyone.

She shook her head, her face etched with pain. Marlow looked past her to the heart, to this impossible thing that had crawled through time and space, that had devoured worlds and pulled holes in universes. And he knew that they had never stood a chance, not really. Like the Devil had told him, this story had been written too long ago.

The heart reared up in front of them and Marlow looked away from it. He wouldn't give it the satisfaction of watching him beg. He turned to Pan instead, ran a hand through her hair, and offered her the last thing he had to give: a smile.

Wherever they were going next, at least they'd be together.

He heard it before he felt it, the butcher's slice of metal through meat. Pan jolted in his arms but there was nothing there, no alien limb puncturing her skin. Marlow looked at himself, wondering if the rolling waves of agony had masked his own end.

Then he saw it, a gleaming blade of dull metal jutting out of the heart's groaning maw. It was coated in black blood, vanishing with a twist before slicing through again, this time bursting out of the side of its face.

"Die, *puta*!"

The heart roared, trying to turn. But it had made itself too big, struggling like an injured bear. The blade was wrenched from its face and somebody appeared from behind it, somebody dressed in rags and dust and blood, somebody armed with a ten-foot spear of Engine metal.

"Night!" Marlow yelled.

The girl pulled the spear back like she was a viper, then

plunged it forward. The creature's blood hissed as the metal touched it, its mouth uttering a gargled howl that was almost human.

Pan had managed to roll herself away, scuttling crablike across the ground to where the crossbow bolt lay. She scooped it up, fumbling it from her blood-slicked fingers, tried again. The heart-beast groaned but Marlow barely heard it. Another sound rocked the air, a screaming roar like there was a 747 hurtling toward him. The cavern shook, more chunks of rock raining down.

Night sliced through the heart-beast, pulling the blade free with a gout of black blood. It punched one of its scorpion-tail limbs at her and she ducked, swinging the spear down and slicing clean through it. She didn't stop, just turned in one fluid motion and jabbed the blade back in. Pan was there too, shanking the monster with everything she had.

A cleft seemed to open in the air overhead, a bolt of lightning that didn't fade away but just stayed there. Something that wasn't light and wasn't darkness bled from it, leaking into the room. It was a glitch in reality, so impossible that Marlow couldn't look at it. Another tore through the ground next to the Black Pool, crackling and spitting. The cavern was shaking so much now that Marlow thought it might give way beneath them, bury them alive.

"Hey," he said, pulling himself up, crouching because he couldn't trust himself to stand. The heart was struggling, spilling its guts, but it was repairing itself almost as quickly, bulging shapes pushing themselves from its wounds, sprouting more limbs, more eyes. "Hey," Marlow said again, a third rift tearing the air in two like it was a sheet of paper. "Guys, we gotta move."

Night whipped the spear around in an arc, slicing open half a dozen of its eyes like they were eggs. Then she grabbed Pan, hauling her away. Another of those tears in reality cracked the

Black Pool in two, a color that Marlow had never seen before leaching from the rift.

"What is that?" Night yelled over the roar, the two of them struggling to Marlow's side. It was like the world had forgotten how to hold itself together, like it was eating itself from the inside.

And suddenly he understood what was happening.

Night had crossed back into the world. She had escaped hell. The deal that Marlow had made with the Devil had been fulfilled.

And the gateway between worlds was collapsing.

"Ah, crappity crap," he said, turning so fast the world seemed to do a 360 around him. He lunged forward, another crack appearing in the air, just hanging there and bleeding its absence into the cave. It was pumping out a noise he couldn't make any sense of, like every single person on the planet had opened their mouth and cried out.

They reached the steps, Night and Pan taking the lead. Pan was losing a lot of blood but she wasn't giving in. Marlow glanced over his shoulder, saw the heart-beast pulling itself after them, scuttling like a giant roach. Its face was just eyes and a gaping mouth and yet somehow the panic was still there. It knew what was happening.

"Go!" Marlow shouted. But they weren't going to make it. The heart-beast was gaining fast. Night stood her ground, bracing the haft of the spear against the bottom step and angling the blade out. Marlow shook his hands, trying to find one last drop of power there. He flicked them, a mist of plasma crackling over his fingers like it didn't know what to do with itself.

But *he* knew.

The heart-beast was there, towering over them. Night swore, thrusting the spear at the creature's stomach. Marlow grabbed it, too, channeling the charge down the metal shaft—a raging torrent of fire that made the weapon glow red hot. If the heart-beast saw it, it didn't stop, running right into the blade. Marlow fell away, Night dancing back as the creature's limbs reached for her. The heart-beast was impaled, its insides sizzling and steaming, its mouth open in a soundless howl.

Marlow didn't stop to see what it did next, limping after the others. The cavern was coming apart, the air shattering like glass. The pressure was changing, wind whistling into the cracks. Marlow stopped as he reached the vault door, sucking in scraps of oxygen.

The pool was folding into itself like there was a black hole beneath the surface, the ground fracturing into dust as it was sucked inside. The motion of the air was stronger now, a current that pulled everything toward that churning mass of dark water. Farther out in the cavern, the Engine was dismantling itself—giant sections of machinery crumbling as they were hauled toward the pool. The heart-beast was pulling at the spear with every one of its limbs but it was stuck fast, fused there.

Marlow ran, managing three steps before he slowed into a walk. The thought of the staircase was almost too much but Night and Pan were waiting for him, and the sight of them there gave him strength.

"Last one up," Pan started, pausing while she caught her breath. "Is a rotten egg."

The last one up would be dead, and Marlow set off, the three of them staying close, helping one another. The entire stairwell was fracturing, the wind screaming past their ears as it flowed down to the cavern. It was making so much noise that Marlow didn't hear the roars from the heart-beast until it was almost right beneath them. He peered over the banister, seeing the monstrosity struggling up, the spear clanging against the rails.

But they were close, he knew that. He could see light up above, streaming into the stairwell. The day was up there, and it was waiting for them. And it was that that did it—not the threat of being trapped here, not the fear of death, not the last vestiges of the Devil's strength that flowed through him. It was the thought of stepping out into the warmth, into the glorious heat of summer, that drove him up the last few flights and out into the corridor.

He slung Pan's arm over his shoulder, dragging her toward the Red Door. The floor was giving way beneath his feet, festering into rot, and sand, and ash. He plowed through it, not stopping even when he heard the screams behind him, the heart-beast crashing out of the stairwell. He didn't stop until he'd opened the Red Door and tumbled through, sprawling in the dirt.

Night was the last one through and she grabbed the handle, pausing long enough for them all to look back inside. The Devil's heart—or what was left of it—was bouldering for the exit, struggling against the wind, against the disintegrating world. One of those impossible whipcracks of lightning sliced through the elevator, chunks of metal and rock flowing down into a widening gyre. Another cut the corridor in half, slicing right through the heart, dissecting it. One half of it fell away like it had been turned to stone, but the rest of it kept going, a single eye bulging from the foaming mess of its face, its mouth drooping, useless.

"Close the door," Pan said.

"Wait," said Marlow.

The far end of the corridor was a whirlpool of darkness, a vortex that devoured everything. The heart-beast was losing purchase, its limbs dragging through the dust, grabbing at the crumbling walls. But still it pushed on, just twenty yards away now, howling silently. That single eye stared, and stared.

"Close the goddamned door, Night," said Pan.

Lightning cracked again, a rift in reality just on the other side of the door—too close for comfort.

"I have to see," Marlow said. "I have to make sure."

The heart took another step, then it began to slide back, dragged by an invisible hand. It fought for all of a second, then it gave in. It rolled away, sucked into the chaos.

It was gone.

Marlow felt himself slide toward the door, the maelstrom pulling them in.

"Close it!" he screamed, but the wind was too strong, Night struggling, losing her footing. Marlow got up, ran to her. He hooked his fingers around the side of the door, pulling. Then Pan was there too, screaming against the pain as she fought to close it. The Nest was almost gone, swallowed by the storm that raged inside. But they pulled, they pulled, they pulled.

Until the Red Door clicked shut.

HELLPUTTERBACKERERS

Silence, other than their ragged breaths, and the deafening drum of Marlow's heart.

The Red Door rattled once, then fell still. They waited for it to open, to be ripped out of its frame by a cyclone that wanted to devour the world. They waited for it to open, the heart-beast clawing its way out, its limbs scything through the air, through them. They waited for it to open, the evil inside the Red Door ushering darkness into the day.

But it was just a door, and it stayed closed.

Until Night reached out and turned the handle.

"Whoa!" yelled Marlow from where he had collapsed to the ground. "What are—"

It opened into nothing—not darkness, not light, but something else. Then even that, too, began to fade. And there was just a warehouse, empty other than some metal shelves and a carpet of dead pigeons.

"Is it gone?" whispered Pan. She was lying on the floor holding her stomach, her eyes screwed closed. She looked like she'd been drawn in grayscale, like she hadn't quite made it back to the real world. Only the metal pieces of her had brightness and color, and they glinted in the sun. Marlow glanced up, the day as bright as ever, no sign of the storm aside from the carnage it had caused. Pieces of debris still rained down but only quietly, like they didn't want to disturb the peace.

"It's gone," Marlow said.

"You think it's in Paris?" Night asked.

There was a chance, Marlow thought. The actual Engine lay there, deep beneath the streets. But something told him that even there the Devil was dead. The gateway had been destroyed, had been utterly obliterated. And didn't that mean the entire Engine? That *was* the gateway, after all. Everything from the Red Door to the Black Pool had been designed to open a breach between Earth and hell, so it made sense that everything between them was gone for good.

"Old magic," said Pan, still not moving. "The Red Door, the Liminal. It kept the explosion inside. I never thought that bastard thing would save me."

"But has it gone?" Marlow asked. "You know, for good?"

Nobody answered. How could they know? Like the Devil had said, this was a story that had been written an eternity ago, one of infinite complexity. For all they knew, the Devil was lying dormant, ready to build itself a new Engine. And what about the other pieces of this creature, whatever it was? The six other Strangers? Were they murdering their way through their own universes, searching for this place? Would they carve their way through the sky one day and crush them all to dust?

Or maybe, just maybe, the Devil was dead.

"Maybe it's over," he said.

A scream startled the quiet, demons still cleaving their way through New Jersey.

"Way to tempt fate," answered Pan.

"*Almost* over," said Marlow. Because they were just demons. Without their master, they'd drop like flies.

Marlow stood, Night offering him a hand and hauling him to his feet. He felt weak, and the pain was like a heavy blanket thrown over him, smothering him. Everything hurt, but that kind of made it feel like nothing hurt. He probed his chest, the wounds there sealed by what might have been Kevlar. When he rapped his knuckles against it, it sounded hollow. He wasn't going to be running any marathons, that was for sure, but he didn't think he was going to die, either.

Pan, though, was a different story. He crouched beside her, pulling up her shirt and examining the wound. Blood was pooling in the bowl of her stomach, and when he wiped it away he saw a wound there, two inches long and open like a mouth.

"How bad is it?" she asked.

"Not bad," he said, and she grimaced.

"You always were a terrible liar."

He wondered if he should squeeze some of the Devil's blood on it. If it worked for him, then maybe it could heal her, too. But that nagging doubt was still there—what if the Devil had been right? What if he was the spawn of hell? The blood could kill her.

So instead he ripped a strip from what remained of his polo shirt, easing it under her and then knotting it across the wound. She swore at him, batting his hands away, managing to sit up.

"Where did you come from?" she said, squinting at Night.

"Found my way back," the girl said, rubbing her face. There was a new scar there, Marlow saw, running from her forehead around to her chin. He didn't need to ask what it was, he could still see Patrick's immense jaw locked around her, biting. "Twice."

"Twice?" Marlow asked.

She nodded. "First time a ghost got me. Didn't see it coming."

"Well, your timing was perfect," Marlow said. Night smiled. *"Siempre."*

They rested there, the warmth of the sun creeping into them—tentatively, like it wanted to make sure they were real. The shrieks of the demons were being chased by sirens, a helicopter thudding its way through the sky. Pan flinched.

"Herc's dead," she said.

Marlow sighed, nodded his acceptance. The statement refused to sink in, but he knew it would soon, and it would hurt a hell of a lot more than any of his physical wounds. He swore, remembering Charlie, but Pan held up a hand to calm him.

"I saw Charlie," she said. "He's okay. Broken leg, you did it."

"Oh," said Marlow. "Whoops."

And suddenly he was thinking of his house. The last few hours were choked with fog but he saw glimpses of the horror there, of what he'd done.

"I need to find my mom," he said, trying not to imagine what it was he would actually find.

"We will," said Pan. "I promise."

Marlow brought his hand to his mouth, chewed on his knuckle for a second before spitting out the taste of the Devil's blood. Pan groaned, Night helping her up.

"You shouldn't move," said Marlow. "You'll bleed out."

"If hell didn't kill me," she said, taking an unsteady step. "Then this little thing won't." She hawked up a ball of crimson spit, launching it at the Red Door. "Besides, we've got a job to do."

"Seriously?" Marlow said. "We've done our part, Pan."

"More than our part," said Night. "Like, way more."

"We need to go rest," Marlow said. "We need to find Charlie, then a hospital."

"Slacker," Pan said. "So long as hell's still out there, we've got work to do."

"You sound like Herc," muttered Marlow.

She looped her arm over his shoulders and he slung his

around her waist, supporting her as she walked. He stumbled, nearly falling, until Night grabbed his free arm and held him steady.

"You do realize that a demon is going to wipe the floor with us," said Marlow. "We look like we've escaped a geriatric facility."

Pan almost managed a smile.

"We're Hellraisers, Marlow," she said. "We'll always be Hellraisers."

"No," he said, shaking his head. It already felt like a dream, everything that had happened since stepping into that parking lot a million years ago. How could any of it have been real? But it had been, he knew. He only had to look at the metal ribs in his arm to know that he'd raised hell, he'd fought hell, and he'd walked in hell, too. It had been as real as anything else in his life, but maybe that was a good thing, because he knew now that the rest of his life *had* been real. Everything. He wasn't sure if he would ever find out the truth of where he came from, of who he was. He wasn't sure if he ever really wanted to. All that mattered was that he was himself, he was Marlow Green, and right now, right here, he was real.

"I think we need to change our name," he said as they hobbled over a railway track. To the south the sky was still dark, but across the bay Manhattan shone, as defiant as it always was. "Raising hell was a bad idea."

"Yeah," said Pan and Night together.

"Hellputterbackerers?" Marlow suggested. Pan laughed.

"Yeah, I like it," she said. "It's catchy."

"We should make T-shirts," added Night.

They stopped, the three of them wheezing, trembling. If anything, Pan seemed even grayer than before.

"Okay," she said, taking a shuddering breath. "Maybe we should leave the demons to the army."

"Slacker," said Marlow.

They stood there, breathing in the smell of the river, all of them watching the water as it flowed silently out to sea. It was oblivious, Marlow knew. It had no idea what had just happened. All that mattered to it was the journey. And maybe they'd all be the same, in time. Maybe one day they'd forget about all this—or maybe not forget, exactly, but learn to be okay with it—and pass peacefully through the rest of their lives.

It was a nice thought.

"Come on," he said, steering them the other way. "Let's get out of here."

"Hellputterbackerers signing out," said Pan.

And together they crossed the ruined street, the sun on their backs, the gulls serenading them. Marlow risked one look back, still expecting to see the Devil striding from the Red Door. And who knew, maybe one day it would—it or something just as foul, just as ancient. The world was a vulnerable place, after all, and the universes were vast and full of terrors.

That was the problem with being who he was and knowing what he knew, wasn't it? That was the trouble with being a hellraiser.

Sometimes you got burned.

But not today, he thought. Not today.

Today they were going to be just fine.